ISBN 978-1-7

Typesetting by Mark Jacobs
Printed by Imprint Digital, Exeter
Concur Books

A CIP Catalogue record for this book is available from the British Library.

TELLING TALES

Voices from the East Midlands

Concur Books

Contents

Introduction to the Stories

Mark Jacobs

This is fun! A gather of writers putting their progress in public view! If one wants to know what goes on inside the heads of writers it is all here, in glorious difference and the sameness of a question common to all: What next? Where to? Why?

The anthology offers a miscellany of stories, some in progress, written by the East Midlands branch of the UK Society of Authors, ranging from chapters of novels in process, to poems, short-stories, flash-fiction, light biography. It is meant to show the kind of work going on in this particular Midlands branch and, generally, others up and down England, some of it peculiarly local in dialect and location, as here in Nottingham, home to Lawrence and Sillitoe, some purely fiction, whether in strictly detective format, science-fiction or spiritual and spooky.

The book is intended to illustrate and to cater to all tastes and present something of surprise as each page is turned – so many minds, so many different heads, buzzing with thoughts! But all having a beginning, middle and end, as all good stories do, even when there is a question-mark at the end, which is simply the appetite for more. Because stories never quite end – there is always 'What next?' as authors mature and move on, just as in life we all do. Moving on never quite ends, questions continue to be asked, which is the richness of literature, or one might say the richness of human beings, since we are all in this together. Like Jack Horner, I would expect some readers to pull out plums, while others will gluttonise the whole book. Whichever way, happy reading!

The Hunter

Antonia Reed

She didn't like the accusing look it was giving her.

I didn't kill you, did I? It was tempting to say it out loud, but she realised how mad that would sound. Instead, she returned the stuffed fox's stare, trying to work out what she was going to do with it.

She couldn't just get rid of it. It was one of the few things Uncle Hugo had left her specifically, like a cryptic message, after years of no contact. He hadn't known how fond she was of them, so if it was a vindictive gesture, it was a subtle one. Today was the day she'd agreed to come and collect it, no going back now.

Aunt Val came back in with the tea, and Georgie shifted to make room on the sofa, side-eyeing the fox through its glass case. From this angle, it reminded her of her old dog when it wanted to go out for a walk. She knew the feeling. Val started talking about a lovely young man who'd joined her hiking group, and how Georgie just needed to get out there more. Georgie nodded along, looking out at the heavy sky past the dark green curtains, and felt a creeping sense of how the world looked to the bright-tailed creature in front of her.

'It's a shame the two of you never had the chance to go hunting together,' Val said, nodding at the duck lying, somewhat flatly, by the fox's front paws. 'The get-togethers afterwards were always such fun.' At least it didn't have the uncanny dead-but-not-really, alive-but-not-really quality the mammal had, its glass eye very much unseeing. Georgie wondered if that was perhaps the more dignified option.

'I'd have never trusted myself with a rifle,' she answered. 'I'd probably have taken out Hugo or one of his friends by mistake.'

Val chuckled lightly and refilled their cups, and George felt her gaze softening, merging into the hard orange eyes of the fox.

It was, admittedly, a beautiful thought. The crimson spray bursting from the men's heads, a flock of wild birds, alerted by the noise, scattering into the sky above.

She felt the fox would approve.

Let Down Your Hair

Antonia Reed

'Have you got everything?' Silkie asks, then scoots around checking anyway.

'Yes, everything's fine.' My calm voice belies how I feel. So much of our lives revolves around keeping things predictable: checking your house supplies once a week, rotas for patrol duty around the village, quotas for how much of what we grow must be preserved rather than enjoyed fresh. Even building this treehouse in the woods was treated like a childish idea, until we pointed out that it would give us construction skills and could then serve as an emergency shelter or guard tower. By contrast, playing this game now feels like stepping into magic, or an old religion, and the lack of logical thinking unnerves me.

Sam checks her acid gun and lays it down for me. 'Just in case.'

'Thanks.' I've never even had to spray an animal, let alone a human. I cross my fingers inside my sleeping bag and hope that nothing larger than a squirrel tries to join me tonight. Nothing's going to happen, I know this deep down. I'm just going to sleep here for a night, alone, as the ritual demands, feeling the treehouse groan around me as the temperature drops, jumping when the inevitable shriek of an owl pierces the quiet. And in the morning, I'll be the same. Perhaps a little disappointed, a little less afraid of the dark.

I don't tell Silkie any of this. She's been planning our rituals for weeks. It didn't work for her or Sam the last two nights, so now she's obsessed with it coming right for me. I think she's just bored, which is always dangerous. We're in our last year of school now; after that we'll choose between expanding our responsibilities here or making the tour of other communities in the network and seeing how we fit elsewhere. As young women we are especially encouraged to do this, in the hope we'll fall in love, stay and help keep the gene pool healthy. It's clear that Silkie is itching to broaden her options beyond the boorish boys from Hardcastle on the other side of the woods, and Sam will probably go where she goes. I also want to see more of the habitable world, but I'm anxious about being under the thumb of another community, not to mention the risk of running into Outlanders while travelling.

Silkie adjusts her leather jacket, more repaired patches now than smooth brown, and turns with her oil lamp to survey the room. An ancient battery torch by my side, acid gun and knife in easy reach, the decorations of plastic beaded necklaces we hung on the walls when we constructed this treehouse years ago. A tin with some bilberries rehydrated from last year's stock, in case the ritual is successful. In case there's someone to share them with.

Sam is starting to move out, sticking her legs through the window before twisting to give me an ironic smile. 'Hope you catch your prince.'

'You'll have to call me Your Highness tomorrow.'

Sam snorts and starts making her way down, leaving me with Silkie. She is tallest of the three of us, looming even larger as she crouches down to hug me goodbye. Her brown hair smells of dust, and when she pulls back her pale eyes almost glow in the gloom, a witch's glare.

'Don't forget to leave the rope down.'

'I won't.'

'It's got to touch the ground.'

'I know!' I swat her shoulder. 'I've got the drill. Don't fall asleep. Let Down My Hair. Snare the prince.'

'Stop rubbishing the magic, Bex.'

'Sorry, I just can't take this seriously...'

A shiver makes me pull the sleeping bag up to my chin. It's cold for May.

'Here.' She presses a small bottle of home brew into my chest. 'For courage.' She winks and starts backing towards the window. 'Just make sure it's not an Outlander, yeah?'

'I'd smell them before they got here.'

'That's my girl.' She grins and clamps the thin handle of the lamp in her mouth, before starting to climb down the rope, leaving the shutters open to the night.

I let out the breath I've been holding and lean back against the car door we used to patch this corner yesterday. The village keeps a couple of electric cars going collectively, for emergencies only because they take endless peddling on the cycle generator to charge, but the fuel ones became scrap long ago. Around me lie the debris of our meeting; a small plastic bag filled with what's left of the squirrels we caught and cooked earlier, our deck of cards that's so worn now you could argue over what individual ones are at times, and the beer I'm already tempted to sip. Silkie and Sam are moving out of the clearing now, pans and knives clattering in their backpacks, shouting good luck, stay safe, and Let Down Your Hair, Let Down Your Hair, Rapunzel, Rapunzel, Let Down Your Hair.

No-one really knows who this Rapunzel was. My grandmother told me she was a figure in a fairytale, but I've never been able to check. Many of our non-essential books had to be burned a decade ago, one winter when the wood became too damp, and the engineers couldn't find a solution. And the few times I've been further than Hardcastle it's been for a wedding, harvest swap or other important event, and sneaking off to explore that settlement's library wasn't a priority. What matters is that Rapunzel won her husband, and her freedom, by hanging her long, rope-like hair down from a tower in which she'd been kept prisoner. And so, in our ritual, every girl copies this as best she can, in the May she ends her schooling. Just in case the right boy happens to come along that night. It's stupid on one level, but it's nice to feel connected to something old and enduring, not rusty or recycled like the stuff our lives are built from.

Now I can no longer feel the presence of the others, the quietness of the night creeps into me. In the village, there is always noise of some sort; my parents talking in the next room, the crackle of a fire, a dog barking after a fox or wanting to be let out, people on watch clearing their throats in the chill air or sharing jokes. Out here in the woods, even the birds are silent. There's just an occasional branch dropping, or something that sounds like a footfall crunching into dry moss, making me go rigid in my sleeping bag. I press myself against the car door. Feeling the hard metal against my back reassures me a little, but I still slide my knife-holder under the pile of clothes that serves as my pillow.

Some people say the Outlanders must all be dead by now, thanks to eating fish from the rotten oceans. That we should send parties out to scout the coast and see what we can salvage from the settlements they've left behind. Others think something worse: that the poison in the water hasn't killed but mutated them beyond human form and perception. No-one can say for sure until someone is brave enough to travel into the Outlands, and so they remain this faceless, formless unknown lurking at the edges of our world.

Despite my nervous thoughts, I can feel myself becoming sleepy. My eyelids are heavy, limbs starting to lose their tension, so I lie down and let my thoughts settle as best I can. A soft breeze is wafting into the treehouse, and I imagine someone gently stroking my cheek, playing with my hair. But then comes the soft and very real sound of something moving nearby, slowing down when it enters the clearing. A deer perhaps, something that knows how to tread so only the most alert hunter will hear it.

My eyes bolt open at what are now clearly human footsteps approaching the tree, accompanied by soft clacks like a zip or button knocking against something. I lurch into sitting as the rope starts to creak. The person is hauling themself up, feet already scraping against the outer boards. This can't be happening. My mind is wide awake now, gut gurgling with nerves, and I grab for my knife, finding the acid gun instead. I shuffle the sleeping bag off me and raise my arms straight, pointing the gun at the open window and bracing myself as the stranger lifts themself through the window, their shape made hulking by their hood and backpack.

'Stay back.'

The stranger gasps, nearly falling back out of the window, but manages to grab the sides in time. Their hood falls back but it's too dark to see them properly. I only heard hands hit the window frame though, so they're unarmed. Currently. I allow myself to release one of my hands from the acid gun and reach for my torch.

'Don't move,' I say, and click it on.

I am taken aback by how pretty the boy is, with a black choppy fringe over dark, slightly slanting eyes and a delicate nose and mouth. His figure under the bulky clothes looks slight too. His eyes flick around, either to check I don't have backup or to gauge what there is to steal, then come back to rest on me.

'Sorry,' he says quietly. 'I didn't realise anyone was here. I just need a place to sleep.'

I wait to see if noises will accompany his speech, see if he has come alone or with others, waiting to attack. But he just stands there, hands raised, chewing his lip.

He takes a step closer. 'I'm not—'

I nudge the gun up and he raises his arms again. In the movement, I see the shape of small breasts pushing against the grey hooded jumper. The pretty face has a different meaning now, the delicate brown hands and long slender fingers. It shouldn't make a difference, being female won't stop her from robbing me, or worse. But I can't help feeling that little bit less afraid.

I lower the gun slightly. 'Are you alone?'

'Yes.' The girl's mouth twitches, trying to look friendly. 'I've also got food, and I'm happy to share.'

I think for a moment, assessing how strong she might be, what risk I'm taking just engaging in this conversation. There are shadows under her eyes I can see now that she's closer, betraying a tiredness her manner has overplayed. I don't recognise her from any settlement I've been to, I wonder how far she's travelled to get here, and why.

'Take off your shoes, and your jacket and jumper. Turn out your pockets and give me your bag. Then maybe you can stay.'

The girl nods and I lower the gun, although she doesn't exactly look happy about taking off her top layers. 'How do I know I can trust you?'

she asks, voice muffled as she pulls them over her head.

'Because I haven't shot you. Yet.'

We eyeball each other as she throws the jacket and jumper onto my lap, and I check them as she bends to unzip the sides of her boots. Inside the jumper's front pocket is a handkerchief and a multi-purpose knife, its once white handle stained green.

'I use that to take cuttings,' the girl says, and our eyes meet again. 'And so that I've got something if ever someone attacks me. Which hasn't happened so far.'

I can't help wondering if *Let Down Your Hair* is really intended as it's been sold to us. With this stranger in front of me now, it feels more like it was meant as a test of courage, a dare. None of us really *wanted* to meet someone out here in the woods, alone, in the middle of the night. And yet here I am, the legend turned reality, with no script for what happens next.

Placing her boots against the wall, the girl kneels between me and the window. I watch her carefully, still gripping the gun, as she starts to unfasten the top of her rucksack.

'Hey.' I indicate the bag with my gun. 'I told you to give that to me.'

'I'm just opening it,' she answers. 'The clasp is fiddly, and you're holding a *gun*. But be my guest.' She finishes opening the buckle, having to slide part of it around to loosen it properly, then places the bag next to my legs.

Pungent vegetable flavours greet me as I loosen the drawstring with my free hand, as well as the smell of fish and salt, sweet rot. Pulse quickening, I peer deeper inside, and there is a bundle of salted fish jerky, dried seaweed, and fried pieces of some tentacled thing I don't recognise. All species you don't find Inland.

I scoot backwards and throw the bag back at her. 'You're an Outlander.'

'And?' Her shoulders are raised, defensive. 'An Outlander who's offering you food. What's the problem?'

I wipe my hands on my jeans, trying to rub away the feeling of contamination. Perhaps this was a trap after all. I go over to the window and listen out, but I still can't hear anything.

'I told you, I'm alone,' she says. 'I wouldn't have hauled myself into this junk heap if I wasn't.'

I pull up the dangling rope and pull in the shutters, swiping down the catch to lock them in place. The hut feels even darker now, the torchlight casting our shadows tall against the wall and roof.

'Seriously, I just want a place to stay tonight,' she continues. 'I'm tired, I've come a long way. Just let me sleep a few hours and I'll be out of your hair.'

My mind seesaws with indecision. All my life I have been told to fear Outlanders. That most of them are dead, but that those who are left are decrepit, immoral monsters who would kill you as soon as they looked at you. But this girl seems so...normal.

Despite my better judgement, I slowly place the acid gun behind me, then pick up one of the rolled-up mats leaning against the wall and shove it over to her.

'Thanks. I appreciate this.'

'That's just so you don't get a cold backside while we talk. I've not said you can stay.'

She gives a half-second chuckle. 'Well, my backside says thank you. What's your name?'

I suppose it can't hurt to tell her that. 'Rebekah. You?'

'Kay.'

She smiles, showing white, even teeth. A rarity in this world. I feel embarrassed that mine are so crooked.

'What are you doing Inland? How did you even get here?'

'I swam.'

'Bollocks.'

'It's true! OK, for bits of it. It's amazing how scared you Inlanders are of water. You guys really don't know how to use the rivers and canals. I got past two guard posts just holding my breath for long enough.'

'But the water's dangerous! Don't they teach you that at...sea school?'

Another chuckle from Kay. 'It's toxic! Unless you boil it for ages. That's why so many of the fish died.'

'They didn't though. Not in the numbers you lot think anyway.'

A different kind of nervousness creeps into me. 'What do you mean?'

'How d'you think I got these?' Kay pulls out the dried fish. 'They're not from Before. My dad caught these a few weeks ago.'

'I don't believe you.'

'You Inlanders don't know anything! And your leaders keep it that way. They probably want you thinking it's dangerous to go Outland, because then you might see that it's *nicer* living by the coast, with the sea breeze on you and a view of the ocean. Then they'd have no-one left to work the fields or get the old tech working again, would they?'

'You don't know anything about us,' I say, although a voice in my head tells me she has a point. That I don't know what I don't know. But doubts like this need to be dealt with in my own time. I can't trust this isn't a ploy to rile me up, distract me from the fact I know even less about her.

Kay's jaw sets. 'Just because you don't want to hear it doesn't—'

'Yeah, well, if the Outlands are so fantastic, why did you drag yourself all the way here?'

'To forage. Some plants we need only grow Inland, and there's loads of old settlements no-one goes to, full of stuff we can't make at home. Looks like you guys managed to stash all the weapons though.'

'We need them.'

'Apparently.' Her eyebrow lifts. She's mocking me.

'Then *forage* what you need and piss off.' I lie down, angling myself so I can still see her, and pull my sleeping bag up around me.

'Does that mean I can stay?'

'Yes.' I give her back her jumper, without the knife. 'But your other stuff stays behind me.'

'Well...thanks. I suppose.'

She settles near me. Too near me. Why is she so confident I won't hurt *her*? Or is this also a ploy of some sort? I close my eyes for a moment to centre myself, listen to the sound of her movements, the swipe of her mat against the floorboards. I open my eyes again and her face is level with mine, jumper bunched up as a pillow. For a moment I am taken in by her eyes, they seem black and endless in the dim light, her smooth high cheekbones and the smell of fish on her clothes. No, the smell of the ocean, makes me think of freedom somehow.

'I'm really not here to cause problems,' she says quietly. 'I just want to help my family, and my community. I'm sure you're the same.'

She shivers then, so I grab a blanket and throw it over her.

'Thanks.'

'No point having you freeze to death.'

She burrows deeper under it. 'You're saying I'd be too heavy to lug through the window?'

I roll my eyes, resenting myself for finding her charming.

'There's not going to be a patrol here in the morning, is there?' she asks, suddenly more serious. 'I mean, you're not going to rat me out as soon as I'm asleep?'

In truth I hadn't considered this, I've been too overwhelmed by her appearance. I know that I *should*, no-one's going to thank me if this does turn out to be a trap. But too great a part of me wants to see where else this could go. What if Kay is genuine, and this is my first true chance of learning more about the Outlands?

I reach out and click off my torch. 'Don't make me regret this.'

Morning light streaming into my eyes wakes me. The window is open, and Kay has gone. On her mat lie various food gifts from her rucksack, and she's used the plastic necklaces to spell out *THANK YOU.*

I barely have time to perform an inventory before Silkie and Sam are hooting in the clearing below and piling up into the treehouse. I swipe Kay's food into my bag and throw the necklaces into a corner, then they're already clambering in and peppering me with questions. How was it? Did a prince turn up? Or one of the Hardcastle boys trying his luck? No, I say, nothing happened, just a few bats flying in and rattling about.

'Stinks of fish in here,' Sam says. 'Is that what they smell like? Gross.'

'Hello...' Silkie says in a tone that unnerves me, eyes lingering to my side. I realise the mat and blanket I gave Kay are still rolled out. 'What's this then?' She steps closer, a grin threatening to burst open on her face.

'Oh.' I try to sound like I've just noticed myself. 'Must have done that in my sleep. Weird.'

The other two look at each other suspiciously, then burst into cackles.

'We'll get it out of you eventually,' Silkie says.

That evening, I am lying in my normal bed back home. My thoughts won't settle, trying to make sense of what has happened. I spent the night with an Outlander, and it was...fine. She didn't even steal anything when she left. But what if *that* was the trick, to make me trust her so she can come back tonight, this time with reinforcements?

Eventually I give up, knowing I can't ignore this uncertainty. I ensure my parents are asleep, then throw on a coat and boots, take the acid gun from its case in the hall, and slip out.

As I near the clearing, I can already see a low, warm light amongst the dark trees. Just a glimmer, bits shining through the cracks in the boards and car parts making up our hideout, but enough to be foolish. Or...it's a group so strong they can afford to be discovered.

The window is ajar, the rope pulled up. There's no talking inside, no movement I can detect, so whoever it is may be alone.

Feeling scared and ridiculous, but also nervous in a way that, somehow, feels good, I hiss up as loud as I dare, 'Kay?' The word spreads into the night, my body tightening until no echoes remain.

For a moment there is silence, then a stirring. The window opens and a small head, haloed by red light and a jagged bob-cut, pokes out.

'Hey.' My chest flutters with relief that Kay doesn't sound hostile. 'Nice place you've got here.'

'I know. It's mine.' I'm feeling vulnerable down here in the dark, the rope out of reach. But I keep the fear out of my voice. 'Not done foraging then?'

Kay reaches inside and throws down the rope. 'Come and see.'

Everything about this feels wrong, reversed. But I don't feel I have much choice but to play the game and haul myself up.

The second wave of relief comes when I confirm that, once more,

Kay seems to be alone.

I pull the rope up again, just in case, and close the window. 'Your light's too bright. Anyone could see you.'

Kay dims her lamp. 'You hungry?'

'Not really. It's probably midnight by—'

Kay opens her bag and presents its contents. Roots and flowers in different shades, nettles and docks, some herbs I don't recognise, all bunched up with string. There are even some mushrooms that I didn't think grew this time of year.

'You got all this in one day?'

'I know where to look.'

'Bloody hell.' No-one I know could find all this so efficiently.

'Changed your mind about Outlanders then?'

I shrug noncommittally. 'You might have robbed an old lady.'

'So prejudiced!' Kay laughs and shoves me backwards. I giggle in surprise, and she becomes more serious again. 'It's not a problem if I stay another night, is it?'

'What, you break in and then ask?'

'You weren't here earlier! Or should I have come and tracked you down in your village?'

'Jesus, no.' But I should be more strategic this time, I don't want her to feel I'm just going to give in again. 'If I let you stay, even though you *said* you'd move on yesterday, what do I get in return?'

Kay hesitates, and then says, 'I'll owe you. Maybe one day you'll need somewhere to stay. Somewhere far from home.'

I swallow hard at what she's implying. If ever I went into the Outlands. If I ever had to run away.

'Fine,' I say quickly. 'But only if you talk me through what you've collected.'

'Thank you,' she breathes, sinking down onto the mat and blanket she's laid out for herself. I find myself pulling out the set I used last night and settling down next to her on the grubby floor. It feels far too easy, being with this stranger, but there is something hypnotic in the way she gently slips her findings from her bag, runs her slender fingers over their purple, variegated or bright-green leaves. This one can help soothe colic, this one you give a baby to chew if it's teething, this one must be fermented before it's safe to eat. I feel strangely calm listening to her capable voice, and before I know it, we have fallen asleep, and the morning has come too soon.

'Hi.' Kay still seems sleepy, as if she's let herself relax a little now that she's spent two nights here safely. Her black hair looks blue in the early grey light, and a bizarre urge to run my hand over it flits through me. Then I remember there is school today, and that it's my turn to check the family storeroom.

Kay shuffles herself into sitting as I make my way to the window, and I realise that, despite myself, I don't want this to be the last time I see her. I want to know more about her, about where she's from. It feels too arbitrary now to think she has an ulterior motive. I steel myself and turn to face her.

'Will you be here tonight?'

Her dark eyes grow tall with surprise. 'If...that's OK? I could do with one more day, to see if I can tick the last things off my list.' She scratches her head. 'Sorry, I probably stink by now.'

I give her a sly smile. 'Not from over here.'

She chuckles and throws her jumper at me.

In the classroom I feel like I am constantly holding my breath. I know I don't look different, but inside me it feels like the Earth itself has changed. What if other Outlanders are like Kay, healthy and friendly? What if we've got it all wrong? What if we've been deliberately lied to? Then I find myself worrying about her, surely staying in this area for so long is a risk she shouldn't be taking. But another part of me thrills at seeing her again tonight. I catch Silkie and Sam looking at me strangely from their desks ahead of mine. I send them a quick smile and furiously continue to copy out the calculations our teacher has written on the board.

That afternoon, I complete the stockroom check quicker than ever before, fudging a few numbers so I can swipe some items into my bag.

By the time my parents are starting to talk about dinner I have my excuse ready. Silkie, Sam and I will cook together by the treehouse again, then we've got some repairs to do and may as well sleep out there.

That night, Kay and I share the dried fish and squid she gave me earlier, plus what's left of her seaweed. At first, I find the flavours too intense and salty, but after a few bites they grow on me, and by the end I quite like the prickling aftertaste. We accompany them with two bottles of cider and a hunk of bread from my house, and for her journey back I hand over a packet of water biscuits, as much dried sausage as I dared cut off, and a jar of pear slices.

'Sorry I can't give you something fancier, but I thought it best not to raise suspicion.'

'No, this is great.'

We lie back on the blankets, feeling the warm buzz of the cider.

'It's not fair that you can't just...come home to my family,' I say. 'I'm sure they'd love you.'

'Not the word I'm thinking.'

'OK. Well, I'm sure they'd find you *impressive*.'

Kay is quiet for a moment, and then her voice sounds nervous. 'I'm glad me met.'

I turn to look at her, and she does the same. 'Me too.' I smooth down the blanket that has bunched up between us. 'Tell me more about your home.'

'OK...' She looks up at the ceiling as she searches for where to start. And then she tells me about her parents, her father who fishes and her mother who runs an inn where people travelling between settlements can stay. How their community also has a network of mutual support, although rather than a ring like ours it runs along a patch of the coast. How she has grown up learning that Inlanders aren't mutated or diseased, but stupid and violent, unwilling to share. I suppose that's not entirely a lie.

'Your leaders will have had their reasons,' I say. 'Like ours.'

Kay just breathes out, neither agreeing nor disagreeing. Then, with an expression I can't quite read, she reaches back to her rucksack and pulls out a folded-up map, so old it has bleached into various shades of blue. My stomach tingles as she opens out a couple of pages and her finger starts tracing a line south from where we are, crossing the boundary of the Inlands, continuing down across unknown land until it comes to rest against a town called *Weymouth*.

She looks at me, cautiously. 'That's me. You know, if you ever...'

Her eyes are still uncertain, but now it looks more like sadness. Perhaps she is thinking the same as I am, that this fairytale must now end. Tomorrow, she will swim back to the ocean like a mermaid, and I will stay, landlocked.

'Thank you for trusting me,' I say, and then don't know what to add. My feelings suddenly feel too big, too confusing, for words.

'Same.' Kay reaches out, running her fingers delicately through my reddish hair, smoothing down my back. Before fear can get the better of me, I edge closer, until her warm breath is on my cheek, place my arm so it's almost touching her. And then she closes the gap between us, soft lips moving against mine, answering the question I've been too afraid to ask.

I wake to see Kay tying up her rucksack. Her eyes are heavy and won't meet mine.

'Morning,' I say, determined we're not going to part in silence.

'Hey.' She turns and gives me a small smile.

I sit up and she puts her arms around me. I bury myself in the worn softness of her clothes, the sea-and-forest smell of her neck. 'Do you want to eat something before you go?'

'I'd love to,' she says, fingers playing with my hair. 'But...I've already stayed longer than planned, and I don't want to worry—'

I cut her off with a final kiss, then pull back. 'It's OK. I understand.'

We don't say anything after that, other than to check she's got everything she came with, everything I am able to send with her. I climb down from the treehouse first to check no-one is around, but the woods seem clear. Then I beckon Kay down, watch how lightly she descends.

'Which way will you go?' I ask, wanting to stretch this moment out.

Kay pulls a compass from her top pocket. 'Well, I came from there originally.' She nods to the path behind me on the right. 'But I'm thinking I could try— '

'Hello stranger.'

We both jump, and there is Silkie emerging along one of the tracks, tailed by Sam and two boys from our class, Martin and Finn. Martin has his crossbow. I quickly step in front of Kay.

'Told you it smelled of fish,' Sam scoffs. 'We'll have to wash everything down.'

Silkie's eyes are bright and vicious as she takes in the sight of us. 'We knew you were lying. But not that you'd be—'

'Please,' I interrupt her. 'We've been lied to about the Outlands. Maybe by accident, but—'

'Cut the crap, Rebekah. Come over here and we'll sort this.'

My heart is pounding, but I'm determined to get Kay away safely. 'Just listen to me!'

But the others rush at us. Kay bolts for the trees and I do my best to stop them, pull at their arms, trip them up, but there's four of them and one of me. I jump on Martin and bring him to the ground, but then I hear Kay scream and launch myself forwards. I catch up with Sam first, but when I yell at them to stop whatever the hell they're doing, she swings round and punches me between the eyes.

I wake in the village holding cell, normally reserved for those who peer too deeply into a brewing barrel at the end of harvest. Silkie is sitting on a chair beyond the bars, calmer now but still looking angry and disappointed.

I sit up on the wooden bench. I'm thirsty and my nose and forehead are throbbing, but I'm most concerned about Kay. For a moment I'm relieved she's not here too, but then I see her rucksack resting between Silkie's legs.

'Where is she?' I croak.

'Taken care of.'

Her acid gun lies on the desk beside her, and there's a chemical smell coming off her clothes. A cold, twisting feeling enters my stomach.

'What did you do?'

Silkie's voice is smooth, a snake wrapping itself around my heart.

'We couldn't catch her before she got to the river, but we made sure she wouldn't get far.'

My dry throat and revulsion launch me into a coughing fit, but I manage to press out, 'Please, if there's any chance she survived, you need to—'

'All that matters,' Silkie interrupts me, 'is that an Outlander who's worked out how to cross the Boundary doesn't take that knowledge home. It's better for you this way too.'

Awful images flash across my mind, Kay tumbling into the water shot full of arrows and acid burns. 'She just came to collect plants for her family,' I say quietly, pushing down my rage and grief, they will fuel me later. 'You didn't even give her a chance.'

Silkie stands up and holsters her gun, this stranger who once was my friend. 'I'll tell the Council you're awake.'

The next days are a blur. I sit, pace, or lie in my cell as the Council, including my parents, take turns interrogating and berating me. I am told how foolish and selfish I've been, how much I could have endangered the community. That I'll be denied the end of my schooling, and the freedom to travel, if I don't share everything I know about the Outlander. I don't even give them Kay's name. Instead, I ask if they knew the Outlands aren't as devastated or diseased as we've been led to believe, why we've been kept in the dark, but no-one's willing to answer my questions either. Kay's bag and its contents are taken away and tested, but nothing more incriminating than her green-stained knife is found, and they're locked away here in case clues to the route she took to get this far Inland can be determined down the line. For now, her map is repeatedly shoved in my face in the hope I'll give something away, and I am happy to see she left no marks on it. I also realise their determination might be because the others aren't sure they injured her *enough*, that there's a chance she survived, and that gives me the last bit of willpower I need to stay silent.

I lose track of the days, but eventually the Council realise, or my parents persuade them, that they're not going to get anything from me, and I am no use to anyone in this cell. Shackles are placed on my ankles, connected by a chain, so I can perform my punishment but not escape easily, and I am to stay within the village, or whatever field I'm assigned, and not 'spread rumours' about the Outlands unless I want to land back in here.

I accept the confines of this new life. They are penance for not protecting Kay better, and I wouldn't trust anyone with the slivers of knowledge she has given me anyway. I scrub the guard block toilets and muck out the pig and chicken sheds without complaint, I sit at my parents' table and fork food into my mouth to stay alive, and I gather and bunch our first yield of straw until my fingers are raw. Silkie, the others and I acknowledge one another if we cross paths, but that's it. I know their cruelty was to protect us, and in line with what we've been taught, but I can't go back to how things were. My mind is mostly elsewhere now, picturing the world beyond the Boundary. Happy images of Kay, who by some miracle has made it back home, swimming in a replenished ocean or helping her father bring in a catch. If nothing else, I know there is life outside our network, and hope.

It is August now, the cool morning air already announcing September's arrival. My hair has grown long, twisting down my back like a rope. It's months since Kay was here, but I can still hear her voice, calling me from the invisible ocean. I need to know.

I have kept my head down, stuck to the rules and not raised suspicion. It has allowed me to put together a bag of supplies over time, stashed in a hollow tree between two fields, and a plan. I have even managed to learn the new combination my father put into our weapons store at home, the key that will launch a chain reaction when the time comes. I made sure to watch him carefully one day, then pretended to be tightening my laces when he looked round. This summer has made a good actor of me.

I know it is time when the heavy rain hits. The sound will muffle my movements and make me harder to follow. Seeing the thick clouds coming, most of the village worked together yesterday to bring in a huge haul of potatoes, so this morning the atmosphere is quiet and sleepy. I won't get a better chance.

As quietly as the chain between my ankles will allow, I dress and sneak to the family weapons store. I take out a hunting knife, attaching its sheath to my belt, and the acid gun. There is no time to be sentimental. I peer carefully into my parents' bedroom, breathe in their smell as they sleep, accepting this decision may take me in a direction that cannot be reversed, and leave the house. In the back garden where I'm shielded by bushes, I hold my breath and release the safety catch on the acid gun, then slowly squeeze the trigger over my chain. The liquid hisses against the metal, and after about ten seconds the links are weakened enough that I can snap them apart. The chain slips from my ankle clasps—I'll deal with them later—and drops to the floor like a dead snake. The ground between my feet has bubbled, and I can't help picturing what damage was done to Kay.

I grit my teeth, no time to linger.

The next stop is the old police station. This time I don't hesitate shooting acid into the lock, then rush inside and make quick work of the storage units until I find Kay's rucksack. I grab it and hurry to the edge of the village, sticking to the low stone walls of front gardens, throwing myself over one when I hear a patrol coming around the corner in front of me. It won't be long until my thefts are noticed, so as soon as they're out of earshot, hunched inside their long coats against the rain, I run until I'm out in the fields and at my final stop, the tree. I rummage in the rucksack I've stashed here until I can pull out a couple of precious, large plastic bags. Then, providing what cover I can with my coat, I pour out Kay's possessions and quickly review what could be salvaged. Just in case, just in case. The mushrooms have rotted into a foul-smelling mulch, but the herbs have simply dried, maybe they're still usable. I put them into one plastic bag with her map and knife, then tie a second around it. Now all that's left is stuffing this into my rucksack, and the route I have memorised over the last few weeks, stealing glances at maps whenever I had the opportunity.

Back in the village, someone cries out. The words aren't clear, but they sound angry, or worried. I'm out of time. I run from the field into the woods, my path going wider than planned but it's too risky to turn back. I must enter the river by Hardcastle, but the rain in still heavy when I get there, sheeting between me and the guards stationed by the bridge. I edge along the riverside, keeping to the trees, until I can sense movement in the woods behind me. Checking the guards are looking away, I plunge into the deep water and under the bridge, letting the water carry me towards what is utterly Outland. I am a fish, I am Kay, I am coming home to where I have never been.

When I climb up the bank sometime later the rain has gone, but I feel numb with cold. The land here is open, bleak and alien. I am trembling from the water, and the shock of what I've done, but I must focus now. This journey will take two or three days, and that's if everything goes to plan. I hurry under the shelter of some yews, strip off my wet clothes, and take out Kay's map.

There are battered-down signs creaking along the last mile, and I drag my feet through the weeds growing through the cracked road as buildings start to appear. Tall and rundown, there's no sense of them being guarded like back home. I have used the old road network to guide me, avoiding settlements and sleeping under hedges at night, but other than thirst and exhaustion nothing has bothered me. Now I feel trepidation though, as I get close enough to hear voices and some kind of machinery rumbling, but then there is the call of a gull and a sea-tang that seeps into my nose, making me want to cry with homesickness for this place I have only known in dreams.

I am too tired to be scared anymore, so I keep walking. People stare at me as I enter under the old arch, but no-one seems hostile. Maybe I look too bedraggled to seem threatening. Their clothes are blue, grey and black, crusted from the sea. I give an old man pushing a barrow full of rope a cautious smile, then stumble over a broken bucket and he catches me just in time. His hands are like shovels, but gentle.

'Are you lost?' he asks, thick white hairs sticking up above his eyes.

'I'm looking…' I croak, '…for the Lin family.'

'Ah,' he says, as if I have told him my entire story.

At the end of the long stony beach is a hut with huge fishing nets hanging to dry in front of it. A man is walking up the shingle towards it with a basket of fresh fish. He looks so much like an older, masculine version of Kay that it stops me for a moment.

The white-haired man taps my arm in parting, and I thank him as he turns back towards the mottled seawalls.

And then my feet are taking me to the hut, the crashing sound of each step announcing my arrival and making me feel sick with nerves. There is no time to prepare anymore, no time to worry if she'll be there, what state she'll be in, if she'll be happy to see me, there is only now.

A new figure steps out behind the blue netting, and my pulse thrums in my ears. Slowly, I walk the last few metres towards her, feeling so light I might be carried off in the wind. There is scarring around her left temple, she was lucky they didn't catch her eyes, and where her pushed-up sleeves reveal her lower arms there are burn streaks where she shielded herself, as if someone has turned parts of her flesh into wax.

I clear the lump from my throat. 'Hi. I'm so sorry for—'

Kay runs forward and throws her arms around me, and then we're both laughing and I'm crying with relief, and she's wiping my tears away with her cool ocean hands. Her hair is longer too, a jet-black ponytail that sweeps the base of her neck.

'I can't believe you're here,' she says, the bright sky above us reflected in her eyes.

'I can't believe you survived!'

'I hope you didn't get into too much trouble.'

'Don't worry about it.' I glance at the scars on her temple. 'I got off lightly.'

She turns serious, and I can feel her father watching us from the hut. 'I have to ask...'

'No-one knows where I am. I swear I didn't tell them anything. That's why it's taken me so long to get here. I was...supervised, so I had to wait for an opportunity. But...I managed to bring you this.' I step away to open my bag, take out of the bundle of plants she'd gathered. 'I don't know how useful they'll be now, but—'

She pulls me closer, and then it's just the two of us, and gulls calling above in the vast, open sky.

From Notorious

Christy Fearn

Act I
Scene One: The Serpentine

It was her habit: Her ritual. On such a morning Amelia would wear her white muslin dress with a narrow royal-blue sash, pin her hair into a hasty knot, drop a handful of coins into her reticule and hurry through the streets of West London to Hyde Park. Dawn had barely broken; the first rays of summer piercing the newly green branches and illuminating the virginal blossoms. 'The darling buds' Amelia smiled to herself. Apart from the earliest risers exercising their horses and the odd page delivering a letter or newspaper, the paths criss-crossing the open lawns were deserted. She caught her breath near the statue of a hero.

'Good morning, sir,' she declaimed as she made a formal curtsey to the figure. High on his plinth, the naked soldier was brandishing his sword ready to strike a death-blow. Amelia adopted a snooty tone:

May I say how fine your weapon is looking this morning?'

She blew him a kiss and continued her progression to the Serpentine.

Amelia picked her way between the trees to the water's edge. She found a spot on the pebbly shore where she hoped she could not be seen. As she unlaced her dress she gazed at the ethereal mist rising from the surface of the lake. It hovered like a spirit; then began to dissipate as the sun climbed above the branches and gilded the water. Spreading her silk shawl on the stoney ground, she weighted the edges with her shoes and large pebbles. Amelia then removed her stockings and placed them in one corner of the shawl with her reticule. Finally she unlaced her short corset and wearing only her shift, tip-toed down to the lake. She waded into the water, the chill rising up through her legs as she moved slowly away from the shore. She knew she would have to brace herself and drop below the surface. Once the water was over her shoulders, she would be comfortable. Amelia drew a deep breath and plunged herself downwards. She counted to three and gasped as the cold water slid over her shoulders. She shivered and then, checking that she could still reach the muddy floor on tiptoe, she began to swim.

A pair of swans appeared, gracefully gliding through the sky, before descending and landing elegantly near the middle. Amelia watched as they pecked affectionately at each other's beaks and dipped their heads below the water to feed. She marvelled at the tranquillity. It was difficult to believe that the park was surrounded by the noisy, smoky city. Her chemise ballooned around her, floating to the surface. Anyone under the water would have a wonderful view, she chuckled to herself. She turned onto her back and floated, gazing at the azure sky. How on earth could Ophelia have killed herself by drowning? Amelia puzzled over the thought. *Her dress bore her up.* Wasn't that Queen Gertrude's line? Surely it was impossible: Unless you had sewn stones into your under-skirt. Amelia frowned; she didn't think Ophelia would have had the presence of mind or forward planning for that. She must have thrown herself into a river, where a current would drag her under. Glancing over at the opposite bank, Amelia wondered if she could swim there and back. Before she had time to properly consider and estimate how long it would take, she became aware of a man's voice shouting from the lakeside where she had left her clothes.

'Madam! Madam, please!!'

He was like a reed: A very tall, thin young man. He appeared to be waving something. Amelia snorted. He looked ridiculous. She trod water for a moment and waved back. The young stranger became almost frantic; his voice a shrill shriek.

'Please madam! Do not kill yourself.'

He dropped whatever he was holding and began to pull off his cravat, then his shoes. Amelia closed her eyes. She wished he would go away. Her eyes flickered open as she heard him shouting again:

'Do not fear!' he cried, 'I shall save you!'

He tore off his jacket.

'Oh for heaven's sake. You idiot,' she hissed. With expert speed Amelia drew herself back to the shore before he had finished removing his shirt. She arrived at a shallow point and stood up. Her chemise clung to her body. The young man paused in his undressing and stared at her. The contours of her statuesque figure were explicitly revealed by the transparent fabric; the warm morning sunshine glowing on her golden hair. Amelia rolled her eyes. She placed her hands on her hips.

'I do not think I need rescuing, do you?'

The young man gulped and looked away. His pale complexion flushed with embarrassment.

'Oh I am so sorry,' he blurted, 'do forgive me,' and began to straighten his shirt once more. Amelia pursed her lips. Then she laughed.

'Do you often rescue drowning ladies?'

The young man shook his head. Amelia surveyed his awkward, gangly frame,

'Actually,' he admitted, 'I cannot even swim.'

'Then you are either very brave, or very stupid,' she smiled, 'which are you?'

'Both.'

He grinned, finished retying his cravat, then sat down to replace his shoes. Amelia stepped forward and picked up the article he had been waving. It was a notebook.

'Are you a hack? Am I going to find a story about me in the newspaper tomorrow? Attempted suicide in the Serpentine thwarted by our brave journalist? No doubt accompanied by one of Mr Cruikshank's amusing cartoons.'

The young man was silent. She opened the book and recognised Blank Verse and Sonnets.

'Oh bravo! You are a poet!' she raised her eyebrows, 'I have never met a poet. I should like to meet Lord Byron,' she flipped through the pages and glanced at him, 'Should I have heard of you?'

He stood. 'I am a poet: But not a famous one. I haven't been published properly,' he paused, 'not yet.'

'Mm,' Amelia hummed, then declaimed one of the verses aloud:

'Soft, my dearest angel, stay
Oh you suck my soul away!
Suck on suck on, I glow I glow!
Tides of maddening passion roll
And streams of rapture drown my soul
Now give me one more billing kiss
Let your lips now repeat the bliss
Endless kisses steal my breath
No life can equal such a death!'

Amelia shot him an approving glance. 'Goodness me, you are passionate, aren't you?'

She gazed at him. He must be several years her junior; about twenty years old? The sun burnished his auburn hair; his light hazel eyes gave him an innocent, almost childlike expression, which belied his sensual nature. His cheeks were now florid with embarrassment.

'If you mean to be a published author, sir, you cannot be bashful about your work.'

Amelia turned the pages and read a little more, from a different poem.

> 'What then are kings? Kings are but dust
> The last eventful day, will level all

And make them lose their sway'

She paused, 'you are also a revolutionary then?'

His cheeks lost their blush and his eyes shone. He nodded.

'I am. I wish for liberty in all things: For all people. Free thought, free speech. Free love.'

Amelia tilted her head to one side.

'And is your wife of the same opinion?'

He twisted his wedding ring and looked away.

'Oh I am sorry. I have overstepped the mark,' Amelia handed him his notebook and began to dress. She laced her corset. She sat down upon her shawl and pulled on her stockings.

'I should keep my mouth closed.' She stood up.

'No,' he moved towards her, 'No, you should speak out. You have a melodious voice.'

Amelia stepped into her shoes. She slipped her arms into her dress and laced the bodice, wrapped the narrow sash under her breasts and secured it.

'Well I am trained to use my voice: I am an actress.' She put out her hand 'Amelia Fitzwilliam.' He took her hand, but instead of kissing it, he shook it firmly, as though greeting another man.

'Percy Bysshe Shelley.'

'Well Mr Shelley, after my swim I usually visit a coffee house and have breakfast. Would you care to accompany me? I feel I owe you at least a cup of coffee in return for your gallant offer to rescue me?'

Shelley drew out his pocket watch: Eight-thirty.

'I am not expected at Mr Godwin's until ten o'clock, so yes, I accept your invitation.'

'Good.'

Amelia picked up her reticule and shawl. They returned to the path and Shelley followed Amelia as she strode through the park, leading the way back to the road.

'Who is Mr Godwin?' she asked.

'William Godwin. The famous author,' Shelley kept pace with her, as they approached Mayfair, 'or rather, the infamous author,' he smiled, 'he wrote *Political Justice* and the novel *Caleb Williams*. Do you know his work?'

Amelia shook her head. 'Has he written any plays?'

Shelley laughed, 'I do not think so. I expect he'd find the theatre rather frivolous.'

Amelia stopped.

'Surely he would approve of Shakespeare? *Julius Caesar, Hamlet* or *Macbeth* ? Or the Greek Tragedies? I had a role in a production of *Oedipus* last year.'

'Oh yes, well that is not frivolous at all. I was referring to the silly comedies.'

Amelia continued her brisk walk once more.

'Comedy is just as valid as tragedy, Mr Shelley. Life is not all misery and drowning.'

He smiled. Amelia opened her reticule and inspected her money.

'I suppose people accuse you of being too serious?'

Shelley nodded, 'They do.'

'Well,' Amelia turned the corner, 'let us put seriousness aside and enjoy breaking our fast together. I prefer to live in the moment, to seize my day and to see my glass as half full of clichés!' She nudged him and he laughed.

'What you need, Mr Shelley, is a strong pot of coffee, and a plate of eggs and bacon.'

'Ah,' he blushed once again, 'I do not drink coffee, nor do I eat meat.'

Amelia arched her eyebrows.

'But I have no objection to Green Tea,' he smiled, 'and a plate of toast.'

They arrived at a building with leaded windows. Amelia pushed open the door of the coffee-house.

'You are an extraordinary man, Mr Shelley.'

Saint George's Day

Christy Fearn

There's my signature on the plans. George Raven. It's a suitably gothic name for an architect; especially one who specialises in restoring churches. Especially this church: St George's in Bloomsbury. I first encountered it as a student, on a field trip to London to research architecture. Churches have always been my passion. Hawksmoor's London churches are some of my favourites, so I grasped the opportunity to work on St George's. It's an unusual place.

I'm staying at the hotel next door. It's something I usually do when working on a building. I like to be as close as possible to the site. To keep my eye on things. I'm pleased that I do this, because some of the stone masons and sculptors have been less than co-operative: all down to 3D printing. Their argument is that it is killing real craftsmen. I can see their point, to an extent I even agree, but I have to argue that it's the future. Well, not even that: it's the present. Their union is dead against it and as a result, they're threatening to strike.

At the last meeting I tried my damnedest to convince them: unless we use 3D printing on this project, we have no means of being entirely certain the sculpture will fit correctly. If that happens we'll be wasting a fortune. Money that has been donated to us. That's another thing: the anonymous donor. No one knows who has stumped up the funds for this restoration. Not even the church. I mean, the funds are managed by the accountants, but they can't tell us whose money it is. 'Can't, or won't?' I asked the Bishop. He shrugged his shoulders. All he could say was that the funds were there and they're more than enough to replace the statue at the top of the steeple. It's a statue of George the First, dressed as a Roman Emperor.

The Royal Beasts at the bottom of the steeple were replaced in 2006. Lions and unicorns, chasing each other around the base of the steeple. They'd been removed in the 1870s by some austere Victorians who objected to them: were the sculptures too frivolous? Or too much of a reminder of the animosity between the two nations? Especially given Victoria's passion for Scotland.

But now King George needs replacing. There was controversy around this, too. Should it be an exact copy of the statue, or will it be someone more contemporary? The donors have stipulated that the funds were dependent on one condition: that they choose the design and it is sculpted exactly as stipulated in the 3D print. Another reason for the sculptors to object.

After the last meeting with the head architectural sculptor I return to my hotel room. I notice I have several missed calls on my phone and a flurry of messages. Odd. I stare at the times of these messages: most of them are in the last couple of hours when my phone was off during the meeting, but the others are in the last 20 minutes. I was here, my phone was on. I was just making a cup of tea and thinking about where to go for dinner.

I scroll through the missed calls. My father. I sigh. He knows I'm working and he knows I can't take calls. I messaged him yesterday about how unreliable the signal is. In the church, that is. The hotel has a good wifi connection and signal, but the church? Forget it! You have to go outside in order to make or take any calls, or even read documents. It's bizarre and very frustrating.

'Hi Dad. Yes, I can meet you for lunch on Sunday. Somewhere near Bloomsbury? Love G'

Bless him. He's nearly 80 and WhatsApp is his favourite thing. He keeps sending me links to articles about the Hawksmoor churches. Yes, I know, they're all a bit weird. Yes, I know Peter Ackroyd wrote a thriller about them. Yes, I know they're featured in a graphic novel about Jack the Ripper. He loves all that: mysteries and conspiracies. Sometimes I wish I could be in two places at once. He's not getting any younger and although he's relatively healthy, I want to spend more time with him. He'll catch the tube on Sunday into the city and I'll take him for lunch. 'My treat' I add to the message. He responds with a smiley face. And a thumbs up. And a GIF of a cute teddy bear eating a cake. I laugh. If the Italian restaurant round the corner is open on Sunday we'll go there. He loves spaghetti Carbonara.

Then I move on to the other messages. Missed calls from an unknown number. Probably spam. I'm about to block, but there are 7 text messages from the same number... they're all asking a question and they're all identical: 'Rex regum et dominus dominantium?' Then there's an image: a tower being struck by lightning.

I call the number. There's a familiar, automated voice: 'I'm sorry, the number you have called has not been recognised'. I hastily type the number into a search app: Who's the Caller?

Nothing. No one else has received calls from this number. I put it into a couple of other similar search sites. Again, nothing. So it isn't a widespread scam. I'm pretty sure I know what the Latin means, but I run it through Translate anyway. 'King of kings and lord of lords?' The image is vaguely familiar. I search for it online. Tarot. I roll my eyes. It's a tarot card. How did they get my number?

I message my dad: has he got another phone with a different number? Has he been sending me stupid anonymous messages quoting Handel's Messiah, with tarot cards on them? Because it really isn't funny.

I regret asking him immediately. He calls me. I pick up.

'Dad, look , sorry, I – it's probably a scam or something, I'm sorry.'

'Are you alright, George? You sound tired,' he, however, sounds genuinely worried.

'Yes, I'm fine, I just thought that you were playing a trick on me. You know, after all that stuff about Hawksmoor and the churches...'

'No. And I certainly wouldn't do it anonymously. Have they said anything threatening? You should contact the police if they have. After all, there are some dangerous people about. And you working on that church, well, we all know how volatile some people can be when it comes to religion.'

I nod 'Yes, I know. It's probably a wrong number. They meant the messages for someone else.' I don't tell him I tried to call it and it didn't exist.

'Block them. That's my advice.'

'I will. I'm doing it now,' I scroll down and click on the block option.

'Good. You do sound tired, George. Get yourself some rest. See you on Sunday!'

'Yes, Dad. I'll message you with the address of the restaurant. See you then.'

He's right. I'm knackered. I'll have a quick supper and get to bed.

It's still dark. I roll over and check my phone. 3.45am. I have another three hours before I have to get up for work. Why did I wake up? I don't need the toilet. My phone alarm is set to wake me, but all other notifications are switched off. The phone screen lights up. I sit up in bed. What the –

There's a message. I pick up my phone and stare at it. It's from another unknown caller. The same message. The same image. I block the number. Almost immediately a different number sends the same message. Angry, I text back:

'What do you want?'

There's a pause of a few seconds. Then a message:

'Saint George'

Just that. I shake my head. What is this? What is going on? I type:

'What do you mean? Who are you?'

The reply is swift:

'Look up'

'Look up what?'

Again, just two words:

'The Steeple'

I try to call the number, but of course, it cuts out.

I don't even bother to get dressed. I pull my coat on over my pyjamas;

shove my phone into the pocket and my feet into my shoes without socks. I ignore the lift; dash along the corridor and down the stairs. I miss the final step, land heavily and my phone flies out of my pocket. I scrabble for it and as I stand up, glance at the reception desk: there's no one there.

Outside everything is still and almost silent. It isn't a busy street anyway and one side of the road is blocked off by scaffolding around the church. My footsteps are loud on the pavement as I walk the few metres from the hotel to the church. The steeple is hidden behind the plastic sheeting that covers the scaffolding.

I punch the code number into the lock on the site door and enter. To the right, there is an intruder alarm. Its red light is motionless. It should be flickering and alternating with a green flash every five seconds. Someone has disabled it.

My phone buzzes. When I dropped it, the notifications must have reactivated.

I remove it from my pocket and see another message:

'Ascend'

It's impossible. There's no signal in here. I activate the torch light on my phone and start to climb the steps up to the scaffolding.

When I reach the top, the air is far from still. I don't suffer with vertigo – you can't fear heights in this job - but I'm feeling dizzy. The wind is buffeting the plastic sheeting and rippling it like waves on the sea. At the end of the platform there's a shape: A figure. There is definitely someone there. They shouldn't be. I call out to them: 'Come down and we can talk about this.'

I'm still trying to work out how they got in. How they switched off the alarm. They turn a corner and they're gone. I follow. On the other side of this platform is the steeple. It's dark, but the light from the moon is sufficient to illuminate the stone structure.

There is an eerie whistling sound as the wind blows through the pipes and the sheeting. It sounds like a distant choir. There he is. At the top of the steeple is a man. The crumbling statue of King George. Is it moving? It must be the light, or the wind blowing the clouds along behind the sculpture. No. It's moving. It's tilting. It's falling towards me. It blocks out the light.

'Mr Raven didn't come down for breakfast and his work colleagues weren't able to get an answer on his phone. Housekeeping had knocked on his door, and when there was no reply, they went in. We're all trained in CPR, but it didn't do any good.'

The paramedics are examining the body:

'You did the right thing, but he's been dead for some time. Have you called the police?'

The receptionist nods. Then a phone buzzes. It's on the table next to the bed. No one touches it. A message flashes on the screen:

'Rex regum et dominus dominantium'

I open my eyes. I'm higher than the rooftops. I can see across the city. But I can't move. I feel heavy, heavy like stone. Below me, far, far below me, I can hear singing. A choir. Handel's Messiah. Lord of Lords. King of Kings. Alleluia! Alleluia!

The Queue

Mark Eklid

The woman struggled to adjust her grip and cursed under her breath. The box was too large and too heavy to hold easily using only one arm, but she needed the other free to reach up and pull down the tailgate door of her black SUV.

The effort of trying to keep a tenuous grasp on the box without dropping it was making closing the door trickier than it should have been. A third attempt proved as unsuccessful as the first two and the door rose on a rush of air as she clawed in vain for a fingertip hold to prevent it going all the way back up. She swore again – out loud this time. This needed a fresh approach. She transferred all her weight on to her left leg, then hitched up her skirt so she could raise her right knee and rest the bottom of the box on her thigh, while wedging her chin down on the top for added security. It made her look like an inelegant support dancer from a UPS-sponsored production of Swan Lake. Balance, though, was an issue and if not for a desperate late outstretched palm to brace herself against the frame of the car, both she and the box might have tumbled into the boot. She wobbled, steadied and, cautiously, reached again to grab the tailgate door before drawing a deep breath and summoning all her strength into one extra-powerful drag downwards. The door finally slammed shut with a satisfying *clunk*.

'Yes!' she hissed through gritted teeth, her lower jaw still fixed against cardboard.

With her free hand, she unclipped the black patent handbag now dangling precariously from her left shoulder and rummaged for the keys to lock the car. After taking a couple of hops so she could stabilise herself against the closed rear door, she found them and pressed thebutton. The car blinked amber lights at her and she dropped the keys back into the bag, relieved to be able to share the burden of the bulky package in both arms and stand on two feet again. Tottering as quickly as she could on kitten heels and in a close-fitting suit skirt, she set off across the supermarket car park towards a row of small shops.

She hoped no-one she knew had been watching and had witnessed her indignity, especially any of the staff at the office where she worked as their section manager. No doubt any one of them would love the chance to entertain the rest with tittle-tattle tales of her struggles with the tail-gate door. Accompanied by video evidence, probably. Enforcing office discipline was hard enough sometimes without having her authority undermined by sniggering behind her back. There were so many kids in the department now, none of them much older than her own, and nobody seemed to teach them respect for superiors these days. Didn't know the meaning of hard work half of them either. With luck, she was far enough away from where they normally hung around at lunchtime to do what she needed to do and escape unseen. She kept her head down and pressed ahead.

The Post Office was the third in the row, between the bakery and the charity shop. The door was open and there were no customers inside. Her luck appeared to be in. But then she noticed the line of people waiting outside. Five of them. None were showing any inclination to move forward to be served at the counter.

'What's going on here?' she asked as she approached the end of the queue.

The female half of the mid-sixties couple who were last in line turned to offer a gentle smile and an explanation.

'They've asked us to wait outside. They're expecting a money drop-off and they said they can't have any customers in the shop when the security man arrives.'

'Health and safety, I suppose,' said the male half. 'They said they should only be five or ten minutes. Mind you, that was probably five or ten minutes ago.'

The female half forced another sad smile and added a what-can-you-do shrug for good measure.

The woman, breathing heavily from the exertion of her trot across the car park under the weight of the box, stared forlornly into the empty Post Office like a flustered commuter watching the last train pull away from the platform.

'But I've got this parcel to post. It's got to go off today.'

Her words met nothing but unsympathetic silence. Even the mid-sixties couple turned their backs to resume their patient vigil.

'And I've got to be back at work in ten minutes.'

Did no-one appreciate her predicament? A rising tide of indignation added more redness to her already flushed cheeks.

'This is ridiculous!'

A tall thin man poked his bald head beyond the threshold of the Post Office door.

'Sorry about this, folks. Thank you for your patience.' His audience of six looked towards him, anticipating news of progress. 'The van is on its way and once they're here, it should only be five or ten more minutes while we put the money away in the safe, then we can let you come back in.'

Update delivered, he was about to shrink back inside when the parcel woman caught his attention.

'Excuse me.'

He checked to see who in the queue had called out.

'Yes?'

'Could I just nip in before the van arrives to sort out my parcel? It won't take a minute.'

The man shook his head.

'I'm sorry. It's security procedure.'

'But it's got to go off today and I need to be back at work in less than ten minutes.'

'I'm sorry,' he replied, grimly.

'This is ridiculous!' She abandoned her attempt to appeal for compassion. It was clearly a wasted effort. 'The last time I came here you were closed for lunch. What kind of a way is this to run a business? You're supposed to be a public service.'

The man stared back impassively, then pointedly glanced down the line at the other members of the queue and said: 'Thank you again for your patience' before retreating back inside.

An elderly black man with a walking stick hobbled in short steps towards them.

'Is this a queue?' he asked, rather unnecessarily.

Parcel woman ignored him, too cross to enter polite conversation.

'They've asked us to wait outside because they're expecting a money drop-off and they can't have anybody inside when the security man arrives,' explained the female half of the mid-sixties couple again.

'The man's just told us it'll be five or ten minutes,' added the male half again. 'Another five or ten minutes.' He rolled his eyes.

'Ridiculous!' muttered parcel woman again.

'Oh, I see,' walking stick man chuckled. 'As long as they've got enough money left for me!'

He shuffled to the end of the queue.

'Not good enough.' Parcel woman was still stewing in the unfairness of it all. 'Don't they realise some of us have jobs to get back to?'

The box was making her arms ache and though she was reluctant to allow what might be construed as an acceptance of her fate, she put it down. She glanced at her watch and sighed.

Come on! How much longer is this going to take?

She leaned to her right to have a look down the line, trying to assess how long the wait might be once the Post Office staff did finally deign to allow customers back inside.

It was hard to tell. None of the first three in the queue appeared to have anything on them as obvious as a parcel to post. They might only be waiting to buy a book of stamps. Quick and easy and off you go. Or they could have a passport to renew and needed help filling in the forms correctly. Or they could be expecting to sort out a year's worth of complicated financial transactions, with the process made even more excruciatingly drawn out by having to communicate each instruction through a thick slab of counter screen glass. That would be just her luck.

At least the couple in front of her were easier to judge. The male half was carrying a shopping bag. She peeked inside it. Four brown A3-size envelopes.

'Is that all you need to do?' she asked.

The female half turned. 'Sorry?'

Parcel woman nodded towards the shopping bag. 'Is that all you have to sort out at the Post Office today?'

'Oh, I see,' came the reply. 'Yes. That's all.'

That was something. Four ordinary envelopes shouldn't take too long, especially if they had identical contents. Weigh one, pay for four, done.

'Would you like to go before us?' added the female half. 'It sounds like you're in a bit of a rush.'

'Are you sure?' parcel woman felt obliged to ask, while moving quickly to pick up the box to make it obvious a change of mind would not be acceptable.

'Of course!'

'No problem,' confirmed the male half.

'So good of you,' said parcel woman, bustling forward to take their place.

Only three more in front of her now. Perhaps they, too, would be sympathetic to her situation.

Immediately ahead was a scrawny young woman, hunched with her head bowed beneath the canopy of a scruffy pink hoodie, her hands buried deep into its pouch. Parcel woman looked the girl up and down and decided whatever she was waiting for was not urgent. Probably collecting her benefits or something.

'Excuse me.'

No response. Parcel woman bent lower to try to force eye contact.

'Excuse me.'

Startled blue eyes stared back at her through the strands of a long dyed-blonde fringe.

Parcel woman attempted a friendly smile.

Hoodie girl hurriedly reached with her right hand to pluck out an earbud.

'Would you mind if I went ahead of you in the queue, please lovie? I've got to get back to work, you see. If that's all right.' Another smile to seal the deal.

Hoodie girl sighed. 'Whatever,' she mumbled and stepped aside, slipping back into her own world by replacing the earbud.

This was excellent progress. Only two more ahead now. Hopes of making it all the way to the front were rising.

The next obstacle was a South Asian woman. In her fifties, maybe. She wore a black coat over the flowing green material of a sari and her head was covered by a purple hijab.

Parcel woman took a moment to consider her approach. A cross-culture exchange such as this might have to be handled more delicately.

She stepped alongside the woman. 'Hello?' she mouthed with exaggerated lip movement, sounding like someone calling into a darkened room because they were not sure if a dangerous stranger was lurking in one of the corners.

The South Asian woman looked back at her, curiously.

'Can I push in front of you, please, dear? I've got this parcel to post, you see, and I have to be back to work in five minutes, so it would be really nice of you if you could let me take your turn in the queue. Is that OK?'

Her head tilted into an expression as condescending as her manner. The South Asian woman shook her head – not in refusal, but to signal she did not understand.

Parcel woman retreated with a sour pout.

'Wonderful. Doesn't even speak English,' she said, making no attempt to hush her words.

The setback demanded a change of tack. She could not impress the urgency of her situation on the next person in the queue, but perhaps she could go straight to the man at the front and get his permission to move up. The South Asian woman would surely not be able to object to that. She'd probably just accept that's the way we do things here.

She stepped up to the shoulder of a lean, tall man in his early thirties. He wore a faded dark blue sweatshirt over black jeans that hung loosely off his slim hips. Long dark hair poked beneath a black beanie hat and the sallow features of his face melted into a jawline covered in not quite stubble, not quite beard.

'Could I...'

'Save your breath,' he cut in with a flash of angry dark eyes.

'Pardon me?' The instant rebuttal startled her.

'Don't even think about asking me to let you in. The answer's no.'

Parcel woman was momentarily silenced. But only momentarily.

'Well, that's not very nice. I only...'

'I know. I heard you. You've got a parcel. You've got to get back to work. Your time is more valuable than everybody else's in this queue. Well, tough. None of us want to be waiting out here, but you show up thinking you're more important than the rest of us and we should step aside to let you go first. Is that it? You know what? If you'd gone about asking in the right way – shown a little respect, a bit of humility – I wouldn't have had a problem with that. I'd have said fair enough, go to the front. But you know why I'm not going to let you ahead of me? It's because you're rude and you're arrogant. What's more, I've decided I don't like you, so you can forget it. Get back and wait your turn.'

Beanie man stared ahead again. Parcel woman felt her ears burn in chagrined fury, but she did not respond. She quietly took a half-step back.

'Not there,' barked beanie man without turning. 'This lady was ahead of you.'

Parcel woman slinked back to third place in the line, seething with embarrassment.

'No need for that kind of attitude,' she fumed, setting down the parcel. 'I was only making a perfectly reasonable request. That's all. And he says *I'm* the rude one!'

Beanie man did not rise to the bait. Quiet fell on the queue, but then all seven of its members stirred at the sight of a bright red security van pulling into a vacant parking space ten yards away.

'Here he is, at last!' chirped the male half of the mid-sixties couple.

'About time,' sniffed parcel woman. She glanced at her watch. Another five or ten minutes meant she would certainly be late back to work, but as long as both counters in the Post Office were open and at least one of the two in front of her didn't take too long the delay might not be so bad. Within acceptable boundaries. She would most likely get back to her desk without her immediate boss even noticing and, if anybody did object, she could make up an excuse about the traffic being bad. Having waited this long, she decided she might as well see it through the rest of the way.

The South Asian woman in front of her started waving to someone making their way towards them down the row of small shops. Parcel woman peered to see who she was waving to. It was another South Asian woman, dressed similarly and maybe a few years older. The two exchanged a few words in their native language as the gap between them closed and the new arrival stopped. But this was no chance meeting between acquaintances followed by a brief catch-up chat before each went about their separate business. The new arrival wasn't about to move on. She was standing. In the queue. Waiting. Ahead of parcel woman.

'Woah! Hang on!' she said as the realisation dawned and her sense of injustice was aroused. 'This is not right!'

She stepped forward to confront the two women.

'I'm sorry, love, but this is a queue. Some of us have been waiting here patiently for a long time. You can't just butt in like that.'

The two turned to each other with puzzled looks, not knowing exactly what was being said to them, but disturbed by the apparent grievance of this strange, angry woman.

'You're going to have to go to the end of the line. We don't allow queue-jumping in this country.'

'She was here earlier,' said beanie man, with barely-hidden contempt and without turning to face them.

'What?'

'I said...' He shuffled slowly around to deliver his explanation. 'She was there before you got here. She went away for a few minutes and now she's back. Her friend held her place in the queue.'

'Well, that's no good,' grumbled parcel woman, not prepared to concede the point. 'Where did she go?'

'How should I know?' said beanie man with distain. 'That's none of my business. Or yours. This lady was in the queue before you. She went to sort out something else for a minute or two and now she's back. End of story. So get back to your place and wait your turn.'

He scowled at parcel woman, compelling her to back down. But she would not. Not this time.

'She gave up her place and now she has to go to the back of the queue. That's the way it works. You don't just get to come and go as you like.'

She grabbed the arm of the new arrival, who yelped in alarm. So did her friend. Parcel woman began trying to drag the new arrival away.

'Come on! Move it! Back of the queue!'

New arrival screamed. The mid-sixties couple gasped. Even hoodie girl looked up. Beanie man moved to intervene.

'What is wrong with you?' he growled as he attempted to prise the two-handed grasp of parcel woman off the arm of the new arrival, who screamed again. Parcel woman would not let go, digging her fingers deeper into the dark material of the coat sleeve. South Asian woman threw her arms around the shoulders of her friend to try to protect her. They both screamed.

'Let – her – go!' commanded beanie man as parcel woman, consumed by righteous anger, clung on for all she was worth.

Finally, the grip was broken. Parcel woman, having committed all her strength to the struggle, stumbled back, out of control. Her right arm, the first to give up its hold on new arrival's arm, flailed as she spun around and struck hoodie girl in the chest, knocking the tiny figure backwards against the large Post Office front window with a thud. The window shook but did not crack. Hoodie girl threw out both arms to try to break her fall. From under her pink top, something heavy dropped to the pavement.

No-one moved for a second. The disorientating flurry of activity left everyone needing to catch a breath. But then all eyes turned to the object that had fallen from beneath hoodie girl's top. Small. Black. Metal. Unmistakable.

'Jesus! It's a gun!' yelped the male half of the mid-sixties couple.

Hoodie girl pounced on the weapon. Ten yards away, a security guard wearing hefty body armour and carrying a sturdy black case, was just about to slide the rear door of the Post Office van back into place when the word 'gun' permeated his visored helmet and sparked him into a rapid change of plan.

'Abort! Abort!' he called to the driver as he jumped back into the protective safety of the red van.

'No!' moaned hoodie girl. She never intended to take on a whole security team. The plan was to point the gun at the counter staff to scare them into handing over the money she needed to pay off her mum's debt to the loan sharks. That's all. The debt was overdue. The lenders were threatening to get nasty. The situation was desperate. But then, when she arrived to do the deed, the staff said more money was on its way and she got greedy. More money meant they really could break the cycle. Get away from here. But now she was exposed. Her cover was blown.

She panicked. Raising the gun in both hands, she squeezed the trigger and a bullet pinged as it ricocheted off the roof of the security van. The unexpected recoil caught her off-balance and rocked her frail body back towards the shop window. As she fell, her finger unintentionally tightened on the trigger again, releasing another shot. An old man who had stopped to watch the commotion on his way back to his car from the supermarket, felt the force of this bullet hit his shoulder with a jarring blow which spun him off his feet, scattering the contents of his shopping bag as he fell.

Hoodie girl, her back pressed against the glass of the window with her hands still gripping the gun, gazed in wide-eyed horror at the pandemonium ahead of her as the security van sped away and terrified shoppers dived shrieking for cover. It was like she was trapped in a video game.

She didn't see beanie man come at her from her left but felt the impact of his considerably larger frame as it collided with hers and knocked her tumbling sideways. Before her tense body relinquished its hold on the gun, she inadvertently fired off another shot.

Less than a yard away, the bullet bit into the shin of the person next in the queue, spitting blood and fragments of splintered bone on to the cracked paving stones. Parcel woman crumpled to the ground. As her initial shock gave way to stark realisation and searing pain, she gawped at the exposed mess of raw flesh, her lower leg buckled at an unnatural angle just above the ankle, and let fly a piercing howl from the depth of her soul.

'Call the police! Call an ambulance!' shouted beanie man as he tried to make himself heard. Hoodie girl was pinned face down to the ground beneath him; silent, numbed and pacified.

Close to the stricken figure of a woman in unimaginable agony beside them, a trickle of blood began to pool against the shiny buff tape wrapped around an unposted parcel.

Winged Messenger

Jasmina Svenne

I nearly leave it there for someone else to find. I don't want any trouble, not now there's a chance I might get the children to safety.

And then the pigeon in the wicker basket begins to croon, a rich, vibrating sound with the warmth of feathers and sunshine, conjuring memories of the dusty air, the rustle of wings, the underlying smell of ammonia in Papa's pigeon loft when I was little.

My hands are stiff with cold, my gloves more darns than original wool. I fumble to unfasten the basket from the miniature parachute that slowed its descent from the balloon that brought it across no-man's land to the edge of the Forest of Mormal.

Silk. Real silk. Imagine what I could do with that. Or maybe I could barter it for some fresh vegetables or a rabbit to make stew for the children. Yes, that would be better. If Madeleine suddenly started wearing a silk dress on Sundays, questions would be asked.

Folding it tight, I tuck it behind my threadbare coat, undoing only two buttons to allow as little warmth as possible to escape. Then, and only then, I lift a corner of the lid of the basket, reaching in to grasp the soft bundle of feathers.

A dulled black eye gazes at me reproachfully. A ray of dying sunlight catches its pink and grey plumage. Beneath my fingers, I can feel the throbbing of a frantic heart. And round its leg, there is a ring.

I've heard whispers about homing pigeons being sent across the front line by the Allies. The Germans, in their turn, have let it be known that anyone, even a child in its teens, caught harbouring an illicit pigeon will be shot.

I can feel how plump the bird is beneath its down, though there's no seed left in its basket. Georges's large, reproachful eyes in his too-thin face haunt me; Madeleine's scrawny limbs, grown scarcely at all since war broke out almost three years ago.

I could wring its neck. Nobody would know. Dead, it would be much easier to hide, in my pocket or among my firewood. I could pluck it and use the feathers to plump the one flattened pillow the Germans have left us. The children would feast like kings tonight.

For me, it would be enough to sniff the savoury aroma of cooked meat; to watch their faces alight with enjoyment; to know that, for once, their bellies will be full when they go to bed, instead of rumbling and grumbling and keeping them awake. And the bones would add flavour to tomorrow's soup and the memory of it would warm and sustain us, for a little while.

As for the leg ring, that I would dispose of somewhere far from home and the note, which must be attached behind the ring, would go into the stove to light the fire to cook the meat...

The pigeon tilts its head, looking at me first with one eye, then the other. It utters an experimental coo. I cannot afford to be sentimental. The permits for us to join the evacuation train to free France might arrive any day – if they don't find some excuse to keep me behind.

And yet I have to fight memories of Papa's birds, the way he taught me to handle them, the way they would land on our shoulders or peck around our feet, even eat from our palms.

Papa, who would suck thoughtfully on the end of his greying moustache and never say very much, in contrast to Maman. Papa, who always came home with some small treat when Maman was upset, even if it was only a new ribbon or a piece of gingerbread.

Papa, who died during this last merciless winter, wheezing for breath, shivering fully clothed under our single blanket because the Boche had requisitioned everything else and we had no fuel for the stove. Papa, who never openly defied the Germans, but nonetheless silently disobeyed their rules whenever he could, going out after curfew to the forest with his snares and returning only when he had a rabbit or a game bird for the pot.

And what about Armand? What would he say if I were to destroy this bird, when perhaps I could save it and send it back across the lines with some small fragment of information that might help to shorten the war and bring Armand back home to us?

Assuming that Armand is still alive. Three years, no, not quite that. He was mobilised in August 1914 and it's now March 1917. I try to count the months, but my mind is dull with exhaustion and starvation. Would he even recognise me if he came back now? My hair has thinned, my face fallen in, the bones too prominent in my cheeks and forehead and wrists.

The light is fading fast. I can't afford to loiter any longer. There are others in the forest, taking advantage of German permission to gather fuel, any one of whom could turn traitor in the hopes of a reward or to deflect suspicion from their own illegal activities.

I can't take the basket with me. It's too obvious. Instead I do my best to shove it deep within an entanglement of brambles. Its barbs penetrate my glove, no doubt leaving long streaks of bubbling blood on my right hand, as I clutch the bird with my left.

I tuck the pigeon inside my coat, wedging it between my flattened breast and my upper arm. Keeping to the shadows, I turn for home, stopping only when I am almost within sight of town to make sure I have my *carte d'identité* at hand, in case the sentries ask for it.

I hurry to catch up with a group ahead of me, hoping for safety in numbers. But fortunately the sentries are bored and cold, uninterested in any of the grey-faced people that pass them. When the bird begins to croon, I feign a cough and then cannot stop. The sentries back off, afraid of infection, and wave me on.

It's this cough that might save me, if the medical officer diagnoses it as the early stages of tuberculosis. If the permits are granted, we could go to free France, to Montpellier, perhaps, or Nice. Somewhere warm. Somewhere where food is, if not plentiful, at least adequate. Somewhere where we won't be dependent on American rations of bread and rice and condensed milk for the children and never anything fresh.

The streets are emptying. Curfew can't be far off. I can't afford to be stopped. I can feel the bird beginning to slip and grow restless, my heart speeding up to match its faster heartbeat.

Mustering the last of my strength, I totter down the narrow alley, letting myself in through the street door. Only then do I dare set down the firewood, unfasten one button of my coat and slip my free hand inside to readjust the pigeon.

But still I have to beware. Even neighbours I've known for years might betray me. Nothing is safe any more.

As if to echo my thoughts, I hear the boom of a shell. The cannonade must have been going on for a while, but we've grown so used to it, since the Boche pulled back to the Hindenburg Line, that we only notice if it's louder or closer than usual.

Maman turns sharply as I slide in through the door.

'Where have you been, *hein*? Cutting it fine as always. The children were convinced you wouldn't be back by curfew. I suppose you would have expected me to take care of them, a poor widow at my time of life, while you explain yourself at the Commandanture...'

'I'm sorry, Maman,' I say, as I unwind my scarf, but she carries on regardless.

'...as if I didn't have enough to do to keep this household running... *Mon Dieu*, what have you done?'

I look up and see where her gaze has strayed. The pigeon has poked its head out from behind my coat collar and is examining its surroundings. Maman lifts her hand to her mouth and she and I both shush the children when they exclaim.

'Where did you get that – thing?' Maman drops her voice to an agitated whisper. 'Are you trying to kill us all? What will happen to the children if you and I are hauled off to prison to be shot?'

Her last words have a paralysing effect on the children.

'Maman?' Madeleine whispers, her eyes wide. 'They wouldn't – not for a –'

'Shush, Madeleine, it's all right,' I say, though unease gnaws inside me like hunger. 'Nothing will happen to us. I don't intend to keep it long. But you mustn't say anything to anyone, you understand? You too, Georges. Not even to your best friend as the most secret of secrets. Because then something bad might happen.'

Their scared expressions make my heart bleed. I don't want to frighten them. But sometimes it's necessary, to keep them safe.

Despite my mother's disapproval, I ask Madeleine to scoop some water into a saucer and set it on the floor. For lack of grain, I tell Georges to crumble up a black crust of bread.

I'm afraid as I set down the bird beside the food that it might take flight and the beating of wings will alert our neighbours. But perhaps it's too exhausted after its ordeal. After a few cautious sips of water, watching us all the while, it retreats into the niche behind the stove.

Though I warn the children to keep their distance – and they do – they remain fascinated by the bird, constantly checking to make sure it's still in its hiding place.

Candles are a precious commodity. Maman and I go to bed at the same time as the children, huddling tight in the only bed that has not been requisitioned. I tell them stories about their grandfather and the pigeons he kept, each named after a legendary figure – Achille, Hercule, Andromaque – until at last they sleep.

Then, and only then, I hear a soft rustle of feathers, the patter of hooked toes, the tock-tock-tock of a curved beak against the floorboards, pecking at the crumbs.

I take the children with me when I go to queue for our rations. Maman protests that I'm mad and they will both catch colds, but it means I can stop quite openly near the railway station, watching the embarkation of Germans troops, counting carriages, memorising insignia. Watching with Georges and assuring him that – all being well – we will be getting on a similar train too, soon, while Madeleine rolls a pebble under her toe, tugs at my skirts and tries to persuade me that we ought to go.

After we return to our room with our meagre gleanings, I print out the information I have gathered in the tiniest letters I can manage, while the children feed the pigeon again and Maman grumbles about having to clean up its mess.

As I tuck the note behind its leg ring, Georges tugs my sleeve.

'Can't we keep it?' he whispers.

He gazes at me with his grandfather's brown eyes.

I shake my head.

'Maybe after the war, we can keep pigeons, like Grandpapa,' I say. 'Now, why don't you and Madeleine open the window and check if anyone is about?'

I intended originally to take the bird out of town, into the forest, and release it there, but Maman hissed at me about taking unnecessary risks.

'If no one is in the street, nobody will know which house or which window the bird came from,' she said.

Still I have my doubts. The bird's eyes are not as bright as I would like. I'm not sure it has the strength to make the journey. But the risk of keeping it is too great. At least when it's free, it can search for its own food; rest when it needs to.

I crouch by the window between the children and peer left and right. The narrowness of the alley is an advantage. German patrols rarely venture here, unless to requisition some commodity we no longer have – iron, brass, candles, cheese, wine, blankets...

But there are numerous windows, in any one of which there might be a face, just far enough back to be out of sight. If anyone were to denounce me, I would never be sure who it was.

'Take our love to Papa,' Madeleine whispers, and Georges obediently echoes her, though I'm not sure he remembers Armand any more.

Once more I feel the rumble of a tiny heartbeat between my palms, its life dependent on me. And then I let go.

For an instant, I'm afraid it will plummet to the ground. Then its wings unfurl and beat, wafting air in our faces, carrying the plump body up, up, above the tiled roof of the house opposite. Away, away, to where my husband might be. If he is still alive. And where we might soon go. If the permits are granted.

The Promise

Moira Hodgkinson

Marsha cursed the warm weather, the faulty air-conditioning, the long-sleeved hoodie she couldn't shake off, and she cursed her best friend. Lucky Becky, in a crop top and shorts. They were in the big Sainsbury's across town. Marsha's budget used to stretch as far as the Lidl down the road, but Becky paid for the groceries now, so Marsha went along with it.

A toddler wailed in an adjacent aisle and the sound bulldozed its way into Marsha's eardrums with a sensation just below the pain threshold. Couples debated the merits of frozen pizza or fresh, and staff stacked brightly coloured vegetables onto racks. Glossy red peppers, orange carrots, knobbles of purple broccoli, a potato that slid to the bottom of the sloping display as Marsha's eyes skirted over the pile. She licked her lips, relishing the vibrancy of the supermarket; the people, the life, and the music that muffled out Becky's droning voice. Becky, the continual presence in her life, buzzing and fussing like an annoying fly she wanted to swat away. She had swatted her once, but it hadn't helped. She wouldn't normally make friends with someone like Becky, someone that brash, loud, and manic, but by the end of their first term at uni, they'd been inseparable. Sharing gossip, swapping clothes, holding back each other's hair at the toilet-clutching tail-end of drunken nights, trading secrets and making promises with pinky-swears.

'I love summer.' Becky's excitement bubbled out in grating tones over the background hubbub of shoppers. 'Pretty dresses, cold cider on a hot afternoon.'

Give me strength. Marsha tuned into the Britney Spears song blaring from speakers in the false ceiling overhead.

'That woman up there's unpacking a box of Pimm's. Are we getting Pimm's today?'

Marsha closed her eyes for a second and gritted her teeth.

'I might get some Pimm's. What do you think? Yeah, good idea.' 'Okay.' said Marsha. 'Fine.'

She followed Becky to Wines and Spirits and two bottles of Pimm's were added to the packets of frozen foods that Marsha despised. An orange and red banner suspended overhead wafted and swung in a frenzy, as though knocked off-kilter by an invisible hand.

Marsha had always had an aversion to the blandness of frozen food and missed the aroma of citrus fruit as the peel burst its tiny spots to spray scented oil, avocado on toast, the texture of bloody steaks. But Becky was paying for this crap, so Marsha could hardly complain.

She traipsed after Becky to the checkouts where they queued behind a woman wearing a yellow dress and a green beret. A beret, of all things. In this heat. Marsha was tempted to knock it off her head.

'Christ, there's enough food in there to feed an army.' Becky said.

Beret Lady turned and glared at Becky, who grinned back at the woman. That was one downside of staying with Becky. Every day brought some fresh hell of verbal outbursts in public places. She wished she'd never made the promise. Sometimes, she even wished she'd never met her best friend. Crazy, insane, inane, and beautiful though she was.

With two years of nights out and giggles and mani-pedis behind them, Marsha made the obvious choice to stay with Becky last summer after the accident. She'd promised, and besides, she didn't have many options. She'd tuned in to late night conversations when Becky's friends came over, watched 1980s horror movies, and random objects appeared in odd places. A decapitated doll's head sitting between yoghurts and milk in the fridge, plastic spiders left in mugs. Lately, though, Becky's relentless narrative felt like a cheese grater paring away her nerve endings, grinding her down strip by strip, down to the end of a white line that inched closer with each passing day.

Aqua's Barbie Girl belched out of the speakers and Becky sang along, getting into the spirit of early summer madness and the promise of warm evenings ahead spent watching lads in nightclubs stripping off their T-shirts, beers in hand.

'Do you mind? The woman hissed at Becky.

'Sorry, love this song.' Becky muttered.

The woman stared at her, venom in her eyes, then, with a shrug, continued to place items on the conveyor belt.

Marsha grimaced. She could have melted into the tiled floor and sunk to the depths below, but Becky didn't care. She'd never been afraid of saying anything that came into her head, no matter who was listening or who she was with, even on her own, that's just the way she was.

'Remember when we went to Liv Dawson's for that party in June, and you got so drunk on Pimm's that you threw up in the sink? Before the barbecue? Sorry, I shouldn't have mentioned that.'

This, again. Marsha screwed her eyes up at the memory. The drunken dancing, bottles of cheap cider passed around in an endless supply, illicit roll-ups and setting the barbecue on fire. Then the sirens and soot and ash. The traumatised Dawsons hadn't taken long to up sticks and build a new life in Luton to heal, far away from painful memories. Then came the funeral with everyone sobbing in snotty wails as a red velvet curtain closed and the coffin disappeared. The bereaved had headed back to the house of the dead young woman for the inevitable buffet of beige food, damp tissues and tearful reminiscences. Marsha had sat next to Becky, a plate of uneaten food between them.

Then Liv's mum had scowled across at Becky and she'd fled in flurry of tears, Marsha trailing in her wake.

'It was an accident.' Marsha said now.

'I'm going to play Guess Who's a Serial Killer.'

The beret lady gave a sigh that was meant to be heard and slammed a loaf of bread on the conveyor and a paper bag ripped open, spilling tomatoes on the conveyor. Red and ripe and juicy.

'Guy over there,' Becky lowered her voice. 'In the Atari t-shirt. Pale and spotty from spending all day in front of a computer. I bet he's one of those blokes who stands in the corner at parties and gets ignored. If he's ever invited to parties, that is.'

'Will you shut up for once?' The words tumbled out in a low hiss.

Wanting to apologise, to appease Becky, to smash her over the head with a bottle of summertime alcohol, Marsha turned to eye up the nerd. She had to admit, he did look like he could be a serial killer. She tuned into fragments of conversation between the beret woman and the checkout worker, desperate to fill her head with some other noise than Becky's rambling.

'That's a hundred and seventy-eight ...'

'Here, just take it.' The woman thrust a credit card at him. 'I need to get out of here.'

'You need to use your PIN.'

Huffing, the woman bent over the card reader to do so. When she straightened up, the beret came off her head, hair flying. With a shocked squeak, the woman grabbed it and shoved it into a bag. She walked off swiftly, sparing a backward glance full of something that could be either concern or disgust. That was nothing compared to how Marsha was feeling right now. She had to tell Becky it was time to move on. Her guts twisted with cramps at the thought of it.

Becky put her shopping into freezer drawers rammed with frost, then took a packet of cornflakes from a cupboard and dumped them into a bowl with milk. No surprises in the fridge today. Marsha was losing her touch. She sat in the lounge with the cereal and turned the television on to watch an old episode of Most Haunted.

'Are you watching this, Marsh?'

No answer, only screaming from the television. She thought of the two bottles in the fridge and her insides grew cold. She'd never drink it all on her own.

'I'm going to give everyone a ring. Jack, Duff, Liv. See if they want to come over tonight. That's okay with you, isn't it? Marsha?'

Grabbing her mobile from the coffee table, Becky rattled off a series of texts and went back to her cereal. The light bulb overhead began swinging and Becky jumped up from the sofa, grinning and punching the air.

'Yes! Yes, I knew it! You're still here. I bloody knew it.' Becky grasped her hands together to stop them shaking. 'You haven't done anything for ages, I thought you'd, you know, moved on.'

Her mobile beeped with a text and Becky scanned the screen. 'Shit, Liv can't make it. She doesn't want a two-hour drive after physio.'

Poor Liv. The cereal bowl tumbled to the floor with a clatter, splashes of milk flooding onto the carpet.

'Someone's feeling guilty.' Becky said. She dabbed at the spill with kitchen roll, eyes peeled, skin tingling with static electricity like spiders crawling over her flesh as she waited for something else to happen. 'It wasn't your fault, Marsha. We did it together, the three of us. Liv was just unlucky.'

Becky and Marsha and Liv, on that long summer's night. Drunk and delirious and high. Marsha taking charge of lighting the barbecue with lighter fluid, Liv sending her flying as she stumbled, the whole thing collapsing as they fell forward onto it. Nobody realised how badly Liv had been burned until Marsha had been declared dead at the scene.

'Sorry,' Becky said now, 'I know you were unlucky too. Try and talk to me again, Marsha. Please?'

She bent in front of the television and focused on the screen, willing the ghost-busting documentary to make way for Marsha's spectral voice.'Come on. I'm waiting, Marsha.'

With an audible pop, the screen went black. 'No, no.' Becky shook the TV, pressed the buttons. She hurled the remote control across the room and it clattered off the wall. She screamed in a rage that came out of nowhere.

'No, you can't disappear on me. We made a pact. Talk to me, bitch!' Becky stood and stared at the blank screen, fire in her eyes. 'I know you're still hanging around, Marsha. I saw that sign swinging over the drinks' aisle today, and that woman's hat went flying off her head like she'd just been slapped. You did that, you did. I know you did.'

She wound her fingers around clumps of her hair and pulled at it, strands coming loose with a pinch at her scalp. Staring at the TV, sitting in tense anticipation for seconds, minutes, hours, she lost track in the silent and unmoving air until she gave up. Resigning herself to playing on her phone and swapping texts with friends, Becky was lost without Marsha. Lost. She filled the void by talking to herself, hoping somebody, somewhere, might hear.

'I bet that nerd guy isn't a serial killer. I bet he's an undercover agent and he works for - '

Noise, buzzing and humming, coming from the radio.

'That potato was me, shampoo, and the tomato bag that ripped.'

'Marsha!' Becky wiped her face and her hand came away lined with damp smears of eyeliner and tears. 'Don't keep disappearing like that, I can't stand it.'

'It's hard, Beckster, so hard.' Marsha's voice echoed, grainy and faint. 'I can't do it anymore.'

'Yes, you can.' Becky crooned. She picked up the radio and cradled it, caressing and stroking the plastic casing. 'You promised, remember?'

The voice in the radio static was broken and stilted. 'You have to ... let me go ... love you.'

'No, Marsha, don't leave me. Please. We promised, you promised me, Marsha. I can't do this without you. I miss you.'

A stream of garbled words came from the radio that she couldn't make out and Becky's ponytail jerked up and down at the tug of a phantom hand. A box of tissues slid in increments across the table and

Becky took one, sniffing with loud tears.

'You promised.'

Best friends for life. Besties beyond the grave, they'd sworn. Whoever dies first would come back and haunt the other. It would be a laugh. Moving things around the house, pulling faces at people, making objects float by themselves.

'I never even know if you're here,' Becky whispered, 'it's sad and pathetic and I miss you.'

'Be happy, Becks.'

The radio fell silent and with it, the voice of the dead. Becky felt it in her bones and in the absence of the eerie otherness that had masked her hideous grief.

The Irizinium Priestess

Moira Hodgkinson

Lace and velvet, glittering jewels, fine draperies and the soft amber glow of thirteen candles adorned the boudoir where Lady Solivante prepared herself.

She perfumed and polished herself, glued long lashes to accentuate crimson eyes, pinned up the silver and copper tresses of her curling hair and let her aides fasten the laces in the back of her corset. Her gilt-tinged arms had become stiff these last few decades and she had long given up trying to reach behind her back to wrestle with the ties. How much longer could she go on like this? Unable even to tie her own laces, she grimaced at the thought of the bleak future ahead. She examined her reflection in a bronzed mirror. Tall and elegant, sparkling. Perfect. The corset would come off again soon enough, but she insisted on looking the part. Her clients paid through the nose for this experience and Lady Solivante took pains to make sure they would never forget how glorious she had been.

'I'm ready.' she said, though with no trace of eagerness. Martin and Monrose withdrew with a bow. She didn't know if they were brothers or lovers and had never enquired; she was just grateful and content they had remained her faithful servants over the long years.

After a few moments, the door opened and her guest walked in, still holding a glass of chilled champagne he had been given on arrival.

She smiled at him and ran her bronzed fingernails against layers of satin and taffeta to hitch her skirts up, giving a hint of shining ankles. Eric Calvanito, the son of a Kra'alin merchant, looked terrified. His eyes widened as they fastened on her ankles and she feared he would crush the glass, so tense he seemed.

'Don't be afraid.' Lady Solivante whispered. 'This is what you paid for, after all. To experience my - difference.'

The Calvanito family credentials were impressive and their wealth considerable, as her high fee demanded, but more importantly, the young man had been judged suitable for her in his manner and temperament. Martin and Monrose were protective of their mistress, and thorough in that respect. She would never think to question their guidance and so far, Eric lived up to expectations - a perfectly mannered, if perfectly intimidated, young gentleman. Though really, she reflected, he was barely out of boyhood. She'd no doubt be free a little sooner this evening than usual.

Lady Solivante unfastened a button at her waist and the voluminous skirts fell to the ground to reveal her legs. Eric made a sound that, though barely audible, she had heard countless times before. She smiled and giggled, raised her eyebrows and cocked her head to one side. Curling a taloned nail towards him, she beckoned. Even that curving of her finger was slow and awkward, like moving through the deep snow of winter. She ought to be enjoying this encounter, it could well be her last, but just as her flesh was being transformed into a cold and lifeless thing, so were her mind and soul. Enjoyment, pleasure, comfort-these things were all but lost to her.

He looked about to speak but instead, the young man's mouth only opened and closed uselessly. He looked at his glass and Lady Solivante gestured towards a side table. He put the glass down and, after an encouraging nod from, her stepped forwards, his keenness evident.

She took his hands into her own to guide him to her corset laces and when the cold, hard surface of her hands touched the warmth and softness of her guest's, Lady Solivante closed her eyes for a brief moment to savour the rich texture of yielding flesh, the scent of his musk and sweat, and with that delicious aroma filling her soul, she shivered.

'Madam?'

She flicked her eyes open at his voice. Had she been holding him too tightly? Every day it was harder to tell, harder to feel. She was in danger of losing sensation completely.

'Go on, dear one.' Being a gentlewoman, and even now at this late stage of her development and transformation considering herself a Priestess, Lady Solivante always took care to be gracious to her clients. Especially those who paid as highly as this one.

Did it matter any longer, she wondered? Their money and sponsorship were worthless to her. No matter how wisely her investors acted on her behalf, the decades of research she financed had come to naught. No amount of coin or treasure could help her now, this condition could not be resolved-her dire fate was sealed.

'Once these are free, we shall have the most marvellous and exciting time.' She ran a hand across the top of her breasts and shivered at the scraping, metallic resonance that ran across her skin like shards of ground glass.

After a few moments of fumbling the corset was discarded, revealing Lady Solivante in all her shining glory. Glistening with pinpricks of light from the candles, her skin glowed with sparkling reflections. Eric let out a gasp of thrilled excitement and wonder at the sight. She nodded at his approval, though little good it did to sooth the regret that writhed below every other thought and emotion. Once revered as the holiest and most high of the Priestesses, she now held barely the status of high-class companion. Desperate to rid herself of these feelings of unsettled disgust at the state of her body, she pulled him close, gathering him into herself as if to devour him completely.

'Touch me.' She whispered, guiding his hands to claw at her breasts and buttocks. She tore at his clothing, sharp fingernails ripping through the cotton ruffles of his shirt and raking into his skin. 'So soft.' She leaned in to smell his odour and regretted the long-ago loss of her own natural scent.

'Are you always this cold?' Eric asked as he found confidence in his excitement.

'Eric, I am cold eternally, but still my flesh will yield to you.'

Lady Solivante let him paw at her, his moist lips giving her metallic skin a thrill of pure pleasure at every point of contact, his warmth lending itself to her, seeping into her gradually. So slowly he would not notice it. Not at first.

'It won't be enough,' she said. It would never be enough.

And perhaps it was time for her to stop trying to make it be enough. The touch of human flesh upon her own was the only sensation she could still feel completely, but it did them no good, her mortal lovers, as her form leeched away at their very life-force.

Her body was almost completely taken over by the living metal spores of the forge where once she had wielded powerful tools and built great sculptures and jewels and buildings and machinery and engines of gold, copper, steel, iron, brass and bronze and silver and titanium, palladium and gelstanium and irizinium. Ah! Sweet irizinium! That living, breathing, flexible metal of her once-home planet. Wretched to her now, that vile substance. What had once been her sole reason for living - oh, the thrill it had given her to be Priestess of that magnificent palace where engineers had held the highest ranks - was now her downfall and would soon be her death.

The young man moaned and she stirred into action, caressing him, returning his touches and clasping him to her roughly as they kissed, smothering one another with fiery passion. She urged him on and the irizinium spores, the now-hated living spores that infected her, parted between her legs and let him enter. An instinctive part of her wanted to close up, not to allow this abomination to happen. If she fed on the iron in his blood, it would leave the man sickly for weeks, perhaps even pass the irizinium infection onto him - it had happened before and killed her guest instantly - but he knew the risk he was taking. Did that make it right? she wondered.

No, Lady Solivante thought, that did not make it right and with this thought her decision was made.

She would not feed on the living energy of this warm-blooded, warm-hearted young man who was paying to experience the wonder of the living metal woman. She would let the irizinium spores take over completely - already they had claimed her legs, her internal organs, chest and arms, even her hair and her eyes, and her power and will to resist it was waning. Let it have me, she thought. I have had enough. Let it be over with.

Two hundred and seventy years of life the infection had given her, a good two hundred more than she had any right to claim. She had roamed the galaxies and funded researchers and engineers and scientists far and wide in search of a counter-measure and had managed only to slow the rate of infection.

'I shall not feed on you.' She said as he pounded in a fevered and frantic rhythm. She wrapped her limbs tightly around him, gripping and crying out against the impulse to seize him in a bloody embrace, fighting the metal-spore urge to sink her nails into his skin, rend it open and gulp down his iron-rich blood in long and greedy draughts.

'I shall not!'

Grunting and panting and coming to his frenzied climax, he said nothing, focused only on this moment of rapture, and with every remaining fibre of her natural body and soul, she fought that urge, the impulse, the desire, the drive, the need, to taste the iron of his vital fluid.

'Let it take me!' Lady Solivante cried out. 'Let it end!'

But still she found the taste of his blood in her mouth and the infectious spores of her once-loved metal, so easy to shape and pleasing to mould, had won out over her humanity again.

Eric, spent and wretched, withdrew himself and reeled as he tried to stand, dizzy and heady with blood loss, climax, and the loss of life energy.

With copper stained tears oozing from deep red eyes, Lady Solivante reached to her bedside stand and chimed a bell to summon her aides.

Martin and Monrose entered the chamber and led the bleeding and dazed young man out of the room and away from their mistress.

Faithful, those two. They would tend to him with care and she knew instinctively that he would not suffer any lasting illness from having his blood taken. She had tasted him and she knew he would survive and thrive.

Lady Solivante rose from her bed, covered with lace, velvet, satin, fur and feathers, luxurious textures laid out to soothe that she could no longer feel, and she picked up her looking glass and gazed at her image.

She drew a finger across her neckline, following the curving line of metallic skin where it had crept up to meet her own skin beneath her chin and the Priestess in her sensed it spreading.

She could no longer rely on the iron of blood to keep at bay the monster of this parasitic metal disease. What was to become of her in the days and weeks and years to come?

Even as she watched, over the course of an hour the bronzing silver of the infection grew and crept unshakably over her face, ripping like razors over her white skin to leave cold, hard metal in its place. The infection took over her cheeks, her brow, her scalp, wormed its icy threads inside her head and in a moment of last movement, she dropped the mirror and rose. And became still and silent. Trapped inside the metal encasement of her diseased body, no longer possessing the will or power to move, only to think.

How much longer will it give me if it no longer receives the bloody offerings of my paying guests? How many more hundreds of years am I to endure this fate, sealed within?

In the grand entrance hall of the Metallurgist Palace stands a beautiful structure, a refined sculpture in the shape of a young woman, perfect in a way no divine hand could hope to mimic. The figure is formed in a silver-bronze metal, with scarlet eyes and coils of silver and iron and copper in place of hair. Standing tall and proud in a pose of strength and pride, one hand stretched out as if to greet a friend. The ghost of a smile on her lips.

Encased in a prison of glass and iron, there is but a single snippet written on the plinth for the visitors who gather to look upon her and stare in wonder.

Lady Arovasta Solivante
High Priestess of the Metallurgist Palace
The Living Priestess of Irizinium
Graceful to the End of Her Days.

Deleon

Mark Jacobs

The next day when I arrived at Beech School, Jim asked me to go to the Year 8 science class to speak to Kathy, a good Scots teacher, to see if I could help with a problem she had with a pupil. Kathy pointed out a black lad sitting at the back. I observed him for a few minutes but there didn't seem a problem so I wandered over slowly, briefly looking at one or two students' work until I came to his desk. He was doodling a picture in his exercise book. I smiled.

'How are you getting on?' I asked, sitting next to him. 'Need any help?' He looked at me.

'I'm okay,' he said.

'Drawing a picture?' He looked away embarrassed.

'Finding it difficult?' I asked. 'Let me help.' Casually taking his exercise book. Apart from rough pictures and doodles there was very little in it of writing or science, and what there was there was not decipherable, or barely.

'Ah,' I said, 'trouble with spelling? Maybe I can help if you'll let me.' He squirmed uncomfortably. As a matter of fact it was instantly clear as the day he was illiterate, couldn't string a sentence together.

'Tell you what,' I said, 'let's take a hike for half an hour. I'll ask Miss if that's okay. Do you want to do that?' He nodded. We walked round the corridor to a vacant office I used sometimes when talking to children. It had an upholstered comfortable bench below a long narrow window and was pleasantly set out. The windows and door were curtained. Apart from that there was little furniture of any kind, which was good because children always look for things to distract themselves rather than talk to an adult.

'So tell me what the problem is, Deleon.'

'I don't understand the work,' he said. He had a bad stutter and I had to wait.

'What, you can't follow the science book or you can't write the answers?'

He squirmed for a moment, looking for that distraction that wasn't there and then looked at me.

'Both, I suppose,' he said, and went back to looking around again.

'Listen, Deleon, I want you to listen to me carefully. Whatever you say to me gets no further than these four walls unless you give me permission to talk to someone else. Also, I'm here to help you, not judge you. Whatever you say is just you and me and nobody else. Do you understand what I'm saying? Just you and me.'

He looked at me, a bit longer this time, then away.

'Okay,' he said.

'So,' I said, 'tell me about yourself. Which school did you go to before?'

'Kingston Primary,' he said.

'Oh, you lived in London?' He laughed.

'No,' he said, 'Kingston Jamaica.'

'Ah! So tell me about that.'

'I was only there a few months.'

So what happened? You came here, to England?'

'Nah,' he replied. 'My uncle took me and my two sisters out of school to live with him on the hill.'

'Oh, but why didn't you go back to school?'

Deleon looked away, frowning, then angry, then uncertain. He glanced up at me again and then down again, thinking.

'You really won't tell anyone what I say?' he asked.

'Promise," I said. 'You can have it in writing, signed if you want.'

He looked thoughtful again, a few moments of silence passed, until he looked up and began telling his story.

'My uncle beat me, every day,' he said, 'and my sisters. Every night he put one of my sisters on his knee, held a gun to her head, and spoke to my mum on the telephone. Every night. Sometimes he would tell my sister to speak to my Mum but she was always crying and he hit her. Then he put me on his knee and hit me on the head so I'd cry. He used to beat me bad with a yard broom. It had a nail in the end and one-time he hooked me under my chin and swung me round the room. Once I came off and went through the window. One of the guards picked me up and took me to my cot and his woman put a plaster on my chin. She wanted to take me to the hospital because I cracked my head bad but he wouldn't allow me.'

He had tears in his eyes and looked away and down to the floor. I was staring at him. I couldn't follow him. What was he saying? Was he making this up? Was it just a confused story? I fell silent, trying to think what to say.

'You don't believe me?' he said.

I shook my head. I didn't know what to think or what to say but he was obviously upset, and that was what was important, not me, so I'd best pursue wherever he was taking me.

'What do you mean, a guard?' I asked.

'There were guards, three or four of them - I don't know how many - but they used to walk round the fence with guns - machine guns. One or two were okay. They didn't bother me and sometimes they looked after me.' His mouth turned downward into a grimace. 'Better than my uncle treated me anyway. I thought he was going to kill one of my sisters one night he got so angry, waving the gun round and shouting on the phone, but he calmed down and started smiling. I was really scared and shouted so afterwards he strapped me bad.'

'Why were there guards?' I asked, still confused, almost unable to take in what he was saying.

'To guard the house.'

'Where was the house?'

'On the green hill outside Kingston. It's a big white house with an electric fence round it with big gates. The guards walk round the fence all day. That's why we couldn't get away.'

'What is your uncle's name, and why was he on the phone to your mother every night?'

'I don't know,' he said. 'He just kept talking about money and bid'ness. His name is Dewey but that's not his real name, it's what everyone calls him.'

I paused. 'So how long have you been here and how did you get here?

'I've been here a year. My grandma got us out, my sisters first and then me, pretending we had to go to a doctor. We went to the airport as soon as we got into Kingston. I flew over in a plane to London.' He stopped, struggling for words for a moment. 'My Mum met me at the station. It was dark. We walked out of the station down the road. There were two men following us and my Mum told me to run so we started running but then she was shot and fell down. I tried to help her up but she was heavy. Then some people were walking towards us and the men ran away. They called the police and she was took to hospital. I haven't seen her since then.'

'Is she all right?'

'Yeah. But I don't know where she is.' He looked down frowning.

'So how did you get here?' I asked.

'Social Services. They took me in for weeks and then brought me here to live with my auntie.'

I still couldn't tell whether what he was saying made any sense, whether any of it was fantasy or all of it. I checked my watch and saw we had been there for an hour and a half. He looked tired and I had other meetings scheduled so I said, 'Okay, let's finish for now - I'll take you back to class and come check on you in a day or two while I think about all this. Is that okay?' He shrugged.

I went straight to see Jim, the Deputy Head.

'Jim, tell me about Deleon, Year 12,' I said.

'Ah,' he said, and pulled a file from his cabinet. 'Strange one that. Came to us less than a year ago. Social services from London brought him in. Let's see.' He riffled through the documents. 'Yes. Haringey. We had a meeting with local police, councillors, social workers and God knows who but it was a bit queer. They really told us nothing, just that his Mum was missing, he was supposed to be staying with a sister and an aunt and they couldn't look after him. And now,' he paused to check, ' he's with his aunt at 12 Melrose Street. Been in a few fights since he's been here, but not disruptive. The other kids call him Ironman.'

'Why Ironman?'

He laughed briefly. 'Because every time they knock him down he stands up again and grins.' He looked at the papers again. 'A couple of other things. He's not disruptive much in lessons but he's backwards educationally and has difficulty keeping up with lessons, doesn't hand in homework, that kind of thing. Gets angry when teachers challenge him about work,' he added. 'That's why we called you in.'

'That's it?'

'That's it.'

I frowned. Something was wrong.

'I'd better call round the house, talk to his Aunt. I can't this week but I'll get back to you.'

My phone rang as I went for lunch. It was Jim from Beech school.

'Can you come,' he asked. 'It's Deleon again. He didn't turn up for a couple of days after you saw him and now he's back he's causing trouble - threatened to hit McArthur with a chair. Mac's okay and can handle him but he's got other lessons to go to and we don't have spare staff. Both our supply teachers are filling in for staff off sick and I have to go to a meeting.'

McArthur was one of the good guys and knew how to handle kids. He was also six feet tall and as strong as a horse and about as gentle as one, too. Deleon would be safe with him.

'Give me twenty minutes, I'll be there,' I said down the phone, and swung away. I had intended to go to Compton to see a slightly autistic thirteen-year old girl who was being bullied, but that was a first meet and not an emergency. I let them know anyway.

I found Mac in his classroom, empty except for Deleon who was sitting drawing at a front desk. I knocked and walked in.

'Hello, sir,' I said, and then pretended to be surprised. 'Oh, I see you've got Deleon with you.'

Mac acted on cue.

'He's just having some time out, Mr. Jackson. Actually, I'm glad you popped in. Have you got a spare twenty minutes? I must go and prep my next class and they'll be waiting for me.'

'Fine,' I said. 'As a matter of fact I'm free for an hour or so, no worries.' Mac scooped up his case and an armful of papers and left, patting Deleon on the shoulder as he went. He wagged a finger.

'Behave,' he said with a grin.

I sat facing Deleon and saw his knuckles were skinned and red and he had a cut over his eye.'

'What happened?' I said. 'Fight?'

'Aw, nuttin',' said Deleon, looking sheepish.

'Nuttin'?' I said, mockingly. 'Nuttin' you with his head was it?' Deleon smiled.

'Nah,' he said. 'Just wanting a fight.'

'Who was it?' I asked. He hesitated for a minute.

'Cole Wuilovsky,' he said finally.

Now, I knew Wuilovsky, a lad in Year 15, a big lout with a crude mouth, head and shoulders above Deleon, who would try to get in on anything going off, but whose character was that of a coward. He wouldn't have set on Deleon without there being a few others.

I nodded. 'And who else,' I asked.

'Ah, just a couple of them, his mates. It didn't bother me,' he shrugged. No, but it didn't set him up for a quiet day either. I sighed. There was I knew no point in asking him if he wanted me to sort it out. That's not how things get done, and hell is paved with good intentions. I decided to pick up the conversation where we left off the previous week, but in a roundabout way. I also learned later, incidentally, that Deleon laid Wuilovsky out flat, which made me grin.

'So, what happened last week? You didn't turn up here.' It was a statement, not a question.

'Just sick,' he said, which is what I expected.

'Sorry to hear it,' I said. 'But you're okay now?' He nodded. 'Good,' I went on, 'because I'd like to come round the house after school and talk to you and your Aunt. I need to ask her a few things.'

He immediately began squirming in his chair and grimacing.

'No, no,' he stuttered. 'You can't do that! If she knows I've been trouble she'll strap me,' he shook his head almost in tears. 'She'll strap me hard.' He was fighting his fear now. I quickly leant forward and put my hand on his arm.

'No, you're not in trouble,' I said. 'That's not what I want to see her about. I just want to see if I can be of help in some way. It has nothing to do with you being in trouble. You're not.' The look of relief on his face was palpable. 'Anyway, are you telling me your Aunt hits you with a strap?' I envisaged a buckle on the end.

'Ah, she strap me terrible if me in trouble,' he mumbled, looking downcast. 'Terrible.' That was not good, I thought. I'd better have a word with her about it if the opportunity came up. But I really wanted to see if she could throw some light on Deleon's story, or fantasy, if that was a better word. I still couldn't make up my mind whether he believed what he told me the previous week was real or not. It certainly seemed like a fantasy to me.

I walked Deleon to his house after school. He was fretting all the way

'If I'm in trouble she'll strap me,' he moaned, 'she'll strap me bad.'

'You're not in trouble, Deleon, I'll make sure she knows that. I just want to introduce myself and chat. There'll be no trouble. I'll even tell her how good you've been.' But it didn't convince him and he was downcast as we reached the door, even more agitated if anything.

A tall good-looking woman answered the door, immediately setting her eyes on Deleon with a frown.

'Hi,' I said. 'My name's Mike Jackson, I'm a teacher at Deleon's school and wanted to say hello.'

'What's he done now?' She looked angry.

'No, no, nothing at all. In fact, he's been very good, no problem. I just wanted to meet you and see if I can help him with his school-work in any way, or if there's a problem you know about that I don't that I could help with, maybe something in his past education.'

She hesitated, looked at Deleon, looked back at me, and briefly smiled, hardly noticeable. I held out my card and she looked at it. She was quite beautiful.

'Oh, that's good. Sometimes he gets into fights and the teachers - they just bring him here and leave him.'

'Nothing like that,' I said. 'Just that I'd really like to talk to you to see what I can do if anything, to help him,' I added.

She frowned. 'Um, I'm not sure it's a good time at the moment,' shaking her head.

'That's okay. I can come tomorrow if that's better, or Thursday if you want. I don't mind.' I wanted her to know I wasn't going to disappear any time soon. She shook her head again as though trying to make up her mind, studied me for a moment and frowned.

'Okay,' she said finally, 'please come in. Deleon, you go upstairs and get on with your homework till I call you.'

She led the way into the dining-room at the back of the house, rather dark it being late afternoon, and asked me to sit on a sofa. I was aware of two people behind me sitting at a table together but not wanting to seem nosey or prying I gave just a quick glance as I settled.

I introduced myself again by first name in case it had slipped by her but hoping she would tell me hers, which she did.

'I'm Sophie,' she said. 'I'm his Aunt. I'm looking after him while my sister's away.' She didn't offer any information as to why Deleon's Mum was away and I didn't ask, thinking I might pick up on it another time. My interest was Deleon.

I was about to ask her a question when the back door opened and two men slid in and stood silent. They nodded to Sophie but didn't speak. They were tall, dressed in dark suits, wearing ties, and both had Rayban's on, despite the dim light. They said nothing, both looked down, slightly to the side, and didn't move, as though they were waiting. Sophie glanced at them, nodding slightly in acknowledgement, then turned back to look at me without speaking.

Boyfriend I wondered? The atmosphere seemed distinctly different for reasons I couldn't figure and for a moment I wasn't sure what to say. If it was a boyfriend it was slightly odd - no particular sign of a greeting or a word, just standing still, heads inclined. Perhaps it was something Jamaican, a nuance I didn't know or comprehend. The two people at the table behind me sat perfectly still. But Sophie looked as though she was waiting for me to say something.

'Well,' I said, casting about, 'I wondered if you'd tell me a bit about Deleon's previous education?' (I'd picked up on the abbreviated 'Deleon'.) 'As you probably know, he's a bit behind on his school-work.' I didn't at this point want to say to her he was almost illiterate, but she might know that anyway.

She sat very straight in her chair, good-looking, upright, dignified. She glanced at her hands.

'I'm afraid he missed quite a bit of education in Jamaica for one reason and another.' She paused, looked up, then down again, then glanced at the two men on my left.

'His school was closed down for quite a while when there were some problems in Kingston,' she went on, 'and when he went back there weren't enough teachers. He might have missed - oh, a couple of years in all, I'm not sure. I wasn't there, you see, but I heard about it. He might have missed more.' She shook her head. 'It was a bad time,' she added. I seemed to recall ructions in Jamaica reported on the news a couple of years back when elections were taking place but I hadn't taken much notice at the time. What she said sounded reasonable anyway and would explain things a bit. I wondered how to approach the next topic.

'Look,' I said. 'Let me explain something about myself. I'm a specialist teacher. I don't actually teach at the school but they call me in if they think someone needs extra help or help of a special kind. I do a kind of assessment, try to find out what the problem is, talk to parents like you to see if you can tell me anything, and then when I think I know something that might help I go back to the school with a report and advise them what to do. It might be, for instance, that Deleon could benefit from a few special classes or some one-to-one help, maybe a mentor to make sure he's safe - that kind of thing.' I was aware I was trying to get her confidence. I didn't want her to think I was a social-worker, on the one hand, or a teacher who might go back to the school and talk too much. I knew from experience how dangerous either of those two scenarios could be. Social-workers could quickly find things got loose from their control: committee meetings could have disastrous post-effects, as they found out to their clients' cost time and time again. I needed Sophie to trust me to some extent.

'The fact is,' I went on, 'whatever you say to me here, or what Deleon says, is entirely confidential, and I won't report anything back unless you or he give me permission.'

I waited.

Sophie looked thoughtful, frowned, studied me a bit more, and then smiled.

'Okay,' she said at last. 'I'll help in whatever way I can.' At that point she nodded to the two men who nodded back and slid out of the door as quietly as they had come in.

It was all very odd but I couldn't, as I say, put my finger on it, nor, I felt, could I ask her a direct question about them because she might take it as none of my business. Which it wasn't. At that time, at least.

It was getting late. A lamp had been switched on. I thought I'd better leave it at that for now and stood up to go. We walked towards the front door and I looked briefly at the two people at the table as I passed them. The man smiled tentatively at me, the woman just stared. They must have been in their seventies. Grandparents, I guessed. I nodded and we walked on. I could hear Deleon creaking about upstairs so I took a chance.

'Oh, by the way,' I said, 'Deleon was worried you might think he was in trouble and you would be angry.'

'I would be,' she pulled a wry face. 'He gets into enough.'

'Well,' I said, smiling, 'he said you'd give him a stropping.' She paused.

'What do you mean, 'a stropping'? What did he say?'

'Well, he said if he was in trouble you'd give him a good stropping.' I turned towards her. 'What? You hit him with a belt?' I made my face non-committal and looked straight into her eyes. She in turn looked disconcerted for a moment and then started laughing.

'Yes!' she said. 'I strop him with my tongue - that's what he's talking about - and if he's really bad I strop him real hard.' She laughed again. I believed her. She was still laughing when I left, vaguely aware of Deleon coming down the stairs.

I didn't know at the time, but I was about to step into the world of the Yardies and the biggest drug trade in England.

Book in progress 2025

The Good Fairy

Mark Jacobs

I drove round town picking up this and that by way of shopping in my two-seater pale brown hybrid when I remembered I must pick up Joe at the shop to take him home. I got lost driving because some streets were closed for maintenance so that I ended up in streets and boulevards where I didn't recognise the shops or buildings and I worried about being late.

When I got to the street where the shop was I had to park in a lane, muddy with rain and slippery. It was an odd shop, with a living room at the front strewn with miscellaneous bits of furniture including a car tyre. Joe was out doing something on a workbench, mending his scooter, I guessed. Mustaphe came through a side-door, a thin man with a goatee beard and long hair. He smiled briefly and nodded and I tipped my head in return. I walked over to Joe and hugged him.

'Come on Joe. Time to go home to your Mum.' He smiled and gathered a few things together and we left. 'Thanks Mustaphe,' I said as we passed him to walk to the care. It was the first time I had met Mustaphe. He struck me as a kind man.

I took Joe home and returned to town to pick up a few things I'd forgotten and then decided I'd go to the cinema to see a new Woody Allen film. Not that I liked Woody Allen but he made me laugh when I was younger when he told stories about protecting himself from bullies by pretending he was even weaker and sillier than he looked so they couldn't eve be bothered with him. It would be like beating up a mouse.

I parked in the parking-lot when Asche rang me to ask if I would pick up Isla, so I drove across to her friend's house. Isla was filling in an A4 sheet full of beautiful coloured pictures by her own hand full of emerald greens, scarlets, blues, and had almost finished. She looked very thin, cold and hungry but was glad to see me.

It had been raining again and when we got to the car it was muddy underfoot. I had difficulty opening the door at first and then thought I had a flat tyre but it had just sunk into the mud.

We drove back through town and I asked her whether she would like to go to the cinema with me and she said yes. When she got out of the car I was again aware of how thin and tired she was but, as always, smiling.

The film was about halfway through. We sat near the front. I pulled her close to keep her warm when I saw tears rolling down her face. I pulled her closer and stared into her eyes.

'What's wrong sweetheart?' I said. She looked at me and smiled.

'Nothing,' she said, and settled comfortably into my arm.

After taking her home I walked across to the wood with a man I knew. It was very wet. We suddenly saw another man ahead who looked like a tramp, with long black hair, dressed in a brown belted raincoat and wellingtons. He was jumping up and down to sink his legs into the mud. He crossed a small shallow stream, laughing out loud, and threw himself backwards into the mud, laughing even louder.

'What on earth is wrong with him?' said Andrew.

'Nothing at all,' I replied, smiling. He's enjoying himself.'

Because of this I discovered the meaning of 'A Fairy Story for Older People', and felt pleased. Tooth and Nail had finally caught up with Her. Geography indeed.

Grown-up Stories

Florida Heat

Mark Jacobs

Jim came the following Saturday. Jim - James F. Mathias - had come to visit for the second week to meet me. He would arrive late by car, Laura told me, and would pick me up and go straight to the motel. Laura had listened carefully the previous day to a small fizzing transistor radio to pick up news of a pending hurricane in order to 'phone Jim and warn him about it that evening, but luckily it had swerved away and she was, she told him, relieved.

He arrived at around nine o'clock in the dusk. We were introduced, he and Laura obviously delighted to see each other, while I sat to one side listening while she caught up with his trip. It was small talk but animated. Then she said he must be tired and he and I ought to go. Back at the motel we crossed the lawn to his room, on the opposite side to mine, where he began unpacking. He was a tall man, slightly taller than me, around six-foot two I guessed, slightly over-weight around the girth but he carried himself upright, probably a remnant of his military service as an officer in the Far East. He was dressed fairly casually in a brown jacket, cream shirt and grey slacks, polished brown leather shoes. He spoke easily and we carried on a conversation about Laura and my stay while he finished unpacking, finally pulling out a bottle of, as I realized later, very good seven-year-old malt whiskey and a box of equally good Cuban cigars, and we settled down to talk. He quizzed me about my week with Laura, what she had said, what we had done, and talked about one or two people we knew in common. Then he began telling me about himself, his wife, Barbara, and two sons, his work, and how he had met Laura.

She had applied for a Guggenheim grant to finish her and Schuyler's book, *Rational Meaning*, and to pay for its typing (by Susan Morris), and was awarded $6,000 - quite a handsome amount of money then. She finished work on the book some time before I arrived, Jim told me, and wrote to him asking how she might return the money she hadn't used, which was around $2,000. He replied immediately to say it wasn't necessary to return the money and he was sure she would find some good use for it in her work. A few days later his secretary came into his office looking nervous to say there was a very strange-looking package just delivered by courier and explaining that she didn't want to open it in case it was dangerous. Jim went out to look at it, agreed that, yes, it did look very strange, and decided to carry it tentatively to his desk to examine it further before calling emergency services, telling all the secretaries to go out and have coffee while he looked at it. He knew a little about explosives from his time as a soldier. As there was no return address on it, he gently pried open a corner of the brown wrapping and saw tinfoil underneath. The parcel itself was very light in weight. He slowly tore off a little more brown paper until he could see it was a tinfoil parcel underneath with a blue ribbon holding it all together. As nothing alarming had happened so far, he went ahead, untied the blue ribbon, pulled back a corner of the foil and, he said, astonishingly, suddenly the whole room filled with the perfume of orange blossom. He realized the parcel was packed with orange petals. On top was a handwritten note from Laura thanking him and explaining how grateful she was to him for the generosity in allowing her to keep the remainder of the money. She hoped he wouldn't mind, she said, this small gesture. Thus began a long friendship of visits and correspondence.

We laughed long and loud over his story. By this time we had finished the first bottle of whiskey and Jim brought out a second which we were a third of the way through. The cigars were very fine, almost mellow. I was pretty unused to drinking and must have been drunk but felt oddly awake - normally I would fall asleep - and we continued to talk. Jim was telling me about his correspondence with Laura and what passed between them on this or that serious or not serious subject, and the more he told me the more warmly he spoke of her, until finally I stared at him and said: 'You're in love with her!' He stopped in mid-sentence, staring back at me for a moment, then grinned ear-to-ear, got out of his chair, walked round to mine and kissed me on the mouth. 'I would never kiss anyone except one of my sons,' he said, 'but I make an exception for you - you seem like a sort of son. You've seen right through me.' He walked unsteadily back to his chair. I was, I must say, very slightly astonished, but then it all seemed sort of natural in a way I couldn't fathom. We smiled at each other for a moment or two and then just continued talking - and drinking and smoking. We were both kind of pleased with ourselves, I suppose.

It was getting towards two in the morning and we were both tired. 'Before we finish up,' he said, 'Laura told me you had to sell your collection of her books to pay for the flight here, which I'm sorry to hear. I'm going to pay for your flight with a cheque.' He leaned across to hand it to me. 'No, no...' I began. 'It's fine,' he cut me off. 'As it happens, I bought my son a car some time ago which he sold recently and returned me the money, so in a way it costs me nothing. And anyway, I can afford it.' He pushed a cheque for $300 into my hand. 'And now goodnight!'

As I walked across the lawn in the heat of the Florida night, I paused to sit in the little pagoda in the middle to collect my thoughts, emotions pouring through my mind. I could have burst into tears if truth be told.

The next morning I was woken by a knock on the door. It was Jim. 'Come on,' he said, 'time to get going to Laura.' What time is it?' I asked groggily. 'Six o'clock,' he said. I groaned out loud and went back to my bed, a hangover crowding behind my eyes. He sat on the edge of the bed laughing. 'How the hell can you get up so early?' I asked. 'I'm heliotropic,' he replied. 'What?' I said, looking through one eye. 'Purple?' He laughed again. 'No, I have a metal plate in my head, right across here,' pointing, 'I'll tell you about it while you get dressed.'

'Whenever the sun's up I have to get up, can't sleep any longer. It happened in the Far East in the war. We were in a village to flush out some Japanese. My colonel ordered six recruits to run across the middle of the square to some huts on the other side to either kill or capture them, and I told him it was a stupid idea and he had no right to ask recruits to do that. They would assuredly be blown up before they could get half-way across. He threatened me with a court-martial if I got in his way and we shouted at each other for a while. Then I said okay, if someone has to do it, I'll do it, so I picked up my rifle and started to run across. Sure enough I ran straight into a grenade and was blown across the square. When I became half-conscious again, I was being carried on a stretcher through the field-hospital and I heard a doctor say, 'Put him outside with the dead ones - he won't last. Half his head is missing.' The next thing I knew they turned around and were carrying me outside. Then I heard someone say, 'Jim? Jim Matthias? Is that you?' It was a surgeon I had joined up with and a drinking buddy. As luck would have it, he was a head and brain surgeon. He had them take me back inside and began work immediately. He saved my life, God knows how. When I shipped back to the States, he had someone waiting for me to take me to the hospital immediately to fit a metal plate in my skull. And here I am! And the sun is up! So come on, let's go.'

Jim spent most of the day going through some letters of Laura's from the 1950s. He burst out laughing at one point. 'What?' said Laura. 'This letter,' he said, 'about your trying to give up smoking! You really had a struggle! And you're nagging me and Mark to stop!' We had walked outside once or twice to enjoy a cigar while we drank coffee and Laura wagged a finger in admonishment, warning us about the damage to our health. We had coffee at the bench-table by the window and chatted. Jim couldn't resist thinking of an Ogden Nash poem, and Laura, remembering the poem, fetched Nash's collected poems, and Jim read aloud:

> There is something about the English
> That makes them when they talk about themselves very nervous
> and tinglish.

This was as much about me as anyone else. We all laughed. Laura turned and fetched a book of Stevie Smith's poems -

Tomorrow I am going alone a long way
Into the jungle. It is all grey
But green on top
Only sometimes when a tree has fallen
The sun comes down plop, it is quite appalling.
You never want to go in a jungle pool
In the hot sun, it would be the act of a fool
Because it's always full of anacondas,
Evelyn, not looking ill-fed, I'll say.
So no more now, from your loving husband Wilfred.

I was surprised she might like Stevie Smith but on reflection I could see why. Then they both looked at me. The only funny poem I could think of were the opening lines of Pope's Epistle to Dr. Arbuthnot:

Shut, shut the door, good John! fatigu'd, I said,
Tie up the knocker, say I'm sick, I'm dead.

'Time for bed,' said Laura, laughing, and we left.

Laura (Riding) Jackson Literary Mayhem 1971-80

Whale Beach

Trevor Watts

'There's definitely something wrong,' I told Mz Bazig, my Dutch fellow-teacher.

'Silly.' She sneered. 'Plane sounds good; is level.' She glanced out the window. 'And still about the same height. We will be at Port Dorsey on time for the connection to Darwin.'

'We're supposed to have a stop at Jakarta first, then Banjar-'

'You P.E, not geography.' She told me. Very abruptly. 'Mr Shelley; he geography; and Miss Gordon, she do all sciences.'

'Yes, but, Jakarta should be more south than we're going. The sun shouldn't be there.'

'So where you want it? On moon?'

All safely seated aboard this smallish propeller-driven plane - a TRA-56Prop. Smooth take-off from Sangkapur, doing a four-stop trip across the whole Malay island group, which has, so the guide book informed me, 17,508 islands. 'That's what it says: over seventeen thousand in Indonesia,' I told my group, 'The largest archipelago in the world.'

I don't know why I let Mz Bazig bully me, apart from her being a foot taller than me, twice my weight, and with a formidably aggressive attitude to anything male. She was also the Deputy Head Teacher of the school - St Clarissa's Prep for 8 to 14 year-olds. Exercising her authority was her life-blood.

I, however, had been employed less than a year, and was smaller and lighter than Patrick and Maria, the two oldest kids - sorry, children. I certainly got on better with our pupils than I did with the three stuffies, as I, and more than a few pupils, thought of the other teachers on the trip.

But, there it was: holiday-cum-field-trip learning experience for four weeks for twenty-four pupils. Six each.

'Where do you want the sun?' one of the girls asked.

'Anywhere except here. It should be ahead of us, not behind, if we're going south to Jakarta.'

'P'raps he's going round a storm.'

'Or mountains.'

'We should have stopped at Jakarta an hour ago.'

'The sun's on our left now.' Observant, some of them.

'Should we be going over such high mountains?' Quite the concerned, or interested, anyway, little discussion group we had going, from two rows forward to two back.

'So many islands... seventeen thousand? did you say, Sir? Look at'em.'

'The cabin stewardess looks bothered. She was talking into her phone just then.'

'She's on her own.'

She was talking in a very worried manner to a couple of rows of locals in business suits, their wifely companions in kebayas and bright batik sarongs. The others from within the country made up two or three more rows, all looking agitated; sounding it, too; dressed in casual western-style trousers, shirts, blouses, whatever.

'I'll go and find out-'

Hand clamped on my knee. Sounded like, 'No, you vill not.'

But I did. I got up, anyway. However, some western men nearer the front had expected to get off in Jakarta, and they were more than cross about whatever had made them miss it. And made it plain to the cabin lady.

One of them was from Java, and he knew the route, and the islands, but not how to control his temper. So that was rubbing off on the three men who were up there with him - sounded American, demanding and threatening.

It seemed that the cabin lass couldn't get any response from the flight cabin. 'Captain Allen and his FO are deaf to my banging and the comms phone.'

The rugby-build-and-mentality four didn't do any better with their attempt at communication - yelling into an unanswered phone. And - well, I mean, those doors are to keep out bomb-wielding terrorists and atom bombs, so four thuggy rugby-type blokes aren't going to get anywhere.

Two of them even tried shoulder-charging the door, but just ended up looking pained; one nursing his shoulder.

Yes, I know I'm a PE teacher, and rugby counts as physical exercise, but I'm more the fly-half type than a second row thunk-head. Fly half and distance running - that's me. Five-two-and-Fast, my nickname in school.

I sat back with Deputy Doom, and waited. Told the nearest kids - Soph and Rupert - what was happening, to pass it on to the others, strap in, make sure they knew exactly which exit was nearest, 'And anything you really value - yes, apart from your phones - put in your pockets.'

Three went to the toilet in quick succession.

Two behind me sounded like they were trying to lose their virginity. I imagine Mz Bazig was jealous, because she turned and raged at them for about four seconds. It was enough to quieten the whole plane.

I think a few passengers managed to get a signal on their phones, but I couldn't hear what they were saying - ordering a pizza, probably.

Made no difference: our two locked-away uniformed controllers with the joysticks seemed to be intent on a ten-thousand mile tour of the islands; the sun wandering in all directions as we gently banked left or right. Four and a half hours, I reckoned, and I thought it felt like we were descending.

Somebody started panicking about it. 'We're being taken hostage.'

'We're going to crash!'

And the cry was taken up all around.

So I got up and told our lot, that, yes, we were descending, but screaming wouldn't help; praying just might; but strapping in would be best. 'I'll stay loose and do a running commentary on our height.' And be ready to strap in bloody quick.

Actually, we were considerably lower by then. And what was outside looked like water and island peaks, not a town with a runway.

So it proved. I did the traditional yell of, 'Brace. Brace. Brace,' sat down swiftly and clipped my seatbelt on. Maybe twenty seconds later, we hit. Yoiks! but it was hard. Very solid. Slammed upwards, jerked to the right, violently - one wing must have caught a wave. So they're all screaming - except me. And Mz Bazig, who's head down and praying silently, by the looks of her.

Something must have worked for her. We slammed again, spun like a mad dog, and rolled. Hearing the plane smashing apart; like a wing or something ripping off. So loud. Stopped - the plane did; the screaming carried on.

Some hadn't strapped in, and had hurtled around the cabin. Worse was the back of the plane, which had almost severed away from the rest - maybe the rear third separated. Water gushing in like a flash flood on waterfall pills. Panicking faces everywhere. I'm up screaming at'em to unfasten, get to me quick. 'Get out. In the water. Stay together.' Except I leapt across to the back bit where the kids were half under water already - getting belts undone - smacked one's hysterical face, yelled, pulled, grabbed and lifted.

Friggerty-foo. It was a yelling, half-panicking chaos, but I knew all the kids could swim - school priority in P.E. Not that it would help much in the middle of whichever sea this was.

Nightmare. Surviving. Clutching together. Kids desperate, but not shrieking - Too busy gasping. Other people - very shocked in the water. Spluttering and struggling.

'Sir. Sir. It's an island.'

It was, too. Rocks and a beach, couple of hundred yards, maybe. Hope, then. Barren volcanic-type peaks; jungle forest; long beach.

We got it made - like an orderly queue. Our kids in twos. Eighteen, I counted, as we started towards this rocky point and a beach. Cursing cursing cursing - Six lost. Couldn't picture who. Really guilty about that - Oh, one - Hazel the redhead. She wasn't with us now. All making our slow way, not rushing. Taking it unpanickingly. Trying to swim along the line; keeping us together. Oh, the Davis twins - they're not here. Gone down with the plane. Shuggit! I was already having horrible visions of that - the kids in our charge, sinking, drowning. I'd have been crying and ranting if I had chance to focus.

The others, the nationals. Yes, some scattered round. Swimming together in pairs or groups; some really messy swimmers. All splash and arms waving. But getting there.

I think we lost two of the non-school lot- Oh Shuggit! - Mr Shelley and Miss Gordon? Didn't see them after the crash. Two teachers, as well.

Totally knackered, staggering through the beach waves, crawling up the sandy beach - coarse, corally fragments; scatter of volcanic black bits among the sand.

Trying to get everybody out the waves - not big waves, but easy to get knocked over when you're my size. Collecting our lot together - flopping there on the sand, all horrified. Crying, asking; and I'm going round the stragglers, looking - shit shit shit. Two more didn't make the swim - missed them - lost them - my fault. I put myself in charge of swimming there, and I'd lost two more since the crash.

Three out the four brute-heads had survived. Demanding, cursing, effing and blinding. Like they were blaming everybody who'd survived. Loud and aggressive.

Had to get our lot together, aware, supporting each other. Move further from the sea. Gathering on the dry higher section, we reckoned the plane was full, and it was a 56-seater; plus three flight and cabin crew - all gone. Out of our party, I'd lost eight children, and two fellow staff members. Ten out of twenty-eight. The other passengers - if it was full - I'm working it out - slow and ponderously, 56+3 crew, so there must have been 35 non-school people aboard, and we now have sixteen of them left, Less than half survived. Our lot? Eighteen survived out of twenty-eight. Around two thirds.

God knows why, but it gave a crumb of comfort in the mass of blank-minded horror.

All this rationalising about being found soon, and shelter and wild animals, native people living there; getting a signal from a salt-water phone. It wasn't my scene - I was half-drowned, focussed on our youngsters and their well-being. Like getting some clothes off to dry; 'No being stupid, Smith.'

That had been mid-afternoon.

By the time the sun was going down, we had decided it was a remote island; probably not inhabited; might be wild animals, insects and pouring rain, 'So we need to find shelter, and food,' I said. 'There's nobody coming for us tonight.'

'So who the heck d'y think you are? Limey?' Comes six-foot-eighter and his two sidekicks - to use the vernacular. He's towering over me by eighteen inches and eight stone; so I judged. With belligerent buddies to back him up.

So I eased into reverse, except Mz Bazig was behind me, telling me to stand up to them, pushing me forward.

He was fast, this guy. Almighty fist, left cheek, and I was going down. Felt a couple of stamps on me; telling me to damn-well stay down. Good job nobody had boots or even shoes on.

Well, they were decisive: they seemed to have decided they were in charge by the time I was capable of sitting up - three or four of our pupils clustering round me.

'You're lucky, Sir.'

'We think they killed one of the Indonesian men who was arguing with them.'

'He hasn't moved since.'

'And it's getting dark.'

It was an awful night - huddled against a low rock cliff at our end of the beach. 'It's the end of a lava flow,' One of our bright sparks informed us. 'It's a volcano.'

'Ought to warm us up a bit, then.'

Lot of sobbing, crying, sleep-talking. Mumbling, shuffling. Mz Bazig one side of them; me the other.

Wasn't actually too cold. 'Warmly humid,' I was told. 'But wet,'

'And the waves are so noisy,'

'I'm starving,' Reggie Buckle kept complaining.

So, getting ourselves together in the morning, it didn't look as if the Evil Triumvirate was organising anything, so we talked with some of the others. Went looking in a joint party for fruit, signs of wild animals, or habitation. Whatever.

Found a stranded whale further down the beach, beyond a small rocky point. It was about twenty feet long; 'Young pilot whale,' one of the Indonesian women said. 'We can eat it.'

All the kids were yeuking and mock-vomiting, but I said, 'If the lady says we can, we can. The Japanese do - Sushi Whale.'

'You're making that up.'

'No. Is true. Can eat it. Wash in sea, Find rock to cut pieces off - black shiny rock with sharp edges.'

'Obsidian ,' says Know-all Alvin Perkins. I thought he was swearing at first, but the others agreed with him, so some of us went looking for such rock among the tumbly bits off the little promontory, and the rest of us set about driving the birds away. Their women saw a fruit tree and went over there.

We didn't find any sharp-edged rock: the pieces were sea-smoothed and rounded. But another bright little lass in Year Six found a large sort of flat-ridged shell.

'It's a scallop,' one of the Javanese business men told us. 'We can sharpen the edge by rubbing it on a rock. 'We did that as children in Tambaksar Guying. We are going home, to Penang. Near there.'

It was dreadful - mostly the idea of it. But we ripped at it and got chunks off. Washed them. Chewed, spat, vomited. Tried the fruit - a bitter-sweet experience.

'Prefer the whale,' said Maryvonne Cole. 'Quite fish-meaty; maybe chicken.'

'More like worms,' Andrews Minor lets the side down again.

'I'm thirsty.'

'So am I.'

'Where's the water, Sir?'

Like I'd know. Except, we could look, when the local crowd shrugged and mentioned taps. 'Right, the school lot, stick together, two groups - looking for streams, puddles - especially in the rocks. Not anything salty.'

So that took most of the day, and we managed on a fruit that looked like dirty grapefruit, and another that resembled potatoes. 'Manggis,' they told us. 'And dukuh.'

But we did find water. On high rocky platforms, on the lava, in puddles. More than a bit dubious, I tried some, and when I didn't die in shrieking agony, like they seemed to expect, they all were on the knees, cupped hands dipping, loads of slurping. 'Not back into it, Jackson.'

There was a steep little black cliff, about fifty yards from the beached whale, almost a cave - an overhang, perhaps, and we decided it would be a bit of a shelter. 'As long as the rain only comes from that direction, Sir.'

'Yes, thank you, Millicent. Let's take a chance, eh? For now.'

They came looking for us, late afternoon. The bully three with the others... 'Er, actually, Sir, the man with the flowery tie isn't among them.'

Oh, yes. I remembered him - round smiley face. Not much taller than me.

'The big American men didn't like something he said. Beat him up. They think he's dead.'

'Well, they're pigging themselves on the whalemeat and the fruits we picked now.'

Bit of luck, it'll choke'em.

Sneering and strutting round; they even came to our group; probably eyeing us up for likely discipline problems - who they'd need to beat up, cripple or kill to make the rest complaint. JK, the biggest one, was built more like a brick tower block than the proverbial shithouse. Swaggering like a failed Giants player with the tree-sized shoulders, suddenly finding himself king of the pile; and a pair of Heavies to back him up.

His buddies-in-brutality - Stevie G and MeanSheen - swaggered and "yeahed" all the time, kept looking up at JK, and gazing over their captives.

'How the hell do they think they'll get away with it? Killing the Javanese guy? With witnesses?'

'Not expecting to get rescued?'

'Blame someone else? One of the other men?'

'Not you, Sir, don't worry - you got more sense than to go against them, haven't you?'

There's confidence-inspiring.

'I bet you could out-run them, eh, Sir?'

Not much used if you're trapped, or on the floor, though. And if this really is a tiny remote island: they'd have plenty of time to find me. No... if I did anything to resist, I'd have to think of some way of hiding.

'So, what? You'd think I'd just run if they threatened me?'

It was the general consensus that, yes, that's exactly what anyone sane would do. 'You are sane, aren't you, Sir?'

'Wonder sometimes,' Perkins pipes up again, 'seeing you on the pitch the other week against All Saints? Chucking yourself around. That hooker nearly got you, though, eh?'

'Too quick for him, I was. He was tight-head prop; and I was Wing - so I'm expected to be fast.'

'And this lot, Sir.'

'Second row numb-brains.'

'Like Mz Bazig?'

To my eternal shame, I didn't upbraid them for their sniggers. Though Mz Bazig looked our way and scowled as if she loathed us all. Which was the general impression she gave in school all the time.

Yeah, the night was pretty awful. We gathered our kids very close - I counted - yes, all there. We pushed them as far under the cliff overhang as we could. 'Stay very close to each. For warmth.' And security. Except Mz Bazig insisted she have the girls on the right side, and I would guard the lads.

A night of trembling, and sudden starts, not much sleep and the occasional five minutes of worry when one of them went for a pee; or the other - that fruit could really go through you if you overdid it. I think Mz Bazig slept well. Didn't notice her move, anyway.

Sounded like some shuffling and kerfuffling with the others, though.

Come morning again, we were intact and all there.

More than could be said for the others - Both western women were looking - I think mortified is the expression. And one of the Javanese girls was traumatised.

Oh, shitshitshit. Three women raped. Claimed. Forced.

'Confiscated,' they said.

There was a body - one of the nondescript western men - Objected to his wife being taken? They dragged him along the beach, and into the sea a couple of hundred yards down.

That made for an uneasy day, to say the least. They left us alone. But beat up two of the men - the Java girl's companion, and one of the western women's, I presumed. They were in no state to protest about anything.

Learn from this, I told myself. I told Mz Bazig the same. 'Keep your head down. Don't attract attention.'

'You coward.'

'And you stupid if you bring their attention our way.'

'How dare you call me stupid?'

'Oh, shut the chuff up. Half our kids are girls, for Godsake. We don't want them noticing us particularly.'

Nothing settled, but they pretty much left us alone. The twelve others - western and local, were cowed. Quiet. Bruised. Tearful, the women.

How the hell can things break down so quickly? Are they not American Footballers? Just my assumption - Could be escaped convicts... Dockers? Celtic supporters?

Two more nights; three awful days - I got kicked in; twice; when I tried to reason and plead with them: once when they were practically throttling one of the Javan men; and once when they were onto one of the women. They both got claimed, anyway. Me and their husbands beaten and helpless. At least they aren't killing anyone now, I was thinking. Then did a count-up. One of the two Javanese men was missing. Done a runner? Buggered, then buggered off? Or strangled and dumped? There was no getting to them and asking.

The days were a sort of pupil-organising and keeping out the way exercise; plus eating, and fetching water.; trying shellfish we collected on the rocks at the point. Wondering how we might catch fish without a net, line or salmon-tickling skills.

That night was the worst so far. There was squealing and protesting; severe grunts and curses. Someone went, "uff" with finality.

I was getting up to see, tremblingly. They sounded rather close. Yes, someone near Mz Bazig, Hard to tell in half-moon light. Heard her protesting - squealingly; indignant. I went stumbling over - tripping over rocky bits and kids' feet.

They were near our kids. The girls!

I went sort of desperately dashing towards them. Frantic - 'No! Leave our girls! They're children! Should have-' I was yelling something.

They query-grunted something back. A laugh in the dark. A fist in my face. Going down. Heavy. Shit, I let'em all down... face in the sand. Stamping on my head, neck... Going blacker, despair...

I think I came to. On the edge of the strand. Beyond despair.

Choking and gasping on sand and salt.

Blurry-eyed with dizziness and pain in my head and everywhere else.

Early dull light; my legs swilling idly round in the wash of waves.

The effort to rise was enormous, merely to get to my knees. The overhang cave was straight up the beach. They didn't drag me far, I thought. Thought I was dead. An example to the others, what happens to those who resist. All huddled there. I didn't dare go closer to see who was still there. Had they molested the girls? Fervently I prayed they left them alone. But couldn't stay there in that state. Blood I could taste, as well as the salt and sand.

So away I crawled, staying in the wash of the waves so they couldn't follow me; around the mini-point that was closest by, and into the little bay where we'd first come ashore. Then gasped and urghed on the sharp-edged rocks, climbing to get in the jungly forest. Twenty or thirty feet above the sands, so dense just there, a few yards in and I flopped down and tried to take stock.

I slept, I think, or just passed out, and awoke around noon. Covered in ants. Silently shrieking I brushed them away and stripped right off and brushed at more. Then picked and gripped and pulled and hated them.

Reddened, stinging and sore, I carefully, pickingly dressed again - in shirt and trousers, still wet from the waves. And needed to eat, or suck at fruit; and find out what was happening on the beach below with all my kids and the others down there with the tyrant three.

Careful, so careful - I crept and eased and squeezed through the lush damp undergrowth, to just above our shelter cave.

Peering down, through fronds and reeds, they were out on the sand. My children huddled together and looking cowed; Mz Bazig among them and looking sour. Probably blaming me, I thought.

They were clustered round something. I had to wait for them to edge and shuffle around. Martina! The fourteen-year-old with the bosom of a grapefruit pair. Wracked in tears, and the others around. Swaggering down came one of the three - MeanSheen, I think, looking down. Talking to them. A sneering, threatening tone I detected, but not the words.

Oh God if he's raped her? Or if all of them did? Or other girls as well?

They split up, sent to find shellfish, whale-meat or fruit with the other adults; threatening calls coming after them from the Three, standing there in triumphant stance.

So what to do? Me, at five-foot-two and ten stones? Half their weight. And on my own. Plus battered and damn-near broken - commiserated with myself over a sticky patch on the back of my head where the ants had gathered thickly. And ribs down the left that grated and severely twinged. I'm not up to doing much at all.

But while I find some fruit and shellfish, perhaps further round the next point, I can try to plan something.

'Sorry,' I said. 'Can't do anything for you just yet,' and backwards crept to search for fruit, or maybe find a wild pig I could wrestle to the ground and kill and eat... 'Stupid.' I told myself. 'Stick to reality - you need to think.'

Found a small animal, grey fur, endearing face. I could kill it and eat it. No you couldn't. With a little face like that? But I've seen the locals eat dishes of ants and other insects. I know where's there's lots of them. But, trying to rest, nurse my bits, and find something, I came across two more fruits that I ate and didn't get cramps or death rattles from. I also realised the sun was almost down. Just hadn't noticed, not under a canopy of trees, and amidst all that undergrowth.

There was a dead tree at a place where an old lava flow had just reached. The whitened bole provided a snug corner beside the lava rock face, and sort of slept, tucked in there. Coldly shivering; and with the deep aches; and with terrible visions of what might be going on with the others - the kids, especially.

They're not going to be much help, I'd decided; not the kids or the other adults. It'll have to be something on my own; and it will have to be very underhanded - I'm hardly up to fisticuffs with those three Cyclopsian Hitlerites.

It took all the next day to work something out, and it was a crap idea.

I watched the shelter from the point of the rock, as the sea gurgled around. As they cuddled and ate and sucked fruit, and the threesome dragged women to their sides - still no fire to warm them or light my way. But I watched where they took their prey: two staying among the others - maybe for an easy change of partner in the dark hours?

The other going twenty yards or so to the right, nearer the remains of the whale.

Still not much moonlight, but enough to pad silently across the beach from the point to where they lay. 'Hi,' I said to his writhing, jerking form as he held her down taking his sadistic urges out on her.

Lying there, engrossed, he turned, twisted to look who had dared to disturb his activities, just as a twenty-pound, glassy obsidian rock smashed into his head. Right eye uppermost, taking the sharp-edged force of all my strength as it pulverised his head, and took his lust to Pluto's Gate with him.

His blood splattered, blackly, almost unseen in the darkness. One of the Indonesian girls. Face of horror. Splattered with blood. And she was gasping and struggling. Great gasping breaths, choking cries, and building up to horror-filled shrieking. So I gave his vile head a couple more smashes, to make sure; and just to show them; and she hadn't broken into full hysterical shrieking yet. So I could; and did.

I was gone by the time she began her real screaming. Along the rocky, jagged face of the low cliff - not to silhouette myself against the moonlit sea. And I stayed deep hidden for the rest of the night and all the next day. Even chuckled to myself at the thought of how it might have been when they came to see what her distraught panic was about; to pull her out from under him; to see the full-pulped glory of his arrogant face as daylight eventually came.

Relieving themselves against the cliff appeared to be the preferred place, or in the undergrowth a bit past the whale, where the cliff was scarcely a yard high.

And that was where they went for Number Twos. Making little feet-pressed trails to private spots to do their duty and use the sort-of leaves and hanging moss to cleanse themselves.

It is so difficult to wait, watch and think through a dozen stupid unworkable plans. And hear shouting - couple of voices I knew from school. And shrieking in the night. And to find out where the vile duo went to crap. The two of them sticking together. Ha ha - careful, are you? warier now?

It would be hard to silently follow them in all that leaf litter and undergrowth; overly-hopeful to ram a sharpened stick into the ground where they squatted. Safer, but so difficult to stay somewhere for hours without moving, it was gnawingly guilteous to wait there for them. Blaming myself for every agony and humiliation they were going through while I did nothing; so penitent and apologetic. One of them would eventually use this tree to squat against. And the other, probably, by that dense sprouting of leafy undergrowth.

Whichever. Not quite in direct sight of each other - twenty feet maybe, for their imitation of privacy.

Sure enough, late morning, they came. One was so close I could almost see up his backside - not a pretty sight. Maybe the idea of the sharpened stick hadn't been total fantasy. But I had my sharpened stick - or snapped and jagged, anyway.

He crouched. Strained. I rose, not three feet behind him, to his right. He sighed in relief; and turned in curiosity as I rustled a foot. My jagged stick-end drove into his face. His right eye. with two or three feet of raging impetus behind it. And deep the stick went. Ramming it; a twist and jerk.

Ur-ur-urfff and down he settled. Stevie G.

'Stevie? You okay? Got some down y'self did ya?' A not-very-concerned voice. Then again, as I was wrenching the stick free, he called again. Stick stuck in his head, dammit. Big Guy was peering round from his crouch. Seeing me. Furious roar; he was ranting and racing at me, massive hands clutching to tear me apart. So fast! And big! And me barely off my knees and going to die. Him fast; his dickie a-flap.

But he stumbled. Trousers round his knees and falling. And down he came onto me with a huge slam and roar just as I got the stick out Stevie's gory eye.

Flattened back, I was helpless under him. I struggled and heaved. He grunted and pawed. Like a stalemate. Why isn't he shredding slices off me; or beating at me?

Until he slowed and quietened to cursing and snarling; and I squirmed and forced from under him. And there! Protruding six inches from his back was the jagged end.

Must have just got it upright as he tumbled. The result was hardly accidental, but the method certainly was - I'd intended to run like the hurricane wind when I'd spiked the first one. Practically killed himself, coming at me like that... and he wasn't dead - stomach-groin spiked, yes, but still conscious and aware; snarling and cursing still, even as I twisted his trousers a couple of times, to act like knots round his ankles, and began to drag him away. You need to be finished off, you maniac. Maybe one of the others might feel the need?

Sheesh! He was heavy. Kept catching, the stick beneath him, clutching at plants. But it was only thirty yards, to the beach just past the whale, and lugged him off the peaty soil, onto the sand.

He seemed to get heavier then, drag-lurching by his feet through the coarse, pebbly patch at the top, then down, through denser grains and coral fragments. With shouts from around, of horror and disbelief.

His dick and his balls on display, he gathered a crowd as I paused for breath amid all their horrified gasps and questions, and lookings-around for the other one. Seeing him writhe and swear and jerk; and clutch and threaten.

'Eff off,' I told him, but had to wait to get my breath as they all stared, kept looking round for spike-face in the forest; and terrified how he, or this one, would take their rampaging revenge on us all. I gave up; no response from them, and started heaving him along again, by his tight-twisted trouser legs. A score-mark down the beach from his stick-out-the-back. To the water's side, and I kept on going for a foot of depth. Easier then; and then another foot deep, as his head was tossing above, and his arms thrashed and tried to stay above the easy-rippling waves. Until I stamped on his chest and forced him down and dropped my kneeling weight on his throat. So maybe I'm only ten stone and he'd toss me aside with ease on a different occasion. But gutted and flat-down in two feet of water. I'm not so easy to dislodge.

Ten minutes or more, I gave him, just to make sure. Then stood and staggered back whence I'd come, to see if Stevie G was fully dead back in the leafy bog.

He almost was, a choking gasp when I pulled at him. 'There are consequences to what we do,' I informed him. Another gasp when I hammered his groin with a rotted branch; and then no more as I stuffed his mouth and nose with excrement and shitty leaves, and watched his eyes go still and blank.

They came for me, still slumped over him. And eased me away, pulling me back to the water. Washed me down, and sluiced off the crap and the ant debris and stuck-on leaves; and I'm stood there in all my five-foot-two of naked inglory in the shallows.

Sure, they sort of looked after me. More scared than anything. Put me in dry clothing. Stood back as though I'd shake myself in a weedy roar and start again.

Filled with fear, they scarcely spoke; the other adults made a comment or two. Mutteringly agape - probably unbelieving mini-Sir could do such things. Mz Bazig was surly and silent, apart from a muttered threat, 'You are murderer. You must pay for this. Is forbidden to kill. You left, and two more girls were attacked because you not here.'

Okay, I never imagined I was the ideal guardian for the girls; which was why Mz Bazig kept them strictly under her own cape. So I wasn't too sure what she meant by that. I hadn't got the strength to tell her to sod off, or to strangle her, so I wandered off. And sat and tried to settle my mind to the terrible things I'd seen and done. I'm outcast myself, it seems.

Comes time to sleep, I went for the place in the cliff shelter where I'd slept before, but there wasn't a gap. They huddled closer together, and I took the hint. The result with the Threesome may have been prayed for, but my method had shocked them to their bones.

A voice came, quiet and soft, a lilt to it. 'Pssst. Come here to me. I have room next to me.' One of the Javanese girls. I'd say the pretty one, but they all were pretty. 'No touch,' she told me as I got near. But she patted the frond-and-leaf-spread ground beside her, and smiled, I think, by the sound of her voice in the near-dark gloom.

And so it went. I was left alone in the following days and nights; scarce spoken to by the other adults, embarrassed, they seemed. Shunned by Mz Bazig, and most of the girls. All my fault, I'd deserted them. The boys were better, but it was like an adventure game to them - "SuperSir fights off the aliens" sort of thing.

My new friend, from Gerokgak on the north Bali coast, was Amisha. Didn't say much, but came by my side when I went to look for fruit, and she showed me another tree with hairy fruit. Part-round the island, we found a bay with pools and rocks, and swirling current, with shell fish and free-swimming fish. 'Ikan berenang.' She charmingly said. We caught a few: a pair of mahi mahi, which I knew of, and two others more colourful. But edible even in their sushi-raw state. 'Not eat too much at once,' she said. 'Or get ill in stomach and back end.'

We shared four more we caught later that day, with the others. And we ate from the communal leaf-bed of fruit, but the talk was muted; topics avoided. Too stunned by recent events. A PE teacher's not what they need, I was thinking, it's a trauma counsellor. I'm seemingly a major part of their trauma, so I kept quiet when we were all together.

I brooded in my silent, solitary times. When - if - we are rescued, I'll be done for triple murders; pre-meditated. No-one here seeming to be on my side, especially not Mz Bazig and her clutch of quailing girls. And Indonesian Law sounds somewhat strict in cases like mine - Foreign, multiple killer. Didn't fancy being shackled to a chair in front of a firing squad, after a couple of years in some pig-pit prison...

In all that time of diminishing hope for rescue, we didn't see a single aircraft that appeared to be searching - just a few five-miles-high 707s every day. And no-one had the get-up-and-go to do anything: organise anything; search the whole island; check the volcano wasn't about to erupt. Or try ways of starting a fire.

They're all content to sink and rot, I thought, or just to vegetate till something happens. I was getting the same - not feeling up to facing all the condemnation to come. So why would I bother?

Amisha was the only one I felt close to - even the lads and girls from school were still wary, The boys were better; they spoke to me, but not of anything beyond where the next cockle was coming from.

We didn't lie together, me and Amisha, in the biblical sense; but we were side by side and close. I wondered if it was her being raped when I stove that one's head in with an obsidian block; but she didn't say. And I didn't ask. Too awful to know-

'A boat! A boat! Out there.'

A miniscule dot, anyway, but it was this side of the horizon, so maybe a mile away. They ran about and jumped up and down as the boat came close - a fishing craft. The crew had seen the remains of our whale, and come to investigate, not being aware of we people until they were close by. They came motoring in then, and everyone was having a festival of smiles and laughing and glowing faces. Clothes and warm food - albeit fish - and on the radio, getting a response. We'd be all aboard and chugging away within the hour. 'Makeldang, this island,' the newcomers said, 'in the Celebes Sea. Manado by evening,' they promised.

Not for me.

I'm better off here.

Live under the snarl of Mz Bazig? Blamed by the girls for not protecting them better? Three raped. Censured by the world for losing eight in the crash and the swim to shore? Condemned by the law for the brutal murders of three fine young men?

Oh, no. Not for me. So I eased away, into the trees and the undergrowth, and watched them getting aboard - I never counted how many of us had survived. As the boat revved up, Amisha was on the stern, looking and calling. Arguing, and waving.

She jumped overboard as they started off, and she swam to the shore. As the boat departed into the slight haze, I went slowly down.

'I couldn't leave you alone.' She came up the beach, a kind of serious smile to that angel face. 'Not forever,' she stood by my side and took my hand as we watched the Ibu Milikku fade away. 'My sister Nyoman; she will tell our brother that we are here. He will charter boat, or maybe helicopter, to take us away. Perhaps a few days. Maybe four or five.'

'And then?' I saw the chair and shackles looming.

'Come with me to Bali. We have hotel, shop, and tourist centre by the temple of Pura Besakih. Do fishing; and farming on low slopes of Mount Agung.'

Sounds idyllic, I thought.

She squeezed my hand.

I held hers tight. I was never letting go.

Being A Writer

Trevor Locke

Trevor Locke wrote, in one of his novels, ' ... writers are not born. They are made.' He was not the only one to believe this. How do people become writers? Why do some people become writers and not others? Trevor turned to his biography in search of answers to these questions. It was his own biography; he wrote it himself, in the third person.

During Trevor's early years he wrote a lot. Many of the documents he wrote, as a child, he still has in his possession, as an adult. He was interested in religion, mainly Christianity but also Buddhism, and in Western and Chinese philosophy. He wrote about spiritual mysteries; topics inspired by his readings of poetry, oriental mysticism and religion. Books he took out from the local library included those about ancient Greek civilisation. He was particularly fascinated both by Minoan civilisation and the wisdom of ancient China.

He also wrote short stories; creative compositions such as Walk under a starlight sky (9th October 1964), The Gentle Spirit was inspired by readings of Chinese poetry and literature (6th November 1964.) One of his compositions was called Travelling Companions; it was an allegory (might have been written in 1963 or '64.)

Trevor's essay Lamment in the morning (sic) was interesting. The piece was about the growth of his knowledge and intellect during his mid-teenage years and how he felt he had outgrown his environment. He used the metaphor of a plant growing in a pot; the plant had become root-bound. The essay stemmed from a realisation that, after a couple of years of reading books from the public library, he was reaching the limits of what he could achieve. Trevor had no sources of inspiration or even of feedback. There was no one in his (home town of) Portsmouth who he could talk to about the things that interested him; he lacked friends or acquaintances who were similar to him, or above him, intellectually. He could not access college courses at that time. There were no groups or societies he could join, as far as he knew.

As Trevor wrote, at the time, 'I used to read all kinds of books; I was interested in everything. My whole life was devoted to the acquisition of knowledge. I grew to be an intellectual, an educated person, a lover of wisdom and truth. Yet, now I find that I am like a plant in a pot: its roots have grown down until they have met the confines of their earthy prison ...'

He came to the realisation that he had reached the limit of what reading could provide him with, without having access to anyone else who could help him to digest his study and to develop his thoughts. He came to a pessimistic conclusion: 'Soon this fine plant will, for want of nourishment, wither and die; it has grown too big for its pot and needs re-potting.' He was adept at taking a metaphor and working with it. His essay was a lament but it did not lead anywhere. No resolutions; no plans, no thoughts about how he could escape. Just a long whine about how awful everything was. Trevor lacked people who he could admire, look up to and learn from.

Around 1964, Trevor read a book about how Michael Ventris translated the ancient Minoan scripts, from Crete, written was in what called 'Linear B' and took out a book by John Chadwick, from the library, that dealt with how these scripts were deciphered. The significance of the work was that it was made at a time when Trevor was studying ancient Greek history and gained a fondness for Crete, Egypt and Greece and felt a particular affinity for languages. Trevor found, from his readings, that the scripts of Linear B were particularly important. He could not afford to purchase this book, so the only way he could retain part of its contents was to copy out sections long-hand. This was long before photocopiers.

At that time, he would have read Homer, in particular *The Odyssey*, which he would have read in translation. There was evidence (in his early writings and archives) of his interest in scripts; take, for example, the letters he invented. He designed 26 letters on a one-to-one match for letters of the English alphabet. The purpose of this was to create a feeling in certain manuscripts he wrote; not to hide the meaning of their content but to imbue them with a certain style, like the manuscripts of antiquity. It was not just about being interested in ancient texts. Trevor wanted to explore their meaning and to understand them by fabricating them for himself. Other boys of his age enjoyed playing with toy trains; Trevor's passion was for historical artefacts and ancient scriptures. That was the kind of boy he was, in 1964.

One of Trevor's early essays - Social life - also employed a metaphor. It used the idea of the bee hive to portray human life and the world of mankind. It reflected, to some extent, the kind of issues that occupied people in the 1960s; over-population, the achievements of science and technology and the growth of civilisation not being matched by increased understanding and international co-operation. He viewed the world as growing out of control. The piece portrayed mankind as a hive of bees, their behaviour driven by instincts of which they were not conscious collectively. From the first light of day until dusk, he wrote, they buzz busily among the flowers, ever intent on attaining the object of their industry, drawn and forced on by instinctive urges and momentum that makes them what they are, that governs and fulfills their lives, motivates their actions and pushes them to their work with ardent intensity. Marvellous though the hive might be, the bee is characterised by being an individual that works until it drops dead.

The achievements of man, Trevor wrote, are as small as those of the bees; the bee's achievements are greater than those of mankind. He continued, look at this world of men, a kindergarten. A mass of infants trying to behave like adults. They have not learned to live together properly. Everywhere there is disorganisation and disruption. In one part of the world people are fed and happy. They have no great social problems, they have health, they are secure and free from strife. Admittedly there is crime, immorality, slums, under nourishment, strained living, noise, abnormally high insanity rates, violence, race hatred ... yet what they do not have is plague, pestilence, famine, drought, starvation on amass scale, unemployment, shanty towns, people living their entire lives in tents, a birth-rate far in excess of a country's resources ... his English might be clumsy but he had grand ideas he felt a need to articulate.

Trevor had a vision of the world, one that contrasts the West with the third world. He would have got that from watching the television. He was nervous about population growth, continual wars, starvation, disease and poverty. These were problems that appeared on the television regularly in the sixties and the younger generation in particular were concerned about them. Trevor mentioned 'the immense swarms of China training for war'; something he had seen, on TV, about what was happening in the far East. It was a dark and pessimistic outlook on the world that was full of foreboding about mankind's future. It was a vision but he had no idea what the solutions might be or what the world should be doing about these problems.

Theodore Sturgeon was an American science fiction, horror writer and critic. Trevor could not remember how he came across Sturgeon's work; it might have been at school or he might have found one of his books at the library or possibly having seen something about him on the television. Trevor's piece Adapted from 'The Skills of Xanadu' by Theodore Sturgeon, references the work that was published in *Galaxy Magazine* in 1956. The story must have been re-printed in a book available in the mid-sixties. Another possibility was that Sturgeon's piece was adapted to form a play on a television or a radio broadcast. Having seen or read this somewhere, Trevor was moved to compose something inspired by it.

In Trevor's essay, the story was about Xanadu. The plot imagined the sun would grow to become a red giant that turned planet Earth into a roasted cinder. As this began to happen, mankind, still around at the time, set off to find a new home somewhere else in the galaxy. This is a concept still being considered today in documentaries and films.

A small group of humans, some of the first to leave in the great exodus, lay frozen and cocooned in a microcosm of their earthly environment, bound for the bright star Proxima Centauri, a few light years from our expanding sun. Around this star revolved a system of six planets each with an array of moons. Only one planet was inhabitable and was as much a lonely place as the Earth. The space craft from Earth lands safely. The story explains that the star shone with a blue light and the planet's plants were violet instead of green and there were no animals or even insects ... the new planet was a perfect replica of the Earth. The human form is so joyously adaptable and such peculiarities would at first be nothing more than novel inconveniences. The craft opened and its occupants walked out into their new world, its beauty and strangeness striking them deeply: the pale blue light was like moonlight back on Earth. Its azure hue on the violet fields and deep red flowers and silver rocks was unnatural but they found it beautiful. After only a few generations the squat and grotesque humans that landed on Xanadu had grown into lithe and graceful figures with long, fine, golden hair and white skin. These angelic pastorals that we see about us on the fields of Xanadu, he wrote, are now classified, by the central government of the human colonies situated on the planet Cherzo (many light years away) as being so unlike the standard human form as to be humanoid ... they never thought that they could be mutants, abominations against the ugly standard human. That story was dated 15th November 1965.

The writing in these early essays was of a higher standard than most of Trevor's output of that time. His handwriting suffered from poor spelling, clumsy grammar and inadequate punctuation but then it would be several decades before he acquired the skills to set type and write to a professional standard. Simply reading books did not give Trevor the skills to write well; his mind was preoccupied with the content and paid little or no attention to how words and sentences were constructed or to the technicalities of putting ideas into words.

Seven days later, Trevor's mood darkened. A piece, in the style of a poem, was headed The Tragic Suttra (sic) (composed on 7th January.) Ostensibly about the world out there, it was an expression of the world inside - his world, his life, his view of inner existence. It was an outspoken statement, a cry from the heart about the shallowness of the world and the blindness of people. It's grieving tone and depressive outlook was directed as much towards the surrounding world as to his inner self.

Behind some of these early works was an attempt to remedy the moods of depression that descended on Trevor. In his review of the year, he noted, under May,'... starting off with the sad tale of Reality Speaks, So Listen, later to be known as Suttra written in the morning. This was a semi-poetical analysis of his life at that time. It was born of depression and accounts for that depression and its origins.

Trevor also read widely from the works of poets. One, in particular, that he liked very much was the allegory 'Time, Real and Imaginary' by Samuel Taylor Coleridge (1772-1834). What appealed to him was its imagery and use of abstruse metaphor. In fact, he memorised the work and could recite it, even in his old age. Trevor remembered reading it when he was either fourteen or fifteen years old.

Trevor discovered astronomy and cosmology. He used local libraries and took out several books that were to have a important influence on his intellectual development. A number of television programmes also sparked his interest in subjects like astronomy, particularly Patrick Moore's *The Sky At Night* series. A programme was broadcast by the BBC about relativity, presented by Herman Bondi (1919 to 2005) the Anglo-Austrian mathematician and cosmologist and this had a profound impression on Trevor. Bondi was of Austrian descent and spoke English with a bit of an accent, which made him all the more fascinating, in Trevor's eyes. His BBC programmes, in 1963, were called *E=mc2*. Trevor found particularly interesting and he watched them avidly. He also wrote away to obtain a copy of the booklet about relativity that was published by the BBC in association with the series. He kept this publication for many years.

Moving to London

In 1967, Trevor decided to leave home and move to London, by himself, but with his parents' permission. Life in Portsmouth had become intolerable for him. He wrote about his arrival in the capital city; he said, Trevor arrived in London after seventeen years of a life that was secluded, cut off, sheltered, lived in obscurity and removed from anything that would make him bigger than he was. He saw himself as a small, shy, ignorant boy from a grim working-class naval port. He had arrived in one of the world's greatest cities and could do anything he wanted. He could meet people, he could have experiences. He could find his own way of life. He could be whoever he wanted to be. There was, he imagined, nothing to stop him. It was a city where the streets were paved with the gold of endless opportunities. Trevor stepped from the train, from Portsmouth, on to the streets of London and his life would never be the same again.

As he walked from the platform at Waterloo station, to the underground, he could not imagine what London would have in store for him. Trevor was a poorly-educated teenager from a dull coastal town and was irrevocably naive. Life had not prepared him in any way for what was to happen to him. But, he had imagination and a zest for living that saw him through the good times and the bad. By the time he left London for good, Trevor had grown. He was deeper, keener, wiser and full of experience. Above all, he was no longer a child.

In 1967, he walked along one of the streets of west London and it literally sparkled with stars. The pavements of Bayswater Road had been coated with a substance containing myriads of tiny crystals that glittered in the bright white street lamps. As he walked back to his bedsit, it was like walking on a carpet of stars. That created an unforgettable image of his life in that great city. One image, in a kaleidoscope of images, that remained with him for the rest of his life.

On Trevor's first day in London, back in 1967, he arrived already having secured a place to live and a job to pay for it. The remnants of world war two were still around. The legacy of Victorian times was everywhere. Rising from these deteriorating remains were the splendours of the new; modern buildings of glass and steel had begun to spring up amidst the gloomy edifices of a bygone era. England's capital city offered the same monumental palaces as any other of the great cities of Europe; it had its museums, opera houses, landmarks, columns, arches, famous streets, iconic statues, parks and broad thoroughfares - just as all the rest. Through its heart ran the great artery of the Thames. Whether walking along its embankments or walking over its famous bridges, the lugubrious muddy waters fascinated Trevor. It was in those days like a river of soup; impenetrably brown, slow-moving and full of garbage.

This was the swinging sixties; though, at the time, few people realised it. That London has gone. Today's visitors would find it hard to know that previous Londons had existed, Londons that have vanished, except in the memory of the old people who once lived in them.

Trevor's dominion was in the West. He started in Chelsea's Cadogan Square and ended up in West Kensington's mansions. In between, he lived in Notting Hill, Earls Court, Bayswater, St. Johns Wood, Paddington and quite a few other places. He thought of himself as an urban gypsy. Between his arrival in London and the time he left in 1971, Trevor had innumerable addresses. He moved from one bed-sitting room to another; eventually he settled into an apartment in West Kensington, as lodger of a friend, and that was the longest period of accommodation he had in his London days. Given the price of even rented rooms in the centre of London, these days, people would find it hard to believe how cheap accommodation was back then and how easy it was to find a new place to live. Bedsits were plentiful and cheap.

Jobs were easy to come by, even for inexperienced teenagers with few qualifications. Trevor did a variety of office jobs until he switched to the hotel and restaurant trade. Office jobs included working for Reuters of Fleet Street, being a reporter at the London Commodity Exchange, in the heart of the city. Doing menial clerical work in Grays Inn and Lincoln's Inn. Working at the Hyde Park Hotel and even the Savoy Hotel. He clocked up some interesting positions in places that had significance. Long after he left London, he returned on day visits and was seen regularly in the Houses of Parliament, Whitehall, The Home Office, The Lord Chancellor's Office, The Natural History Museum and a variety of other locales that were important. Oddly enough he never went to Broadcasting House during his time in London. The BBC either did not attract his attention or vice versa. It was only much later in life that his path crossed the threshold of the BBC. That is worth mentioning because, with Trevor's background and interest in books and entertainment, one might have seen him trying to get into broadcasting. He used his experience of life in the capital to write his longest novel - the trilogy entitled *The Streets of London*.

Life in London would have been a distant memory were it not for the fact that Trevor kept a daily diary; in it he wrote details of what he had done, where he had been, who he had met, the plays he had seen, the books he had read, the films he watched. The best kept of his diaries were those of 1968 through to 1971. He wrote down a lot about what happened to him during those days in London. Without his diaries and journals, Trevor was unable to recollect much about those years in the sixties and early seventies. Those who have read about the London of the 'swinging sixties' in books (such as *Swinging London: The Inside Story* of the 60s Capital of Cool) might think that he led his life in the centre of what was happening. Nothing could be further from the truth. It was true that he visited places that were cool and hip: Carnaby Street, the clubs of Soho, The Way Inn at Harrods, but he was not fashionable. Even though Trevor was in almost continuous employment during those years, he never had really well-paid jobs. There were times when he struggled financially; even though accommodation was cheap and prices were low. A loaf of bread cost about nine pence while a pint of beer was even cheaper. He subsisted on the low-paid jobs that were easy to get. He had no rich parents to subsidise his existence. Like tens of thousands of other urban emigres, Trevor got by (with a little help from his friends.) London was a magnet that sucked in the dispossessed of the world. He met many dozens of people from England's towns and cities that had gone to the big smoke in search of something that they had failed to find at home. The London of those days was full of young people; people of his generation. People who had gone there hoping to find something. Some of them did. They made it. Many did not but they often found what they were not expecting. Sometimes that was good; sometimes it wasn't. That happened to Trevor. As he wrote, 'Life is random. It just happens to you.'

It was the obscurity of Trevor's earlier life that made everything about London so overwhelmingly impressive. Had he been much more intellectually sophisticated, he might not have been so impressed by the people he met and the things that he did. Life in Portsmouth had not prepared him in any way for London. Neither had his poor, simple parents. Neither had his poor, simple education. All those books that he read about philosophy, science, history, art ... they gave him knowledge but not the kind of knowledge that was needed on the streets of London. On the streets, a knowledge of western philosophy was of no use to him; even though he could hold his own in a conversation with an amateur philosopher.

In those years, train fares were cheap and he could catch the train up to London on a day return ticket.He went there a couple of times with mates who he knew from school. So, you see, little had prepared Trevor for the streets of London. And yet it was through his experiences there that he grew and developed both personally and intellectually and began to write in earnest. It was in his teenage years that he yearned to travel.

First Steps Into Europe

In July 1966, Trevor changed himself. He left the legal profession and went to work in a travel agency. Doing that changed him as a person and opened up for him a world of new experiences. He went on a tour of European holiday destinations, a trip he got through work. His school friend persuaded him to accompany him on a package holiday. They chose to go to Italy and booked a two week holiday in the Adriatic resort of Cattolica, near Rimini. That was an experience that had a profound affect on Trevor. He wrote about it in his novel *Holiday* which later became a fictional story, published under the title The Road to Ancona.

Trevor wrote extensively about the year 1969, one of his milestone years. In his Journal, he referred to it as being remarkable. In fact, the whole period of his life in London, from 1967 to 1971, was, for him, a golden age. He had shaken off the yoke of his troubled adolescence and had became mature enough to enjoy the great vitality of the swinging sixties. The London in which he lived was one that has now passed into the realms of history. It is clear from Trevor's writings that it was a London that really swung for him. It is little wonder that he based his three-part novel *The Streets of London* on this period of time. 1969 was a year that saw Trevor doing many new things. He began to study for his A-Levels to gain the entrance qualifications for university (having come to the conclusion that he really did need to go to University.) In February, he got a job at Reuters, the international news agency which then had its headquarters in Fleet Street, in what was then the heart of the newspaper industry. Trevor regarded his job at Reuters to have been the first serious job he had. It was when working there that he decided to go to university.

The Undergraduate Years

Having gained his university entrance qualifications, Trevor accepted a place at Bristol University and moved there in 1971. The University campus was set in the heart of the city, unlike some Universities, Lancaster for example, which were on their own separate campuses, quite some distance from the nearest town. The ornate Wills Building, with its imposing tower, was the main academic building, located some way from the administrative hub, the Senate House. Trevor's course centre was the Sociology Department in Woodlands Road. He had to find all these places during his first days in the city.

The freshers all looked fresh. Mainly composed of eighteen year-olds, who had gone to university straight from school, they all looked younger than Trevor. At 23, he was almost a mature student. His path to academia had been very different from theirs. His GCEs were taken over a period of time, after he left secondary school and began to study at a variety of further education colleges in Portsmouth and London. The six year difference between him and most of them, meant a lot at that time of life.

In his first year at Bristol, Trevor studied sociology, philosophy and politics; these subjects were subdivided into modules about social institutions and the structure of modern Britain, British government and political theory and (in the case of Philosophy) metaphysics and the theory of knowledge, logic and ethics. Trevor joined the University societies for philosophy and for sociology, soon becoming an officer in each of them. He became a reporter for the student newspaper, *Nonesuch*. The first article he wrote for the newspaper, was about the value of two year science degrees, which were being proposed at the time. Trevor reported on the issue but in an uncritical way that did not reflect the controversy behind it.

Trevor's studies, in the second year at Bristol, were organised into a series of subjects, including education, medical sociology, comparative institutions, self/family/society,theory, privacy and community, social movements and methods. Trevor wrote copious notes on sheets of lined foolscap paper. Allied to this part of the course was statistics. It was his worst subject, mainly because he could not do mental arithmetic. As far as he could remember, they did not have pocket calculators in those days. He remembered sitting the statistics exam and being totally unable to answer the questions because he could not do the mathematics involved. He spent the time, during the examination, writing what he knew about the theory - of which he had a fair grasp - and in the end they decided to condone his miserable failure, although he came close to being kicked out of the course. He thought they were cautious about throwing students out because it would reflect badly on the department's reputation. The staff must have been fairly satisfied with the rest of his work to forgive his numeracy problems.

Trevor was not regarded as being a radical and he rather liked his studies of the tribes of Africa, such as the Nuer of Southern Sudan. He also enjoyed the seminars he attended on public and private spheres, which included readings on things like the quality of private life, the ethnics of love and friendship, a subject that frequently occurred in Trevor's journals during his life in London. One of the set books, of his sociology course, was Eric Fromm's *The Art of Loving*.

Another topic that interested Trevor was medical sociology. It focused on a number of topics such as the social construction of the sick role and how culture affects the perception of pain. The sessions on mental illness were particularly interesting and he recalled his involvement in the People Not Psychiatry movement which was protesting against the use of ECT and the incarceration of mentally ill people in hospitals. As part of his involvement in local campaigning groups, Trevor visited one of Bristol's big lunatic asylums to witness some of the shocking conditions that were evident there. Alongside the huge wards that accommodated older people (who suffered from a variety of conditions) there was a small experimental unit that looked after younger patients, offering them a variety of the new therapeutic approaches that were being introduced from North America. Trevor continued with his studies of medical sociology when he was at Manchester doing his first post-graduate course.

One of the memories Trevor cherished most was that of his attendance at the Rag ball in 1973. Rag took place in March and its associated ball took place on Friday 9th March at the union building in Queens Road. This was one of the great social events of the year. The whole building has been decorated with coloured lights, exotic displays made from paper and all manner of amusing trappings to transform it into a fairy-tale castle. This year's event was less formal that in previous years. Student life valued informality whereas, in years gone by, the occasion would have been taken very seriously; formal dress would have been obligatory but to contemporary students that would have been intimidating. The students of the seventies were a more varied bunch than their forebears who would have been drawn from the classes where formal evening attire was considered obligatory. The seventies emphasised equality and the breaking down of class barriers and a desire to make everyone feel comfortable and relaxed in their times of enjoyment. In 1973, the student rag was run on a city-wide basis involving all the local colleges alongside the university; students from the polytechnic and the technical colleges were not used to formal occasions and student from those backgrounds preferred fancy dress to formal suits.

Trevor wrote a great many essays during his time as undergraduate; some were about the academic issues he was studying but many were about his personal experiences and reflections on the world in which he found himself. He continued to write in the Journal that he started in London.

The Post-Graduate Years

After gaining his degree - an upper second honours in sociology - Trevor enrolled on a post-graduate course at the University of Manchester. It was unfunded and he struggled financially, supporting himself through a variety of poorly-paid jobs. Eventually he got a well-paid job and abandoned his course. He had little time to write. Most of his life was devoted to the constant round of struggles to keep his head above water, finally. His only writings were about the people he met and the campaigns that attracted his interest.

Moving to Leicester

Life after Manchester changed dramatically when Trevor moved to Leicester. Having gained a position at one of England's prestigious Quangos, writing became part of his professional duties. In his Journal, Trevor commented about his early days in the Midlands city: In the 1970s, Leicester was a rather dull market town. It was not until much later that it developed into the cosmopolitan environment that we know today. When I arrived, it still held a cattle market once a week and had a somewhat market town ambience. There was little, at that time, that distinguished the place; even its cathedral was unimposing. Its shops were unremarkable. It's people mainly white, working-class, although there was a large Indian community. I soon got fed up with the grotty bedsit in East Park Road and moved to a new one in Sandown Road, off London Road, one of the main thoroughfares into the city. The room was at the top of a Victorian Terrace but I liked it more than my previous digs. Renting a room in those days was inexpensive and there was a ready supply of such furnished accommodation. The large room had two single beds and a couple of arm chairs. A window looked out towards London Road.

In October 1980, Trevor wrote, 'Mounting excitement.' A desire to rid myself of destructive problems and achieve something really worthwhile. I have become unable to organise myself effectively. Perhaps, that has always been my problem. I lack creative energy. Work routinises energy but creative force cannot be turned on and off. Skilled journalists can write well, when they want to. That differs from being motivated to write about an issue and from being expressive or brilliant. I have failed to make writing my craft. My writing has been self-indulgent, child's play. Being a master of writing requires careful study, long practice, precise knowledge of the language and rules of grammar and the execution of style. Being fluent in written language is like being a musician. English is a flexible and highly communicative media, when used artfully. It is a poor technical language but, artistically, it is very rich. However skilled a writer might be, his work will attract no interest if he had nothing to say. Creative energy comes from the mind, from intellectual struggle and excitement. Admittedly, our culture suffers from a poor readership. Television has killed the book, not in terms of quantity but certainly in terms of quality. Most television is a degenerate media, controlled buy businessmen and bureaucrats and scripted by cadres of uncreative, mediocre minds. I seldom see a film, play or documentary on the television that stimulates and excites me. If we stand back from television [programming] we find that really it has little to tell us. It may have quite a lot to show us but its ability to use words is little.

In may 2018, Trevor wrote in his journal, A few weeks ago, I started a course in drawing. Every Monday morning I go the Adult Education Centre to do a course in drawing and sketching. If I learn to draw, will it make me a better writer?Will I become a more able novelist? ... Much of my fiction writing uses images and pictures. Writing a story is, for me, like making a film. Instead of calling sections of my book chapters, I call them scenes. My hope is that learning to draw will help me to see the world around me, to visualise it and above all to observe it. In sketching we need to employ high levels of observation- there is one way of seeing which we do with our eyes partly closed - squinting - seeing only rough shapes, proportions and relationships. Then we open our eyes and look at the details. We also have to observe colour, shades, tones, shadows and textures. Drawing helps me to do this. It helps me to observe what I see. If I can see the world - or people - as an artist would see it, I might be more able to describe it through words. ... As a writer, I want to take my reader to the place I am telling them about. I want them to see it as I see it. After all, none of my books will have actual pictures in them. It is very easy, these days, to insert a picture into a text document. If you happen to have the right picture. If I was to become an expert painter or sketcher, I suppose I could draw any scene or face for my book. This has been done by a few authors who have illustrated their books. I am not sure that is likely to happen in my case. Of course, I need to leave something up to the reader's imagination. I can show them something - a person, a scene - but I should not want to spoon feed the reader. I give them an outline and leave the rest up to their imagination.

Another journal entry gives further insight into Trevor's thinking, 'Being a Writer'. Friday 17th June 2022. I was asked the question, What are some reasons that one should write every day? In my reply, I said, 'I have to eat every day. I have to write every day. There are some things you just cannot do without - eating, sleeping and writing. It's what makes us what we are. Every day. Not just now and then; a few times a month. A writer *has* to write. It's not a matter of choice. Those who take up the pen a couple of times a month are not *writers*. They are simply people who can write. It's not a matter of asking if I *should* write every day. It's something I cannot avoid doing. This has been my life for many decades. Since I was a teenager, in fact. It has resulted in a vast back-catalogue of work. I keep everything. No matter how bad it is. No matter how poor it might be. What I have written is *me*. I write to live. 'A day that passes without being recorded is a lost day.' He continued, 'Writing needs to be a daily routine for someone like me. It is my way of life. Actually, I live to write. I get up, make a mug of tea and start writing. In this instance, writing means original, new composition or editing that which already has been started. My technique is to write quickly to create a draft and set the structure of a piece. I return to that piece many times to edit, proof read, correct and, sometimes, to expand. The first part of the morning is done without there being access to the internet. I switch that on later when I need to access the search engines. When writing an essay or journal article about something that requires considerable research, I need to have the internet at my disposal to find information that I can use. I also added this comment to someone else's post: Writing is NOT just another form of communication. That belittles it. It is life-affirming. It what we are. Who we are Not merely communicators, like everyone else.' Taking up the pen is not a matter of choice. It is a vocation. My responses to questions of this type drew on a lifetime's experience of writing. Admittedly, there were many days in my adult life when I was too busy with professional work to write for myself, about myself. Being a family man and having a pressurised career, meant that I did not have the time or the energy to engage in writing that was not part of my job. My various employments required me to write but that was all technical stuff that would appear in reports and sometimes articles in periodicals and eventually in a book. Now that I have retired, I write every day, for my own pleasure (if one can call it that.) I have become a writer and am not very much else. One's being is subsumed within the condition of writing. Writing is what makes one what one is.

It was when he retired from paid work that Trevor became a novelist. He had the time to write and penned a series of novels, only one of which has been published. He continued to work on his draft books and has even begun to write new ones. He writes for his journal on a daily basis.

This brief summary of the life of a writer shows how being a writer is something that colours one's whole life. People are not born to be writers. Everything in Trevor's life, as a child and young person, militated against him being a writer. It was life itself that compelled him to write. Life and a series of chance occurrences, such as becoming a member of his local library. In his old age, Trevor concluded that his whole life had been about being a writer. A lot of people do writing but living with writing on a daily basis, he believes, is about being a writer.

Mr Graydon

Trevor Watts

It's not as if we're friends in any way. He's not that easy to be friends with, but he's amusing in himself; and in what he says and does, independent of anyone else. Does things to be a bit different. I think he knows I know, so he occasionally makes some not-very-nice comment on his way past me. But I know he only does that because I know; so it's not like he means it.

Alright?

We work at the same place, and I've seen him in Market Cafe as well, where I go for lunch on Tuesdays and Fridays. He's in some office meetings too; the first-Monday-in-the-month ones. In the meetings, he's so dry; like a mite sarcastic with Boss McClinton. He sort of comes the know-it-all; but subtle with it. Almost entertaining on occasion. So I have to be careful to keep a straight face if he's getting under the boss's skin. I'm sure it's stood in the way of his promotion; whatever position he holds. Although I overheard him months ago saying he didn't want to join the higher echelons of staff, and lose all touch with reality and humanity. Right: he stands need to talk - silver-gold waistcoat like a croupier, and a moustache straight out the Salvador Dali catalogue. Come back reality - all is forgiven.

Anyway, I was looking at this brochure one lunchtime, in the third-floor coffee corner. I was quite taken with the look of this river cruise along somewhere desert-and-palm treesy, called the Alnahr Alqadim. We'd just booked a twelve-night tour there, with my history group. Not my history group - just the one I belong to. Coming past, he must have glanced at it on my lap, and decided the only spare seat was the one the other side of the low table from me. From there, he could have a gleg at my brochure. And my legs? I wondered, slenderly-exposed from mid-thigh to ankles, as I put the brochure on the coffee table.

It was an intrusion, I suppose, all outlandish moustache and vivid-patterned socks - commenting that it looked rather interesting. 'That river traffic looks fascinating. Are they the stopover places? Looks somewhat appealing. Those are the day trips, are they? My sort of landscape, that. And that market there, too; so colourful... mystical.'

That was him being silly now, because the first thing he said, before he sat down, was, 'Mmm, Cyrus the Great... Achaemenid Empire. Sumeria... Persia, hmm? Lydia and all that, eh? Beautiful rugged area.' So all that about the brochure pics looking alluring, and the souks - playing the innocent. He obviously knew as much about the region as our history group. Trying to kid me.

'I'm Alison,' I told him. 'Alison Teake. My family came from East Leake, in Nottinghamshire. But I'm not-'

He coughed - so falsely. Wanting to shut me up.

Hmm. I do not go for that. 'You have a first name?' I asked him.

'Not at work. Miss Teake.' He got up to go. 'I'm Mr Graydon.' As if it meant something. Taking a note of the company's name on my brochure - i.e. a pic on his mobile, he took his coffee somewhere else. From that angle, he was piccying my knees, too. 'Thank you, Miss Teake... ah, Mystique, hmm?' Big smirk.

Huh; peasant in silly clothes. I didn't bother watching where he went.

A few days later, he came over to me at coffee, and said he'd studied their brochure online, and booked a trip, same one as we looked at, 'Next Easter.'

'Oh,' I said. I almost brightened up. Dunno why - we were merely workers in the same offices. Scarcely even acquaintances. 'Er, I think that's when we've booked. The girls down the Kettlefurth Historical Group. We do one a year; famous history places. Last year we went to Custer's Last Stand; stayed at Fort Shaw. Machu Picchu before that.'

Not one word did he respond with; nor any kind of look, like peed-off or pleased. Total neutral. So I assumed he didn't care either way.

Unreadable, our Mr Graydon. Didn't even sit and have his coffee at my table. So I ignored him at the next meeting, when he seated himself next to me. And neither of us mentioned it over the next few months - we didn't cross paths a lot, anyway. So it wasn't like deliberate. Just nothing, really.

Along comes Easter, and we were there, together - The Joomer Girls, as we call ourselves - or Jumah Girls, actually: Jilly, Ursula, Marjorie, Alison - that's me - and Hannah. All excited and all that; little drink to get in the mood. Didn't see him at the airport; or on our plane; or on this near-endless jouncing bus ride from Gatur airport out to where the boat was moored-up at Zagrnya. Not that I was thinking about him. We were too busy having a laugh, and moaning about the awful road and the dust.

But it was such a welcome arrival, the captain himself in his posh white uniform; trays full of drinks - a whole spectrum of them in colour and temperature range.

There he was already! Drink in hand, chattering with some of the up-decks crew. First name terms, did I hear? Laughing like old friends - You're never like that at work. Bloody Misery-guts.

I approached him, prompted by the faintest thought of basic politeness. 'Here already?' I spoke the obvious.

'I came a few days early.' He seemed much more aloof with me than his Turkit pals. 'Rang ahead, knew there was room, and they were moored here. Wanted to walk the Hregon Ridge, the Alp the other side of the Tirrit.'

'Walk the what? Dressed like that? You're Joe? One of your new, er, friends called you? Never heard your name before.'

'I am,' he pontificated, from the silly heights of his sailor-cap and Greek nose, 'Joe to the crew only. I have four days of close drinking history with them. Eating, too. And two evenings at a sukhu bar - the music and all that; dancing; hookahs...' he faded off, as though it was obvious what he was on about.

'I suppose you may call me Joseph, for the duration of this holiday.' He sniffed as he turned away. 'Mr Graydon, otherwise.'

Sod off, then, Lord Snotty. I was vaguely affronted. Treating me - a work colleague - like that. Except, I reckoned it was his cover. A pretence. Hiding the inner him - like he did at work, talking down at me from his ridiculous plus-fours, boots and leder-jacket with an edelweiss embroidery on the breast pocket. How entirely naff!

Back turned to me, I was dismissed, and we went off, the girls giggling about what a snooty prat he was, and needed to grow up. And at me, for being "like that" with him. As if.

There aren't many of us on the vessel, not in our section, anyway; doing our trip. Four married couples; two fellers closely together, and a gang of others; acting like a stag party, but just studenty prats. A few other women were aboard; and about eighteen or twenty Asians - sounded and looked Japanese, but I dunno; bit darker-skinned than the average, I would have thought. Might have been a mix. Plus we five girls.

A couple of days down the river, the cruise was settling - the people and the routine; getting on with the crew and where to meet up for visits to touristy sites. The trips ashore, for our FH Group, were super - all these temples and palaces and stuff that we were doing about all this term. 'Seventh heaven,' we agreed. Yes, I know, it doesn't ring true for a pack of silly girls - but I'm the youngest at twenty-five, and Marjorie the oldest at fifty-four. We just call ourselves "The Girls" cos we act like we did back in our youth, when we've had a few together.

I imagine Mr Graydon did his own thing, too. Didn't see him. Didn't care.

The other folk aboard did whatever they fancied, too - the markets, art galleries, some shows, and like a camel rodeo. A wild animals and plants desert park... Except these two fellers, Garry and George, who decided that history was too boring, and people in general were not to be mixed with, unless it was on a personal level; and they decided that we needed their attention.

Jilly and Hannah flirted back, and they all drank inordinate amounts of Sirah - some local spirit with an aniseed-orange flavour. Some people find it quite addictive whilst on holiday, and can't help themselves doing whatever. As I told them in very clear terms, I don't.

In the case of Garry and George, the Tottenham Twosome, or Tits, as I thought of them, their thing, la loro cosa, as the Italians say, became taking the mick out of Mr Graydon. My Mr Graydon. Like I felt responsible for looking after him. My Joseph.

They objected to him being so formal and humourless. 'Staid and stuffy,' as Hannah - our headteacher member - agreed with them.

'Come on,' George argued. 'It's so obvious that this snotty, know-it-all did it. Look at him: loud socks, T shirts and Zapata moustache.'

I thought back. Yes, it was a Dali, now it's a Mexican Zapata.

'Thinks he's so superior to the rest of us. So he does things like dropping tea bags in the coffee grinder; because he thinks he'll simply get away with it.'

'It was him who poured maple syrup all over the boiled eggs-'

'And chucked the crusty bread overboard.'

'It was him who switched the milk warmer off.'

'Yeah, what's he gonna do next, eh?'

'Don't be silly. Mr Graydon just wouldn't do things like that.'

George and Garry put this sort of performance on two or three times a day - like breakfast; late afternoon bevvy when everybody returns to the boat from wherever; and any time in the bar in the evening. Slagging him off whenever; blaming him for whatever; I'm sure they were doing it all themselves.

They gave him hell - George was direct with it. Accused him straight and loud, to his face. Garry more behind his back - muttering, insinuating and suggesting; all as though he was making a joke of something serious. But getting the idea across.

'You're looking for trouble, picking on him,' I told Hannah. 'You should get them off him.'

'Me? One laughing mention in the bar the other night, and those two just took off with it.'

'He'll never be able to cope with your mercilessly vindictive womanhood prompting two idiotic fellers to carry on like this. You started it. Stirred them up. You should stop them.'

I told them about a couple of occasions at work when he'd bettered his colleagues. But the next thing I know is, they're teasing him even more, and I'm so embarrassed because he saw me with them and probably blamed me for it all. God, the way he looked at me - like, you know, the smacked spaniel face on him.

I shrivelled.

Trouble is, his accent and his tone of voice are so distinctive; so easily mimicked; and the stiff way he walked; and the nineteenth-century explorer clothes. He was just asking for it.

And he got it, the fourth night, when George and Garry did an impromptu/well-rehearsed skit on him in the bar - to much entertainment for all.

So it got worse over the next couple of days, with stuff going missing, changes to the itinerary on the board... all him, obviously, so their rumour-mongering went.

But it was water off a duck's back. He just carried on - quietly superior and swanning along with his above-it-all comments when anybody said anything. 'He just isn't taking it seriously,' Jilly said. 'He's not doing anything to help himself.'

'Probably thinking why should he bother with a pair of twats.'

So the piss-stupid twosome from Tottenham upped the ante, and really started giving him gyp.

'Fire! Fire!'

Middle of the night. Near panic. Everyone was up on deck. But no sign of fire. The Asiatic lot were looking at us; and we were looking at Mr Graydon. Like, all of us - his voice was too distinctive not to recognise, even in the dark of night, yelling about a fire.

He collected a mass of condemnatory comments, abuse and dire-looks from virtually everyone present. Although I thought Garry and George were overdoing it with their snickering and smirking. So I wondered about them.

But, he said nothing, maybe smiled inwardly? Was it him? Maybe sixty-forty on the chances. Well, I wasn't taking sides. If it was Mr Graydon, good luck to him: they deserved it for laughing at him and taking the mick all the time. Although their skit on him had been funny, if you'd had a drink.

The crew didn't know any better and a pair of them were chatting amicably with him; so I took him a beaker of kaffe, and didn't mention why we were out there - the alarm and fire and everything. 'Mr Graydon,' I said, offering it. 'Joseph.'

He almost grimaced at me, and carried on talking with Pietr and Yonki - the two most-frequently-visible room stewards, deck hands and trip escorts. He sounded almost fluent; then someone interrupted, for their attention and I grabbed the chance to speak with him. 'You speak Turkit?

He looked at me like it was none of my business, 'Four weeks with Mr Google, and a series of deep sleep-tapes. I needed it for the walking part on my own.'

He clammed up as Pietr and Yonki turned back to us, and I nodded and smiled with them a bit longer. One of them spoke a couple of dozen words in English; the same in German, Japanese and something else.

We swapped words until I had a get-by vocabulary; and then I fetched another Kaffe, and I thought he didn't seem so weird when he was talking with them in pigeon Turkit-English. Almost like a normal person- Or, no, not that much of a loosening up. Yonki and Pietr were much more normal. Then an officer-type came and announced they were 100% certain there wasn't a fire. And we all went back to bed. Separately. I did, anyway.

That day, we went out on a two-hour bus ride to an archaeological dig in the desert. A Gilgamesh-era sort of place with sand-worn columns and steps and toppled giant heads. I mean, that's like two hundred years BCE! And I'd read a translation of the Epic of Gilgamesh poem, and sort of knew loads of bits about him. Seeing this fallen-over bas-relief of some heroic type was awesome. Like fifteen feet high, or long, seeing as it had fallen down in the sand.

I thought we were interested - the girls from the History Group; and so were Garry and George - though I did wonder about them, when they seemed to be more captivated with Jilly and Ursula than bas-reliefs and inscriptions. But they reckoned it was what they'd come for. Jilly gave them the brush-off, but Ursula wasn't excessively discouraging.

The Langtons, the only married couple to have bothered coming on the day trip, were bored; and so were the two holding-hands chappies. Eyes for each other and Stuff Gilgamesh.

Yonki was very knowledgeable about it all; and the Japanese/Asiatic crowd never stopped yacking and selfy-ing and grinning like happy Anime characters.

'Ooooh, it's wonderful,' I kept telling Pietr. 'Exciting.' And we were pointing and taking pics and reading the brochures and bits out the guide books. Some workers were behind the tape, and clearing sand out with their hands, or brushes; or sometimes little picks and trowels.

We heard whisperings about some newly uncovered inscriptions; and there was an update info board about it all. Word and glyph panels carved and painted on an interior cellar-type wall that had been sealed until very recently. So that was really good. Like fresh and bright colouring.

So, comes five o'clock and we're wandering back from all that newly-dug rubble and scaffold pipes to the minibus car park, and Jilly, right behind me, lurched forward like a randy drunk, pushing me off the planking pathway. So I go stumbling into all these loose rocks and scaffold clamps-things; felt my ankle turn sideways and under, and I thought, Muck! Jilly had gone on her knees, and got a bad graze on the right one. When she stood up, all apologies, saying someone had bumped into her, 'Felt like a push.' And I crawled up holding on to her. My ankle really tender. Clutching each other. Looking accusingly, but most of them were striding past to get on the buses.

'Bloody women! Sodding typical,' from married guy, who gets a poke from his wife.

Mr Graydon and Pietr helped Jilly to the buses, and were starting to wash and wipe her knee by the time I got there, with Yonki and a couple of the Asian lot half-carrying me; I couldn't put any weight on my ankle at all. So then they were squeezing and wrapping it really hard. 'To stop the swelling.' I felt something like click and crunch and it made me really squawk and grab onto somebody.

Two of our buses had gone by then, and we all just got piled onto whichever one they pointed us to, or practically lifted me into.

So I end up with Yonki and a dozen Japanese people. Actually seeming to be concerned for a while, with my very epicanthic helper checking on my poorly ankle; adding to the bandage with a stretchy one out the bus's first-aid kit. And pressing at me from time to time; before re-attending to his very pretty wife. Most of the ladies were, actually, attractive.

Yonki poured coldish water on it, and they were all really nice to me, mumbling about my ankle, and me in general, nodding and shrugging. 'Foot not broke,' says my Jap Chap. Gazing with these super-seeing eyes; and a voice like Sean Corrony on honey.

'I doctor,' he smiled. 'Of archaeology. But is okay. I am Nippon - Japanese.'

'I thought you were, your group.'

'We mostly from Hokkaido and north Honshu. Different accents and skin shades, but all sons and daughters of Nippon.' He gave my calf and ankle a double-handed farewell stroke, and backed away with a smiling bow.

So it was a much-suffering me who was helped off the bus, one bouncing, rocking hour later; throbbing, aching and needing a drink of something powerful. At least it wasn't the two hours it had been getting there: the boat had moved downstream during the day; but the track was even rougher than the one out there.

To be honest, it didn't feel too bad in the retrospect of ten minutes later, foot up, and in the bar. 'We give you sedative,' one of my new Japanese friends tells me. 'Now we go drink whisky and shochu other end of bar.' And off they chattering went.

A gentleman from the boat staff came and poured something aromatic on my ankle bandage. Liquid morphine, by the effect it had. Probably Ibuprofen, really. 'Come to clinic ten o'clock tomorrow. Deck Two. We be in Slangyaki by then. Overnight down river. Have half-way rest there. You put feet up two days on boat. No walking, hmm?'

Jilly hobbled in not long after, with Pietr in very attentive tow, followed by Mr Graydon. Huh - him. Not bothered about me, huh? Joseph, indeed. Hadn't see him all day.

But he acted like he only just knew about it; and my foot-up and bandaged. He smiled. You pig. And then came and joined us. 'So, you've crippled yourself, and been dumped, have you?'

I glowered my best hate-stare, and that swine from work smirked and was paying attention to Jilly, and practically stroking her leg. 'I'm the first-aider at work,' he said. 'Fully qualified.'

Fully qualified Nerk, I thought, and nearly jumped out my skin when my Japanese arkio-doctor nipped back to see I was alright. 'Should not jump out such beautiful skin.' He had this really nice smile; and I smiled back and stroked his hand, just once, to dent Mr Graydon's apathy. I bet he didn't know that my Son of Nippon was married and just being doctorly nice. Even if he is an archaeology doctor, not a medical one.

So I was getting settled with Jilly and some of the unattached lot; couldn't face a meal. Just a few drinks. The Langtons came in. 'Typical Bloody Bigmouth,' I happened to say in an over loud mutter. Followed by George, with Garry still eating his extra cake slice from the meal. Pig.

A couple of my Arkio Doc's friends joined us, like they were pleased to get a foot in, conversation-wise, and were chattering away about the ruins and the wonderful insights - all three spoke some English. And Yonki and Pietr stayed at the invitation of "Joey." Joey indeed! And with him speaking some Turkit, and Japanese, too! Hub of the conversation, he was - huh, him, now wearing an embroidered Egyptian bath-keeper's jacket and sequinned trousers. Prat.

No wonder Garry and George were sniggering and making comments. They raised a few smiles, but mostly were ignored; and I thought they were studying me and Jilly a lot, as well as Ursula and the two Japanese ladies. Very roving eyes, they had - ought to clear off with the stag-type lot, not be polluting our atmosphere. But, anyway, we were all getting on pretty well, and some of the other folk in our group joined us, pulling a couple of tables together, and I really liked the attention and they were so nice - all of them. Except Yonki was all overboard for Ursula. And Mr Graydon was super-sweet with Jilly, with a most un-first-aiderly-like hand resting on her grazed knee - etc. So I glowered at her, too, and focused on Haruto, my Arkio-Doc and his friend. It was a little bit of an “any port in a storm” situation with me. I needed some company, not to be ignored just because I had a swollen foot and was sulking.

Well, with the sedation, pain-killers, bandages, attention, and several more large drinks, I was getting over it, and everybody was chattering and drinking, and two more of the Japanese came over - and then two of their ladyfolk - I think one was in charge. They were briefly - but sincerely - asking and checking about our injuries before they brought bottles and glasses across, and some spicy crackers and goat’s cheese crunchies. Pietr came out from behind the bar and joined in - all big smile and so-white teeth. It was Yonki’s turn at the bar for a while, and the Langtons admitted it was their 21st wedding anniversary and they were drunk already and bought a round for everyone - some Turkit semi-fizz that smelled like camel dung and tasted so warm inside. ‘Powerful stuff,’ everyone said, eyes watering.

Yonki put some music on, and the married ones were slow-dancing - and staggering; and the Progeny of Nippon started doing a different dance to it, and the two very-good friends came in to see what all the revelry was, and within five minutes, they were so relaxed and smooching. And I was nearly wetting myself and had to totter off, using a bar stool like a Zimmer frame to get to the toilet - except they called it the hoshtoi - something like that.

But it was fine, even though my foot was aching again, just a bit, and Pietr came and helped me sit down, and checked the bandages - loosened the binding a little and it felt better - and there was a couple of pills. I know they were dihydro-morphine or something like that: it said so on the packet.

It’s a bit of a blur after that - somebody was very attentive, and really nice, and such white teeth - and vivid blue eyes - I think that was one of the very friendly guys from the stag lot. And I remember I was fancying Haruto really eversuch a lot... but Pietr... or maybe Yonki, was there. A voice was saying, ‘Don’t do it.’ But I don’t know what, or who to.

I got really cross with somebody. I mean, I was only going to get up and dance and have a laugh. But some interfering No-hoper made me sit down, and said I'd damage my ankle. I remember some of them looked disappointed. Wanted to see me up and dancing; with the gay abandonment that our two hand-holder guys were doing. I really wanted to get up and flaunt it and be happy.

'No. Stay.' Like I was a poodle. Somebody telling me I would regret it. And my Arkio-Doc was laughing about something and his dark-eyed lady wife was there and she was so beautiful - like a classic painting. Another someone was saying, 'Yes, yes, be alright... Come on.' That might have been Ahmad or Mahdi or whoever...

Oh, irritating God! That clamped hand and unbrookable command. 'Do not get up, Miss Teake.'

But I had another drink or two from somebody - maybe Garry or his mouthy oppo. And some well-meaning soul was asking if I wanted to dance, with the others on the floor; and was helping me to get up and saying really nice things and I was all warm for him. Then some interferer was being nasty and annoying, and pulling me... and I didn't want that. I wanted, I dunno, something...

'Come with me.'

I wasn't going to be bossed round. It was in that, "you must do vot I say,' tone of voice, not that, 'Mmm, darling Mystique, come with me,' silken murmur. I mean, I was the invalid who should be looked after, not bullied round. But this meddlesome man sounded really bossy, and not letting me do what I wanted. It was so insistent and I just couldn't struggle against it; and I just sagged out of it by then and lord alone knows. Wheee! that drink was good stuff.

I remember short and long snatches thereafter - the stars... a warm breeze... smell of something like jasmine, and I was singing that Seals and Croft song. There was somebody really irritating there, but we were on deck, like on our own, and I cuddled him a bit. I recall that much, sort of fluffily... and wrapping me up in a deck blanket and telling somebody to go away... and I was singing Summer Breeze all the time. and I was away with the stars and I felt just magic and I knew everything was perfect.

Ahhh... and it was.

I woke up sometime in the morning, wrapped up in the blanket on a lounger on deck. I was on my own ,and thought, 'Everyone left me? On my own up here on the deck? Oh, no. A lounger right next to mine. Same blanket over both. Omigod! Out here? Did I?I never-' I am so stupid.

Looking round - different mooring. Of course: they said we were moving on to Slangyaki overnight, for a mid-cruise break. Couple of days based here.

'Ah... you're awake? I brought you a coffee. How are you feeling?' Such a slimy solicitous tone.

'You! Mr Graydon?' It shouldn't be you. It ought to be Bonki or Peetie or Arkio-Doc... or the other stag-do feller, thingy. I burned inside to think of-

I heard the words from last night... 'You'll regret it.'

Remember thinking, Would I? The heck I would. Or would I? I wasn't thinking. Intending to do... something. My ankle felt warm and stiff - I tried to flex it. And my head was swimming.

Oh my God. Had I-? With him? Him! Mr Weird. Oh, Lord - how could he? Destroyed my... my what? Oh, Lord. What have I done?

I was struggling to throw the coffee away - awful stuff; and untangle from the blanket; and stand up on this soddin ankle. And flee from the whole excruciating place.

Jilly found me. 'Been looking all over for you, Alison. What you doing in the laundry? One of the crew told me you were here.'

'It was the only door that wasn't locked, or didn't have people in the room. Go away.'

'What? What's happened?'

'Him. That Graydon man. He... And me. On the deck, all night.'

'And you think? Oh, Alison.' She sat on the towel-filled floor next to me.

'They would have let you get up and dance like a wild thing. Long-term injury to your ankle, that would have been. It was Garry who gave you those pills - should never have alcohol with them. And your Arkio-Doc? Pouring something in your drink. You'd have done yourself permanent damage. Or fallen overboard.

'I heard Garry and George plotting something to get you on one side - get you sloshed. Down the back end under the canopy, where there's sunbathing mattresses. And, boy, were you lapping it up - all the attention.'

'You saying I was putting myself about?'

'You were putting everybody about, including the married bloke whose wife goes to bed early. Even Mr Langton fancied his chances. Yonki was hovering kinda close, as well. The two spare stag fellers thought they were in there, too-'

'In there?'

'In the queue for you. But Garry and Greasy George were pretty much counting on it first. Your Doctor of Archaeology friend was enjoying himself immensely; and his two friends. And his wife was permitting it - saw them conspiring and laughing. Hate to say it - but his designs on you weren't exactly Gothic, Doric or Ionian; much more Sukiya-in-bed, methinks.'

'Him? But he's-'

'Yes, I know, a Son of Nippon. The Rising Son of Nippon from the looks of the bulge in his pants last night.'

'Oh, God. What have I done?'

'Well, how's your ankle?'

'Seems not to be any worse.'

'In that case, you probably haven't done anything-'

'But him, Graydon?'

'From what I saw, Alison...'

Jilly and Ursula pushed me at him, late afternoon. He'd been to the souk, by the look of his bejewelled turban and over-braided sash. Like a Haile Selassie in market-mood, sitting in the corner of the bar, playing Pasur on his own, with a pack of traditional sahra' cards.

'I... I...' didn't know what to say, not after I'd slapped his face and hobbled off post haste this morning. 'You... you...'

'Yes?' he looked up at me. Really neutral.

'What? Where? Where's my romance gone.'

He smiled! The pig!

'Your romance? Miss- or perhaps Alison, now we know each other a little better, hmm?'

Oh, God. It was true

'You still have your romance,' he said, 'and whatever degree of virginity you had before, remains intact. You're fine.'

'Jilly's claiming you saved me from a fate worse than death?'

'Oh, Miss... ah, Alison, a) There's no such thing as worse than death, and b) You may have thoroughly enjoyed a night of rampant passion with a dozen fellow travellers, but c) I took it upon myself to believe you would prefer to be sober and conscious when you made the decision.'

'So? What? You did? Out there? Behind the deckchairs?'

He just sighed. 'It's been a busy day, and a disrupted night. I have things to do in my room.'

He was gone.

Oh, Lord. What an awful evening. We Joomer Girls stuck together; or they stuck with me, warding off all-comers. 'Could do with some police tape round this corner,' Marjorie said. I sank back and sipped my coffee and watched the sun go down, palm-tree shadows lengthening, the sand reddening, water darkening. Mood blackening.

Mr Graydon and I had this massive horrible row. Well, I did, anyway: he wasn't there; throughout my third drink. Then the others were coming up on deck and in the lounge and bar, laughing and looking forward to the next spare day exploring this place, after today's distractions around Slangyaki- Except! Tomorrow is the optional trip to the fabled - I like to think - palace of Giryilga. It's visible through the shallow waters of the river. We'd done two sessions on it this past term, and I just had to go, and I'd been resting my ankle, in the washing room, and the after-deck, and our room - me and Jilly. I did us all a favour, took a sleeper, and left them to it.

Having done my time of rest, in the morning, I joined the group to take the minibuses out to the flooded site. Very delicately - ankle not feeling too wonderful - the on-boat doc had said there was severe tearing of the tendons, and there had been a temporary dislocation of the tarsal bone and something. 'It replaced itself almost immediately, aided by the bandaging that was applied at the time. But you must take the pills I prescribed for ten days. They will reduce pain; and the swelling. Rest it.'

'I will,' I promised, fingers crossed. After I've been to the Giryilga palace.

So I was waiting, keeping my head down among the others. Bloody Garry and George sniggering, crude in language and gesture. 'Tottenham Turds,' I told them, and they kept going on about Mr Graydon and me 'shagging away on the deck all night, eh?'

In the face of that, and weaponless, I made sure I was well away from them when it came to loading onto the minibuses. Very delicately having to stand to join the queue-

'No. Not you. You're under doctor's orders to stay off your feet.' Mr Graydon! My nema-bloody-sis. He needn't come the masterful bit with me...

'You must,' he said, 'completely rest that ankle for at least another day. I heard what you were told- No no no... you have to give it chance. I'll stay here with you.'

'You will not! I'm not stopping on this boat another whole day. Especially with you.' Except my ankle was hurting and aching already - just five minutes standing. Dammit, I suppose he's right. He would be, wouldn't he? No no no... noooo. I've looked forward to it for six winter months. I was in floods of tears. 'Giryilga. I'll miss it. Nooo.'

He held the bus up from departing. 'One moment.'

Back two minutes later, he was pushing a bloody wheelchair, serious smile, and a deft hand at jerking it into the folded position, dropping the push handles, and helping me to the three steps aboard.

'No more tears,' he ordered. 'We'll see if we can get a bit of plywood under the seat, if you need to elevate the foot.'

It was fabulous. The water was so clear, and all the gorgeous photos and posters they had for sale; and the pics we took. The artefacts they'd assembled in a free museum. And you could hire glass-bottom buckets to look down more clearly. And go on boats with a glass bottom. And get the most super buffet for next to nothing. He made me pay, because he was doing all the work, he said. Chelo kebab, ghormeh sabzi and all sorts - like tahdig. No alcoholic drink, though. Just as well, really. And seeing Jilly and the others every now and again. Going in the shade, and along this palm and statues avenue. Being accosted by the Tottenham toerags irregularly and most embarrassingly. Nasty, they were with Mr Graydon; crude with me.

I sagged at the sight of them at the minibuses.

But at least they weren't on our bus, and the trip back, after a couple of painkillers, seemed to pass quite dreamily. But Joey! Huh! Joey Indeed! Had been there all day and hadn't let me go anywhere standing up, except to the toilet; and moved my chair everywhere I fancied, sun, shade, then the riverside to see the water traffic... and the dockside to see the passers-by, and the street sellers.

The meal felt so relaxed when we got back to the boat - another new mooring we had to find. With drink. Alcoholic bliss! So tasty, a local Shiraz. I eased a fraction towards my Joey when he came back in the bar with some Turkish Delight nibbles to share with the others as they came wandering in later. 'Pavement trader at Giryilga,' he told them. 'Did a smart line in silk carpet slippers, too.'

The bar was slowly filling up; Hamuto and wife; the stag-do five; the other loose ones and marrieds from our group.'Thought George and Garry would be in here by now,' someone was looking round. 'Said they would be - had a great idea for a show...'

'Be in their room, I expect.'

'Been a long day; probably crashed out. Be in later...'

Mr Langton went and asked Pietr if he knew anything. He went and checked; back to us in ten minutes, 'There has just been a call from the Zagrnya office. They have just arrived there, Zagrnya.'

'Eh? How'd that happen?'

'That's two hundred miles north - near where we started.' Bafflement all round.

'The office says it would be another week before the next boat downriver.'

'So... they won't be rejoining us, then?' A touch of enlightenment all round.

'How did that happen?'

'What did they do that for?'

I saw him smile. He knew something. I waited. 'What?' I said.

'What what?' he avoided.

I poked.

'Oh that...' The most innocent, smiling shrug. 'Two thousand karanty and they'll put anybody on any minibus you want. Shush, hmm? Twenty quid well spent, methinks?'

Sanctuary

Julie Malone

The quiet nightshift followed a stormy evening at home. The row with Kate had been on his mind all night and he felt drained. Finally, this was his last fare and all he wanted was to get home, have a mug of tea, breakfast and bed. Nothing else mattered. If Kate was in a mood, she'd have to get over it. It was her problem, not his.

He announced his arrival with an impatient blast on the horn and was rewarded by a twitch of the curtains, closely followed by a woman emerging from the house, her eyes concealed by enormous dark glasses. Short on tolerance, he guessed she was hungover and muttered an expletive when she stopped at the gate and peered cautiously up and down the street. But then another look told him this pick-up was not what it first seemed. This woman was wary, guarded, she was a frightened rabbit on the lookout for danger and ready for flight. He knew the signs. She was running away. From what he didn't care but if this meant trouble he wanted no part of it. But her fear transferred to him and he cast a quick look through the rear window. The street seemed to be clear other than a couple of women approaching, one of them pushing a toddler in a buggy. No one, as far as he could see, was peering secretively from behind net curtains, and there was no sign of a Bailiff's van trundling down the street to catch her before she run.

He wished she would hurry up so they could get going, and was relieved to see her turn, satisfied all was well, and beckon towards the porch. A pretty, dark haired girl in her mid-teens struggled from the house lugging some black bags. Close behind, a small boy, blond haired and bespectacled, half lifted, half dragged a heavy holdall towards the car. The girl urged him to speed up just as the driver joined them at the back of the car.

He grinned at her as he opened the boot. 'You doing a moonlight?'

'Something like that,' she replied flatly.

His attempt at chirpiness obviously not appreciated, the driver hefted the bags into the boot then turned to find the woman behind him with two more holdalls.

'There's another couple to come,' she said, her tone preoccupied, detached, her mind elsewhere. She turned towards the bay window of the house, looking for something.

'You won't get any more in there,' he chuckled, 'or the lad'll have to sit on the roof.'

She didn't respond and his eyes were drawn in the direction of her gaze. He caught a quick twitch of the curtain.

'You're not expecting to get anyone else in there are ya?'

She shook her head.

'Thank the Lord for that or they really would be sittin' on the roof!'

He tried flippancy again, but it went unacknowledged as the woman once more glanced quickly up and down the street, then returned to the porch and collected the remaining luggage, the boy trotting in her wake, lifted something and clutched it tight. A teddy wearing a striped pullover and a bobble-hat. Cherished and reassuring, the lad held it close to him and grasping the woman's skirt came with her back down the path.

At the window a little girl in a pink pyjama top, her dark hair tousled as if she had just got out of bed, pushed back the net curtain and waved cheerfully at the woman as she ushered the boy, still hugging the teddy, onto the back seat next to his sister, squashed in with three black bags, they huddled together like sardines in a tin.

The front door of the house opened and a young woman, looking very like the little girl in the window, ran out. The driver noticed her feet were bare.

She blew a kiss to the children then turned to the woman, her expression one of concern. 'Take care of yourselves and let me know when you're there, safe.'

'I will and...thank you...for everything, Fiona. You've been a true friend.' The women hugged. The driver did not rush them. Back in the front seat he looked through the rear view mirror at the children in the back. The boy was still waving at the little girl in the window, but his sister watched their mother anxiously, clearly eager to be on their way.

'We've got to get going,' the woman told her friend, 'and you'd better get back inside. We'll be OK and thank you again. We'd never have got this far without you.'

The women separated and, with another quick look, the mother then climbed into the front of the taxi. Her hands, clutching the hold-all on her lap, were trembling, the driver noticed but looked away. Whatever this was about, it was none of his business.

Her friend walked slowly back to her door but did not go inside.

'Right, where are we off to?' he asked, making another attempt at lightening the atmosphere. 'I promise I won't tell the rent man if he asks!' he laughed, but with no responding smile, gave up. It was only when she muttered the address that he finally understood.

The younger woman watched the taxi until it disappeared around a corner before going inside and closing the door.

Tiny specks of rain dotted the windscreen during the silent, ten minute journey as the taxi weaved its way through the crawling, morning rush-hour traffic in the business section of the town.

Already looking forward to that first coffee of the day, workers battled against the tide of people on the crowded pavements, their collars turned up and umbrellas at the ready for the threatened drenching. Drivers yelled abuse at dare-devil pedestrians who risked their lives darting across the road between lanes of fast flowing traffic, trying to save the few seconds it would have taken to walk to the crossings.

Children hurried to school. A motorbike roared past, car tyres squealed. A police siren came blaring up from behind. The woman turned to watch it approach, fearful, ready for flight...

'It's alright, love,' the cab driver said. 'Look its gone past.' He reached out to touch her arm, intending reassurance, comfort. She flinched away.

Pulling up at their destination, a non-descript shop front, the girl jumped out telling her brother to wait. Pale and drawn, she cast anxious looks at passing pedestrians before beckoning him out but keeping him hidden, safe, between her and the car. Their mother did not move. Although unseen, her eyes seemed fixed on the darkened glass frontage of the building. Her hands still shook.

He had spent just ten short minutes with this tense family and was dog-tired, but the driver had enough sensitivity not to rush her. Although he tried not to look, he had noted the half-moon purple bruising high up on her cheek, and the red mark between her left eyebrow and the top of her nose, showing livid above her glasses. He wondered what he would have done had she been his daughter, or sister. He guessed she was forty-ish and probably fairly attractive but what disfigurement was she hiding?

Her children were growing fretful, but still he did not hurry her. He tried to find some encouraging words, but everything he thought of sounded trite and over-used. What could he say? That he had seen it all before? Had dropped many women and children at this place and watched them pass through the door? There was no point in that. Anyway, he usually put them from his mind as he drove away, never saw them again or knew their fate. He didn't dwell on their problems even though a few stuck in his mind, and he sometimes found himself wondering about them. He thought of his own family and how lucky he was and, on impulse, decided to buy Kate some flowers on the way home.

The girl opened the passenger door. 'Come on Mum.' Her brother still clutched his teddy bear and his sister's hand as if his life depended on it. 'We got to get inside. It's raining!'

The woman nodded, reached for her purse, took out a note and paid the driver. It had not taken long for the rain to become a steady downpour but she welcomed it; rain meant lowered heads; less likelihood of being spotted.

The driver unloaded the jumble of holdalls and black bags onto the pavement. The woman's trembling fingers slipped on the wet plastic as she struggled to get a grip on the heavy knotted bags. She was close to tears.

'It's alright,' the driver said in a tone of fatherly understanding. 'You and the kids'll be safe in there. You go on in. I'll see to this lot.' He waited for an elderly man pushing a woman in a wheelchair to go by before hefting three of the heavier bags across his shoulder, then effortlessly picked up two more and headed towards the office.

Still she hesitated, her hair now in wet rat-tails, her feet splashed with rain, apparently reluctant to enter. Until this moment she had been strong, but the enormity of the situation, of what she was about to do - had already done - hit her as solidly as the blows from a few nights before. That and the sympathetic kindness of the cab driver finally brought the tears to her eyes; compassion had weakened her resolve.

'Mum?' The girl handed her brother a couple of smaller bags while she struggled with the wet and awkward bulk of three more. 'Mum?' she repeated. 'Come on.'

'Okay, let's do this,' the mother said, taking a deep breath and following the girl as she shepherded her little brother ahead of her. At the door, they met the driver on his way out and moved to one side to allow him past before they entered. The mother, assuming he was about to leave, stopped to thank him. Her surprise was genuine when, with a wink, he pushed the fare she had just given him into her pocket.

'Don't tell anyone else or they'll all expect it,' he joked, and then in a more serious tone said, 'but, I think you need it more'n I do.'

Tears, never far away over recent days, slid down her face; she was unused to kindness. She tried to thank him but no words came. He gave her a knowing nod and briefly gripped her arm.

'We're not all bastards,' he said gently, 'though sometimes some of us come close to it without realising and it's me who should be thanking you. Not the other way round.'

He walked to the driver's side of the car and opened the door. 'Get yourself inside, Ma'am. You've a grand pair of kids there, and a courage that does you proud. You've done the right thing. You'll be safe there.' He got in the car, gave the woman a half salute and drove off without looking back, leaving her staring after him, her fear of being seen on the street forgotten in that one magic moment of rarely experienced humanity.

The woman, the mother, felt inside as if she were a frightened little girl. Courage? Yes it had taken courage to tell the neighbours her bruising had been caused in a car crash and, yes it had taken courage to defend her children against his yelling and ravings. But was it courage she had needed to secretively pack as many of their belongings as they could carry, to call Fiona yesterday afternoon and arrange to stay with her last night? Was it bravery or fear that made her finally pick up that phone and talk to people who could help her and the children?

She smiled at a memory. Yes, it had taken courage to face Gregory's Head Teacher, keep her nerve and tell bare-faced lies to get him out of school without any awkward questions being asked.

But was it weakness or courage to give up on vows and commitment? She pictured his face. He had made those vows too. He had made that commitment to love her and take care of her and he had betrayed her and the children. Now she was lucky to be alive, the children were safe and they were leaving forever. The hardest part, the walking away was done. That was achieved.

What came next would not be easy. There would still be fear, doubt and uncertainty. Tears and struggle; yes all that was still to come. But if she took one step at a time, held her head high and told herself freedom was awaiting just around the corner, and in its wake, smiles, happiness and laughter, then this first step was going to be worth taking. Surely they deserved that. No, it would not be easy, but was anything worth having ever easy?

One step at a time. She took a deep breath, lifted her head high against the pouring rain and took those few steps forward towards sanctuary, went through the door and closed it, firmly, behind her.

Freedom

Julie Malone

Now, when I look at my week-old baby son, I thank God he will never experience what we went through when I was a child. As long as I live I will never forget that Tuesday morning thirty-one years ago, and Mum was holding my hand as she walked me to school.

Cars sped by; drivers with or without passengers headed to work. Some were friends who hooted and waved to us as they passed and, in the distance, the constant thrummm of vehicles on the dual carriageway echoed across to the busy school road.

The closer we got to the school, the more impatient parents in cars became, slotting into spaces other drivers wanted. I heard more swear words close to the school gates each morning than I ever did anywhere else. Usually my Mum would tell me not to listen but, on this morning it was she who didn't seem to hear.

The pavements teemed with children in blue and grey, mothers chatted to friends about what had been on the television the night before, or what they'd had for dinner. Mostly the children walked themselves to school, their Mums ignoring them being too busy chatting as they walked two or three abreast, blocking the pathway with their pushchairs and prams.

I remember giving a little smile as the mothers, forced to step into the road to get by the obstruction, gave filthy looks and muttered swear words as they stepped back on to the pavement. To be honest, there was always some aggravation around the school gates in the morning; it blended with the chat and laughter.

In a few minutes, groups of happy children would be running around in the playground together, and the equally happy mothers, free of their offspring for a few hours, would be on their way to work, a shopping trip, coffee with a friend, or for those very unlucky, back to the housework. Every school morning was the same, except this one. Well it seemed to be for everyone else, but not for us.

For some reason, although my mother always held my hand, on this day her grip was tighter than usual and she seemed tense, was very, very quiet, it was totally unlike her. We normally talked about what I was going to do at school that day, what I wanted for my tea, what Dusty, our Old English Sheepdog, had been up to. We would just talk...all the way to school, about anything, and she usually made me laugh. Not that there had been much to laugh about over the previous few weeks. And certainly she was not laughing that morning. She seemed to be so deep in thought she didn't even notice her friend Ruth call out, and she missed seeing our neighbour, Sally, wave as she went by on her way to work. At least I think she missed them. She never mentioned having seen them, but then later on we had too many other things to think about, I suppose. But it seemed strange that she turned her head in the opposite direction as Ruth called. That was very unlike Mum. She really liked Ruth and I couldn't understand why she had ignored her. I remember being a little frightened by that. I wanted to say something but stayed quiet; she didn't seem to want to talk, not even to me, and we were almost at the gates. She suddenly stopped walking.

'Mum, what's the matter? Mum?' I remember looking up at her. She looked so...so serious. I was scared. I was about to go into school and wouldn't see her until later. I was going to Davie's house to wait for Dad to collect me, and all I wanted was to see her smile before she left.

Then, as she gently pulled me to one side to stand against the school wall to allow others enough space to pass, she gave me that smile that meant everything was alright and she crouched down so her face was level with mine.

'Move your foot forward and I can pretend I'm tying your shoe laces,' she said, turning to look either side. I put my right foot out and she started playing with the laces. I could see the red mark and bruising between her left eye and the side of her nose over her dark glasses.

'I know I've been a bit quiet but I had something on my mind.' She undid and re-tied my shoe lace, looked up at me and smiled. 'I want to talk to you before you go in and then I have to go to work, but this has to be just between us, you do understand, don't you?'

I nodded; I remember thinking that I knew what was coming. Her face was close to mine and I reached out my hand. She flinched. I drew my hand away for a second then reached out again. This time she didn't move and let me run my finger gently along the still livid, red scar that ran from her left eyebrow to halfway down the left side of her nose.

'Does it still hurt, Mum?' It looked as though it should, and she still had what was left of the bruising that had been all around both swollen eyes, but was now yellow-green saucer-shaped lines low down on her cheeks. I had seen the fading black-blue marks moving lower and lower down her face over the last two weeks. Looking back I now realise it was the blood going to the lowest point and pooling.

It had been seven weeks since that night, the stitches had been taken out and her nose straightened, but the evidence was still there. I will never forget how she looked in the ambulance on the way to hospital. Helen had shoved my big teddy into my arms to cuddle for comfort but she kept her arms around me as well while the paramedic was looking after Mum. The scar still looked sore.

She shook her head. 'Not any more, love.' She took my hand away from her face and held it, waited for a group of four women, two prams and a number of children to go by. 'Sweetheart, if I have to make a decision about...' I looked down at the chipped and cracked grey paving slabs of the pavement and the muddy green moss between them. Then Mum stood up and I thought she wasn't going to say any more, but I was wrong.

'Greg, you're a big boy now and you know what happened. I've been thinking that I need to make a big decision about the family. Will you trust me to make the right one?'

I remember a feeling of such happiness I couldn't speak. I was right. I did know what she was talking about and I threw my arms around her waist. 'You mean leave Dad? How soon can we go?' I was so pleased. We were going to get away.

Gently she released herself from my hug and took my hand again to lead me towards the open black wrought iron school gate. Most of my friends were already in the playground and there were only a few chatting parents left.

'How did you know?' Mum asked. 'How could you be so understanding...at your age?'

'I was hoping we'd leave. He frightens me. When are we going, Mum?' This was so exciting.

We stood back to allow the Macdonald twins through into the playground. Mrs Colston and Miss Mackie were the first two teachers who came through the main doors, whistles at the ready to see their classes line up.

'You're going to have to go in now. Your sister and I have been talking and we're trying to plan things properly. It might be a few days yet, but I'll let you know when I've been able to sort everything out. Remember, it has to be our secret. Can you do that? You must not even tell Davie.'

'. . . but will it be soon, Mum?'

'Yes, love. It'll be soon but Dad mustn't know or he won't let us go. You do understand that don't you?'

Oh yes! I knew that. He would never let us go and everything would get worse. No, I wasn't going to say anything to him at all and I promised her I wouldn't. 'But what about Helen? She's coming too, isn't she?'

'Oh, yes, of course. Helen will come too.'

I just knew that everything was going to be alright. Mum hugged me. 'You'd better go in now and I'll see you tonight.'

I had just gone through the gate and Mum was a few steps away down the pavement. I had a thought and ran back. 'Mum! What about Dusty and the cats? We're not leaving them behind, are we?'

She turned back to give me one last hug.

'No. No-one gets left behind,' she smiled. 'Now, off you go or you'll be late into class. Don't forget, you need to get on with your schoolwork today. Just remember, everything has to seem normal. This is our exciting secret. No-one must know...'

'. . . .especially Dad.' I finished her sentence.

'Do you think you can be brave enough?'

'Yes. I don't want to live with Dad anymore. He scares me.'

'Come on, Greg!' Davie yelled. The classes were all heading into school.

'See you later, Mum,' I said as I ran back into the playground. Inside I felt as though I was glowing and hoped it didn't show. It was our secret and no-one would know.

-oOo-

All through the morning, I tried not to think about what Mum had said, but I couldn't help it, and it was just really hard trying not to say anything, especially to Davie and my other pal, Alex. It was difficult to concentrate during classes that morning, but I managed to get through and by lunchtime, I had almost forgotten about it. Outside in the playground, running around with my mates had felt so normal. Then it was time to go back into class for our reading lesson and I got stuck into my book, got a gold star for reading out loud and for understanding, and then it was afternoon break.

I remember we had only just gone back into class and taken out our Geography books when the door opened and in walked Mrs McMurdo, the Headteacher. She looked in my direction as she walked to the front of the class to talk to our teacher, Mrs Livingstone, who stood up. Teachers always stood up when the Headteacher entered their classroom.

By the blackboard, they turned their backs and spoke quietly. Angus, sitting at the desk nearest to them stretched forward as far as he could go, trying to hear what they were saying but sat back sharply as they turned around.

'Gregory,' said Mrs Livingstone. 'Collect your things and go with Mrs McMurdo, please.' I remember being so surprised at hearing my name that, for a moment, I didn't move.

'Come, boy,' snapped Mrs McMurdo and the whole class turned to look at me. I stood up, shakily took my jacket off the back of my chair, threw my books and pencil case into my school bag while Mrs

McMurdo, who now seemed very impatient, her arms folded and in what we always called her cast-iron cardy mood, watched from the doorway. You didn't keep Mrs McMurdo waiting.

'What's up?' whispered Davie, as I squeezed by his desk.

'Don't know,' I muttered, hurrying to join Mrs McMurdo and aware of the silence of my classmates as they all watched me leave.

When I stood in front of her, Mrs McMurdo smiled at me. I don't think I had ever seen her do that before and it was quite frightening, to be honest. She laid her hand gently on my shoulder and ushered me out of the door and into the corridor where I found my Mum waiting for me. I went to speak but Mum gave me an almost imperceptible shake of her head and took my hand.

'I'm glad to see you looking so much better after that nasty car accident,' Mrs McMurdo said to Mum. 'I hope you're feeling better too.'

'Yes. Yes, I am. Thank you for asking.' Mum smiled very sweetly. 'I'm sorry I have to take Gregory out of school for a few days but as I mentioned, my aunt and I have always been close and there's no-one else, you see.'

'Oh, I quite understand, family must come first, but of course Gregory seems a little confused.'

Mum looked at me. 'We have to go to London for a few days, Greg. Auntie Connie has been taken ill and...do you remember her son, Keith?'

I shook my head.

'No, well perhaps you wouldn't, it's been a while since you saw them. Anyway he's in the army in Germany and can't get home until the end of the week, so we're going to look after Auntie Connie until he can get home.'

She turned to Mrs McMurdo. 'Thank you so much for letting me take Greg with me. Unfortunately, as I mentioned, with my husband working shifts...'

That's when I knew she was telling lies. Dad was just starting the second year of his college course. He didn't have a job, let alone working shifts. But I said nothing, although I was dying to ask.

'. . . he can't look after the children, so they're having to come with me. All being well Greg will be back on Monday.' She looked at her watch. 'Oh, is that the time? Sorry, Mrs McMurdo, we'll have to catch a train so we need to get home, get a few things packed and be on the 5.15 train to Euston.'

Mrs McMurdo just looked down at me. 'I don't think there's too much to worry about with young Gregory being away from school for three days. You're up to date with all your work aren't you?' I nodded.

'And you have your reading book.' I nodded again. 'Then we'll see you on Monday. Right, I'll let you get on your way. Have a good journey.' And with that she walked away, her footsteps echoing on the tiled floor.

'What's happening?' I asked.

But Mum just took my hand, winked, but said nothing as we headed towards the cloakroom. I can still remember our footsteps sounding as loud as Mrs McMurdo's had as we walked the length of the corridor towards the main door; any sound seemed to echo more loudly along that long passageway.

When we reached the cloakroom, Mum looked around. There was no-one in sight. Everyone else was in class. 'Quickly, get your coat and PE bag.'

I remember standing at the door and starting to ask... 'But...'

'I'll explain when we get outside. Go on, quickly. Give me your school bag. I'll wait for you by the main doors.'

'But who's Auntie Connie?' I asked.

'Just hurry up...come on.'

I ran in, snatched my coat off the peg, grabbed my PE bag from the cage underneath the seat and ran out. Mum took hold of my hand, we darted out of the door and just beyond the gate I saw a big, black taxi. Helen was inside and she seemed to be a bit squashed in. She waved and beckoned.

As we ran out of the gate, Mum said. 'I couldn't say any more this morning, but Helen and I have just packed up everything we need. We gave ourselves an hour to take just what was necessary. We've left home. You won't be coming back to this school. I had to lie to Mrs McMurdo to get you out.'

Inside the taxi, a very excited, tail-wagging, Dusty almost threw herself at us, but Helen held her back by her lead to let us get in, then the silly dog jumped all over me. I can still feel her licks making my face wet now.

Piled up against the other door were four cases, a couple of holdalls and some black bags and our two cats, Strider and Sophie, sat miserably in baskets on the floor. There wasn't much room for Mum and me, I can tell you.

'Right then,' said the driver, 'where noo?' He started the engine. It was such a relief when we moved off.

'Can you take us to the vets by the Johnny Walker Distillery, please. We have an appointment there and then there are two more stops. Is that going to be OK for you?'

'Aye,' he said, and I've never forgotten this. He turned to look at us. 'Ah think ah ken wha' yer doin' an' ah'll help. Yeh'll pay sumthin' but ah'll no charge yer the fu' fare, hen.'

Mum smiled. 'Thank you. That's good of you.' She moved over to the pull-down seat and spoke to the driver through the gap in the screen where people paid their fares. 'Can I ask you a favour please?'

Keeping his eye on the road he didn't look round. 'Aye. Yer can ask,' he smiled.

'I just wondered if. . . if anyone. . . '

'If anyone gets in touch with the comp'ny tae ask aboot yer, dinna fash yersel' hen. Ah ne'er saw yer. Thass nae problem, hen. Ah've tekken lassies like yersel away from bad lives afore.'

Mum sat back beside me, and it was then I asked what had happened to my goldfish. I had two in a big bowl with plants and a little castle-thing. Mum told me that she'd given them to the little girl next door. She wasn't leaving anything behind to suffer. I didn't mind that. I liked little Debbie.

Soon after we were at the vets. Mum took Strider inside to have a vaccination booster while we waited in the car. Then we drove to a kennels where they also had a cattery section.

The driver waited while we booked Dusty and the cats in, and got Dusty settled in the dog section where she had a large indoor kennel with an outside run, and the cats were housed together in the other part of the building.

I can't recall the exact conversation between Mum and the woman at the kennels, but I know Mum asked if they would keep it a secret that our pets were there, and I know the lady agreed. She said they would only deal with Mum, and I saw her write something on their notes.

It was horrible leaving Dusty there. The cats didn't seem to mind too much, but Dusty cried and whined and ran at the door of her run as we left her behind. I remember Helen crying. Mum hugged us both and I do remember what she said to us then, word for word. 'We'll get them back as soon as we can and we'll visit, but remember they're safe and that's what counts. We'll get them back when we have somewhere to live. Now we have to get to Fiona's.'

No-one spoke as we walked back to the taxi. We were all too upset at leaving our pets behind. But Mum was right. They would be safe there and we would get them back when we were settled somewhere.

Fiona was a work friend of Mum's and we were to stay at her home that night. Dad didn't know her so would have no idea where we were, or where to begin looking. As we unloaded all our bags, the taxi driver got out to help. He even took some of the bags inside for us. Then, when he was ready to leave, Mum went to pay him and he refused to take any more than five pounds. To this day I can still remember his face. There are some kind people in the world.

Neither Helen or I had met Fiona before but she was amazing; beautiful and really friendly. Mum said she was a little like a cross between a Hippie and a Goth. I thought she was fantastic and Helen loved her style. I can still remember her now. Long, black shoulder length hair, and sparkling green eyes. Mum said later that she used emerald-colour contact lenses but her eyes were naturally green.

Once we had settled, Mum then explained that we would be going to the Women's Aid the next morning and they would help us. She and Helen had made plans for us to go straight there the following day, while

Dad was at college, but when he came home on Monday afternoon, his timetable had changed and they found out he would be at home on Wednesdays. That meant we had to leave earlier than they had planned and Fiona had offered to let us stay at hers overnight.

It was after six o'clock that evening that Mum phoned Dad's brother to let him know we had left, were safe but she wouldn't tell him where we were. I heard her say that if he didn't know where we were staying, he couldn't tell any lies.

That night, I slept in Fiona's little boy's room. I can't remember his name but he was a lovely three year old who was very excited at having someone sleeping in his room. Mum slept on the sofa in the living room and Helen slept in Fiona's bedroom. Not that any of us got much sleep that night.

Because I found it hard to get to sleep, I heard some of the conversation between Fiona, Mum and Helen. At one point I heard Mum say: 'Jim was pleased we had left and was going to go and see him. He said the best thing I'd done was to get Greg away from his father's influence.'

The next morning we went to the Women's Aid office and stayed for a few weeks at their refuge in the same town, then moved to another town sixty miles away where Mum had friends. It was there we changed our surnames and 'disappeared' through their system. We never saw my Dad again and I wasn't sorry.

Of course, I never went back to that school. For about six weeks I went to another primary school in the town. Mum paid for a taxi to take the other refuge children and me to school. She never admitted it, and I realised afterwards that it was because she didn't want me to be at risk, but going to school and back in the taxi and then straight into the refuge meant I was never out on the streets where Dad might see me. She was protecting me you see. Helen was older and wanted to keep attending her college. She travelled by bus, and was always careful to keep an eye out for him.

When we moved away, I went to another school close to the Women's Aid refuge. All the primary school age children went there and they were expert at keeping us safe.

We found out later from Uncle Jim that Dad never went back to college. Well, he did but just once - to pick up his grant cheque.

Sometime later Mum met another man, they married and he became the best father I could ever have asked for both Helen and me. He legally adopted me when I was twelve years old. Helen took his surname legally but she was over the age of adoption.

Over the years, what Uncle Jim said has come back to me. I liked Uncle Jim but did he really think that Dad's violent streak would come out in me? That what I saw would make me act like my father? If anything it had the opposite effect. I have no time for any man who hits a woman. Being drunk is no excuse. It's a power thing. I'm sure of that.

And my son will never know the fear and misery of living with a monster. We had freedom to live our lives in peace and that's how I want it to stay.

Motorcycle Emptiness

James Ellson

Kerr opened the front door to the postman. He wasn't expecting anything, definitely nothing in a box the size of a motorcycle helmet. It wasn't his birthday or Christmas, so had to be a mistake.

The postman lingered. He was tall with long arms. Kerr wanted to imagine it was because he'd carried too many parcels.

'Where's Jack?'

The postman shrugged. It made the sleeves on his jacket ride higher as if his uniform had shrunk in the wash. Explained - disappointingly - his long arms. Behind him, a pink-edged sky promised a day Kerr could do something with. Go for a walk in Lyme Park or visit Chatsworth, or take the boat tour through Speedwell Cavern.

'See you later,' said the postman, then turned and walked back to his van. It wasn't a standard red vehicle but a dirty white Transit.

Kerr shut the door and shunted the box into the kitchen. His name and address were written in thick black pen on the top of the box, but there was no stamp or franking. He twisted the parcel to inspect the sides but found no markings. He turned it over. No return label or identification there, either.

He sat back on his haunches. If it was a helmet, he could buy a motorcycle. He pictured a red and gold helmet, and black leathers with a dragon on the back. Racing up Snake Pass, double de-clutching through Sheffield, hooning back to Manchester. He'd not had - not felt like having - a mid-life crisis, but everyone was living longer, so he thought perhaps the mid-life crisis came later.

A motorcycle! He could already feel the wind whipping tears from his eyes; smell the burning rubber; experience the stomach lurch of acceleration. He would attract the stares of young women as he pulled into the Grindleford cafe, and the scowls of his neighbours when he returned home in the early hours.

If it was a helmet, he'd buy a motorcycle.

He would.

He really would.

Kerr searched the internet. Motorcycle dealers, second-hand bikes, riding lessons. Motorcycles were kings of capitalism. Beasts of polished chrome with sleek lines and fat tyres. Cockpits like fighter jets; exhausts like shotgun barrels; drive chains like belts of machine gun bullets. They were red and silver and black, the palette of speed and daring. Scantily-clad women sat on them, clung to them, rode them.

He glanced over at the box.

On the back of an envelope Kerr scribbled names - Dancer, The Devil, Z43, Red Dreams, The Searcher - and prices and phone numbers. The nearest riding school was in Salford, and courses started every week.

Opening the box could be like walking through the back of the wardrobe, or climbing the beanstalk, or enchanting a broom.

He was no longer a child, but —

He stabbed a knife through the strip of packing tape across the top of the box, and dragged it back and forth. The flaps sprung open. He peeled back the tape, and balled it up.

Inside the box was another box protected by a nest of bubble wrap. He took out the inner box. He flattened and rolled the bubble wrap, and put it in the cupboard under the stairs. He flattened the outer box and put it in the recycling. He had all day, and tomorrow. The whole week. Nothing planned for the rest of the year, no day-trips or weekends away or holidays. Occasionally he considered a few days in Blackpool or Colwyn Bay, but the last time he'd been to the sea was as a child. Since leaving work, he'd not even bought a diary.

Lessons in motorcycle proficiency. Definitely.

The inner box was sealed with more tape. Kerr stabbed again with the knife, and slit the box open. Again, the flaps sprung wide. He half-expected a third box, but instead, there was a tartan wash kit, a paperback, and an alarm clock.

Bomb?

He drew back, but quickly laughed at himself. There were no wires, and no pot of nails or screws to cause injuries from flying shrapnel. He'd seen the news. Some days he watched the six o'clock and the ten o'clock bulletins. Occasionally, he watched the weather. Shortly after retiring, he'd read a book on poker, and daydreamed about a trip to Las Vegas. Even visiting the Stockport casino would be okay. They offered a happy hour and ten pounds of free chips if you stayed until midnight. But - he didn't sleep well if he went to bed after eleven.

The wash kit was fastened with a scrap of cord — a section of pyjama cord if Kerr had to guess. He didn't have to. He didn't have to do anything now he'd retired. That was the beauty of it. He'd had a programme on his work computer which counted down the hours until retirement. When his colleague in the next cubicle had shown it to him, Kerr's countdown had started at 10,276 hours. To begin with he'd checked every Friday, but it had quickly become a daily habit. Derek had changed it to show minutes and seconds and made it appear in the corner of the screen.

He pulled open the cord and inspected the wash kit. The razor was stained and the blade filled with stubble. The toothbrush was knackered, and the tube almost empty. There were packets of ibuprofen and condoms, and a bottle of peppermint mouthwash. A carton of cigarettes. No doubt, the police would be able to identify the owner through DNA analysis of the hairs or spittle from the toothbrush. But they would only laugh at him and send him away because a crime hadn't been committed.

Kerr sat back. No bomb, but no motorcycle helmet. A mistake, but a peculiar one: Kerr's name and address were correctly handwritten on the larger box. Someone had intended he receive the parcel. Maybe, there had been a list of addresses, and someone had made an error. But what list, and why was his name on it?

He disliked baffling and inexplicable events. Why the backdoor now stuck, the whereabouts of the potato peeler. He didn't believe in ghosts or UFOs or God.

The dirty white Transit pulled up outside.

The postman climbed out and manoeuvred a ramp into position at the rear doors. It had upturned striations like a pastry cutter. The postman climbed into the back of the van and wheeled a motorcycle down the ramp and into Kerr's front garden. He set the bike on its stand.

Kerr opened the front door.

'I didn't order a motorcycle.'

'Is that your name and address?' said the postman, proffering his smart device.

Kerr nodded.

'Well, then.'

Kerr wavered. A parcel of odds and ends was one thing, but a motorcycle worth thousands of pounds was quite another. It was his name and address, but keeping it might be considered theft. He could safeguard it, and make enquiries. Contact the police. Meanwhile, he could buy a helmet. Plummeting down Woodhead Pass, the wind whipping his teary eyes might become a reality.

The postman signed the device. He drew a large K with his finger, then a squiggle. 'See you, Kerr.' He climbed back in the van and drove away.

Kerr inspected the motorcycle. The bike was shiny chrome and metallic black. He caressed the bulbous fuselage, and felt the firmness of its leather seat. He read its numerous dials and ran his fingers over the forest of switches. He glanced up and down the road, then heaved a leg over the saddle. He gripped the handlebars, ducked his head, and made a revving noise.

He climbed down. He could buy a helmet.

Wednesday was his normal supermarket day - to beat Thursdays' pre-weekend rush - but he'd go a day early. Opposite the shop was a motorcycle showroom and outside stood an oversize Harley Davidson for children to clamber over. If he'd been married with kids, he might have taken them. Derek once told him typing-pool Sue had asked if Kerr was single. Kerr had thought about taking her out.

After lunch, he'd buy a helmet.

He would.

He really would.

In the kitchen he opened a cupboard crammed with pilchard tins. Too fidgety to wait for toast, he made a sandwich. He hadn't been this excited since his twenty-first when he'd entered a betting shop and placed a five-pound bet on a horse. Bright Outlook had lost and he'd never returned.

Fingering up the crumbs, he wondered if the motorcycle club at work was open to former employees. They rode alternate weekends out into the Peaks and toured several times a year, occasionally abroad. Kerr didn't own a passport, but he could apply. The Vikings organised summer barbeques and a Christmas party.

He boiled the kettle, but couldn't decide between coffee and tea. He settled on a glass of water.

He checked the backdoor and the windows were locked. The sky had darkened, rain a possibility. He put on a coat and went out.

At the gate he returned for an umbrella. He unlocked the door, grabbed the large brolly, and locked up again. The sky seemed a touch brighter. He unlocked the door and replaced the brolly. He hurried down the path and onto the pavement, heading for the bus-stop. No one entered a motorcycle showroom carrying an umbrella.

At the bus-stop he perched on a small, angled seat.

If he bought a helmet, he'd also need a set of leathers in case he fell off. Boots, too. He would need insurance in case he had an accident. Which wouldn't be cheap because he'd never owned a car. At night, the motorcycle would need to be secure - he'd need to buy a heavy chain and a padlock. Or an alarm? Or both? Maybe a tracker. A tracking device would no doubt involve a monthly subscription. The costs were mounting up. He began to make a list.

He had savings - he'd never spent much - but the future was an uncertain and unpredictable place. When he'd retired he'd missed the counter on his screen showing the minutes and seconds remaining in his job, so he'd set up a graphic with his money. It seldom changed which was the way he liked it.

There was no sign of the bus.

Another thought struck: where was he going to park it? On the road would leave it vulnerable to scratches from vandals and chips from stones thrown up by passing traffic. In his front garden would invite theft. He neither owned a garage nor a shed, so he'd need to build a shelter in the back garden. Then there were would be lessons, fuel, servicing.

He walked back home the longer way around the estate. It wasn't even a supermarket day.

As Kerr unlocked the front door and stepped inside, the dirty white Transit pulled up on the road. The postman climbed out of the passenger side and walked up the path. He held a small holdall, and no longer wore his uniform jacket.

'Another delivery for me?' said Kerr.

'Not exactly,' said the postman, stepping into the hall.

Kerr took a pace backwards. 'What're you doing?'

'Coming in — I'm your replacement.'

'For what?'

'All of it.'

'All of what?' Kerr began to panic. He was about to be robbed, or beaten, or worse. The news was full of it.

'Listen, Kerr, there's a procedure I have to follow. Let's sit in your front room, and I'll go through it. Otherwise they can be funny when I'm reporting back.'

'The Post Office?'

'Let's sit.'

They sat. The postman on the far side next to the sideboard which Kerr had been intending to move to investigate the damp patch on the wall. Kerr sat opposite the postman - if, as now seemed unlikely, the intruder was a postman. The stranger who'd unloaded the motorcycle. Kerr's replacement? He pulled his chair out and sat sideways, ready to make a move for the door. Or for a weapon. He could throw a dinner plate, or the picture on the wall. He'd been meaning to put another one up and also some family pictures. Which reminded him he should visit his mum at the nursing home. He hadn't seen her for over a year. Then again, he hadn't seen his sister and her family for over three years so perhaps they were the priority.

'Who are you?'

'I told you, I'm your replacement.'

'And the motorcycle?'

'It's mine,' said the stranger. 'It could have been yours, or one very like it. But apart from a half-hearted attempt to visit a motorcycle showroom, you did nothing about it. It's the story of your life.'

'I made a list.'

'Lists, schlists.' The stranger took out a packet of cigarettes, and lit one. He inhaled deeply.

'Do you mind?'

The stranger ignored him, and tapped ash into the top of the open packet. 'Are you familiar, Kerr, with the four givens of existence?'

'Should I be?'

The stranger shrugged, and continued to tap more ash from the cigarette. 'Freedom of choice?'

'I suppose so, vaguely.'

'We all have freedom of choice, but it can be both a blessing and a curse. You can decide whether to study hard at school, or bum; to join a gym, or sit on the couch; to study to become an electrician or an accountant, or sit at a supermarket checkout.' The stranger inhaled on the cigarette. 'Sorry if I'm sounding like an instruction manual but we're obliged to tell you all this. It's like the police caution. On the course, they made the point over and over.' He tapped off another section of ash. 'So anyway, later you retire and then your time is all your own. You can do anything, go anywhere, even if you haven't much money. Take long walks in the country, visit free museums, borrow library books. But you have to decide what to do, and you have to act.'

Outside, someone in the van hooted.

'They're getting impatient.'

'Who are?'

'The drivers. They're waiting for you.'

'Me?'

'Don't be disingenuous. I told you, you're being replaced.'

The doorbell rang.

'They want to get away. Beat the traffic.' He balanced the cigarette on the lid of the packet.

'And where are they taking me?'

The Replacement shrugged and stood up. 'They tell us it's to work on a farm, but none of us believe them.'

The letterbox flapped up and down. It was as if Kerr's house was on fire. 'Tell me one thing, I assume it's your wash kit, but why bother delivering it an hour earlier?'

The Replacement nodded. 'They like to give everyone a final chance. But we got the packages mixed up: it should have been a motorcycle helmet, but it didn't matter, the box still triggered the same response.'

There was a burst of hammering on the front door.

'Alright!' shouted the Replacement. 'Anything else, Kerr?' He picked up the cigarette, and glanced around. 'I'll have to get some ashtrays.'

'Can I have a puff?' said Kerr, 'I've always wondered.' His replacement passed him the remainder of the cigarette. He put it to his lips, and inhaled a snake of smoke. It tasted like burnt toast, but with a hint of something sweet. He wanted to inhale again, but instead passed it back.

'Right then,' said the Replacement, tamping out the cigarette.

Kerr stood up. The Replacement took hold of his arm and escorted him to the front door. Kerr pulled it open. Two men who looked like club bouncers waited. Nods were exchanged. The Replacement escorted Kerr to the van and waited while he climbed in.

'Last thing, I need your keys.'

'Really?' said Kerr. His voice sounded strange, and he was beginning to panic.

'Really.'

Kerr handed them over and the door slammed shut. He sat on a bench and looked out through the small square window in the back. The Replacement donned motorcycle leathers and strapped on a gold-coloured helmet. He locked Kerr's front door.

The van started up and pulled away.

Kerr stared out: at identikit houses on the estate, scruffy front yards, wizened trees. They turned onto the A6 and into a line of vehicles. They stop-started through Hazel Grove, High Lane, Disley, past Lyme Park. Finally, they reached the dual carriageway and the countryside. Sheep dotted a field, moorland beyond.

In the distance, a sudden buzz - increasing in no time to an untrammelled roar.

A motorcycle glided up behind the van. The Replacement was hunkered down, his padded leathers like polished armour, his golden helmet catching the sun. With a throaty rip of throttle, the bike slipped out of the van's slipstream into the next lane.

The motorcycle surged past.

Leaving only a whiff of fuel.

And a mounting quiet.

To the Devil, a Doctor.

Julie Malone

It was Halloween, and browbeaten by the constant nagging from both of my children, I had given in and promised to take them Trick or Treating. The trouble was that we were incredibly busy at work, and I needed a really good excuse to get away early. So when my business partner, Luke, double-booked his appointments again, I volunteered to get him out of trouble by meeting one of his clients at their property in the pretty north Nottinghamshire village of Wensborough, on the condition that I could go straight home afterwards. A prime location affordable only by the very wealthy, Wensborough was on my way home, so it was really quite convenient for me. Thankfully, Luke was grateful enough to agree.

Having shown the clients around the house a little over two years ago and remembered how delighted they were with it, I was struggling to understand why they wanted to sell up. They had adored Wensborough Hall on sight when they viewed it, put in an offer, which was accepted immediately, and indicated that they never intended to move again. Thinking back to that time, it occurred to me that the previous owners had not been in the house more than a couple of years either.

I arrived at the house early, before the client, so had time to flip through the leaflet on the property again, reacquainting myself with the house while I waited.

Of Georgian design, stone built, with five bedrooms, three bathrooms, standing in half an acre of formal garden and with a very attractive front aspect, I would have given my eye-teeth to be able to afford this dream house. Why on earth were they selling?

I had been there about ten minutes when Mr Phillips arrived, and looking like he had no time to waste, signalled me to follow him inside.

Previously calm and affable, this was a very different Mr Phillips from the one I met before. His hands shook as he fumbled with the keys, then he dropped them, and cursed.

As he picked them up, he said: 'I'm all fingers and thumbs today. Too much rushing about.' He gave a hint of a smile, it was more of a grimace, I thought and, as he straightened up from retrieving the keys, it seemed that he couldn't look me in the eye.

'Look, I hope you don't mind,' he said, opening the front door, 'but I rather want to get this done as quickly as possible.'

I smiled. 'Oh, that's perfectly alright with me, Mr Phillips. It just means I get home in time to take my young tyrants out for Trick or Treat this evening.' I laughed. He didn't.

'Good. Right let's get on with it' He turned at the doorstep and appeared to take a deep breath before opening the door. Where I had thought this would be just another job, I was now picking up on his stress, and I wondered what I was in for.

It took just ten breathless minutes to go through the house, starting upstairs, while I struggled to take shaky notes of the changes they had made; more double electric points, new decor, shower cabinets and bathroom suites, hallway and landing walls painted pristine white and so on; the only room he passed by was the downstairs study.

When I mentioned it, he muttered something about having lost the key and that he had another appointment to attend. The tour was over, he locked the door, threw me the keys and almost ran down the steps to his car. His relief at leaving, was evident. But instead of driving away as I expected him to, he appeared to be rooting through the glove compartment for something. He opened the window and called me over.

'Look I'm really sorry to have been brusque and rushed you through that.' He seemed more himself as he handed me an old, worn golden-brown leather book. In the centre of the front cover was a faded embossed symbol. It looked like a kind of rod with two snakes wrapped around it. It seemed familiar but I couldn't recall why.

'Read this. It will explain why we want to get shot of this house. Neither of us will be returning. We'll send a removal team for our furniture and belongings.' He turned on the ignition and the Jaguar purred into life.

'But, Mr Phillips, what's so wrong with the house? I thought you and your family were happy there.' I still needed an answer and, although he said the notebook would explain everything, I wanted to hear it from him.

He looked sadly at the house. 'Oh we did. We loved it but...but...it... it's evil.'

I must have pulled a face because he said: 'Yes, everyone we say that to looks at us like that...you see nothing ever happens when other people are around...but there's something sinister...' He turned away, shook his head, then slumped forward and rested his head on the steering wheel for a moment. When he turned back to me his expression was one of a beaten man.

'Look, until you've read those notes, you will never understand. My wife, Myra...she's...she's on medication. She walks around in a...a...oh, never mind. All I can say is that Myra and I realised that this house will never truly belong to anyone. It's been such a...I just don't want to talk about it anymore. We'll consider any offer, even if it means losing thousands. We just want to be rid of it.' He put the car in gear and, as he drove away, he called back. 'Read the damn book!'

I have to admit, his bizarre behaviour spooked me, but even so it was such a beautiful house, I found it hard to believe there was anything wrong with it. I did some quick, and ultimately pointless, calculations to see if we could raise enough money to buy it, but even though he wanted a desperately quick sale, and would sell for a low price, I knew it was beyond our means.

Back In my car, I put my bag and the book on the passenger seat planning to look through it later and fastened my seat belt, but when I reached across to the glove compartment for my favourite Pink CD, the book caught my eye and I just had to pick it up. Without opening it, I examined the soft leather. I stared at the symbol on the cover trying to remember where I had seen it before, and I kept seeing my husband, David's face. Then it came to me. David was a GP, and I had seen this image in some of his books; it was a symbol of healing and medicine, The Rod of Asclepius! Well, that puzzle was solved.

The book felt warm, alive in my hands, and I had the strangest feeling of being in a dream, almost as if I was watching myself in a film; nothing seemed quite real. I put the book back on the passenger seat ready to drive away but somehow it drew me back. I undid my seatbelt and switched off my mobile phone. I opened the book, briefly wondered why the handwriting oddly sloped to the left, and began to read.

October 31st

This written record of my life is not meant to be my confession for there would be little purpose in that. It is nothing more than explanation of how I came to this day, for I know this is the day I will be held accountable for my misdeeds.

I have never robbed a bank or committed a murder, but I have ignored terrible deeds when they were committed in my name. I have consciously benefitted from deceit and, whoever reads this, please understand, I know Evil has walked with me.

My name is Oliver Bartlett and I am, or rather I was, a doctor; a good and successful one too, but I must acknowledge here and now that little of my success was achieved through my own efforts. I could never have attained my privileged circumstances without Un-divine intervention. Did I sell my soul? You can decide that for yourself.

To help you understand I will start at the very beginning. My family were affluent pillars of Bristol society, and we lived in a large, detached house just outside Keynsham. My father was an accountant and mother, who received a Trust Fund allowance, looked after me and my younger brother, Ralph, and involved herself in local charitable activities; we were, as I then thought, a happy family. Then a little after my tenth birthday our father embezzled a small fortune from the business and absconded with his cousin's wife.

Happily for me, I resembled my mother but Ralph was not so lucky. It was his misfortune to look remarkably like our father, reminding her daily of her humiliation and how poor Ralph suffered for it. Looking back, I suppose it was immature self-centredness, but I took advantage of our mother's favour by using it to get away with anything I could, starting with talking Ralph into joining me in raiding an orchard. Ralph was caught but I escaped and hurried home, sneaked up to my room, changed my clothes and was innocently reading a book when I was summoned downstairs. Poor Ralph had been slippered, but the little sympathy I felt at seeing his stricken tear-streaked face, was not enough to make me admit my guilt. In fact, I lied through my teeth and got away with it. Ralph never trusted me again and I can still see his hurt expression at my betrayal, but it had proved just how gullible our mother was, and how clever I was. The pattern I followed for the rest of my life had begun.

From then on Ralph avoided me whenever possible, his hostility and moodiness justifying mother's belief in his 'bad blood'. Naturally, there were times when he had an alibi, and then mother sought another culprit, never me. I recall a weekend when Ralph was at Air Cadet camp and I 'borrowed' £200 from mother's hidden stash. I had heard about a 'cert' in the 3.30 at Cheltenham. I fully intended to replace the money from my winnings before she noticed. Being under eighteen years old at that time, a friend put the bet on and found it very amusing when the horse refused at the starting post. I did not! What was I to do? Mrs Clemmow, our elderly cleaner, was sacked without a reference, and I was in the clear again.

I continued lying, cheating, stealing. Time and time again poor Ralph bore the brunt of it and, when he could not prove his innocence, knowing protest was pointless, he took my punishment stoically. I felt no remorse or guilt.

At college I achieved straight A's in Chemistry, Biology, Physics and Maths at GCE 'A' Level. Ralph's only interest was aircraft. Eventually I decided on Medical School and Ralph joined the R.A.F. On the day he left, I alone watched him go. Our mother chose to be elsewhere. He did not say goodbye or look back, his warm farewell was for our housekeeper. Later we heard his plane was shot down by a Patriot missile during the Gulf War. We had grown so distant his death hardly affected me, at that time.

I excelled at Medical School, with first-rate exam results and correct practical diagnoses, my tutors said I had a brilliant future ahead. With little effort on my part, life was good. There were always parties and nurses to flirt with, and I took full advantage, broke some hearts, or so I was told, apparently not all of them female. There I met Sally Ridgeway, a sweet girl, a great nurse and entirely trustworthy to cover for me on the odd occasion when I screwed up - usually when hungover - because she loved me.

But luck runs out and the morning after a very late night at a friend's booze-filled party, my lack of concentration caused the death of a four-year-old girl in AU. I will not go into details, but my career was in jeopardy, and I needed to find a scapegoat for the enquiry that would surely follow. I convinced my consultant that I was in shock, was unable to concentrate on my duties, and was sent home.

For hours I walked the foggy streets while I searched for an answer to the mess I was in, but every idea ended with my attendance at a medical tribunal. Sometime later I arrived home to find a man waiting for me; it was to turn out that he was the answer to my prayers, righteous or otherwise.

Shrouded by the blanket of fog, his deep and soothing voice seemed to come from nowhere, or thinking about it now, perhaps everywhere would be a better description. He emerged behind me from the haze and followed me to my door commenting on what an awful night it was. I grunted some sort of response and fumbled in my pocket for my keys. I hoped he would take the hint and go but he offered to help. I told him to leave me alone, but he persisted and asked if he could do anything to make me feel better. I muttered something about if he pissed off, I'd feel loads better, but what he said next rocked me to the core.

'Poor, poor Oliver. In trouble and no-one to blame this time, eh?'

He knew who I was! He knew what I had done! I remember the feeling of sheer terror and the urge to run, but my legs would not have worked if they had made any attempt at flight. His hand reached forward, calmly took the keys from me and opened the door. It was only when he turned the light on in the hall and turned to look at me that I saw his face for the first time. He looked like me! His face was my face! I had no spit to speak, which he found very amusing. I had no will of my own and followed him up the stairs like a puppy on a lead to my first floor flat, and it was then I noticed a smell about him, similar to bad eggs, it was overpowering; I felt sick.

He let us both into the flat and went directly into the sitting room drinks cupboard as if he owned the place, and poured two large brandies, one he handed one to me. My trembling eased as the warm liquid slid down my throat; what was there to worry about? There was a strange feeling of comfort in his presence. We stared at each other in silence or rather, I stared at myself, which by that time seemed perfectly normal.

When I asked who he was he said his name was unimportant, but it was what he could do for me that mattered. With a smile that chilled the marrow in my bones, he told me about the dead child and said he could help. He then described my childhood in detail, he knew what happened to Ralph, and how our mother treated us. He knew it all.

The whole situation was totally preposterous. Surreal. I was in my own flat surrounded by normality, drinking brandy and talking to myself sitting across the room. I knew my worries must have unhinged me. I was going mad. He did not exist, could not exist. I went to the window and looked down; the fog still obscured the road. Convinced I was hallucinating, I did not react when he stood up and joined me by the window. I did react when he punched me in the back. I fell forward and hit my head on the window frame. It hurt. He laughed and said that proved he was real and I should just accept it.

He drained his drink in one swallow and I watched with complete acceptance as the glass refilled itself. He raised it in a mock salute. My head hurt like hell and my back ached. He apologised and touched my forehead. The pain lifted and my backache eased. It was then he explained what he wanted was me. I remember being angry at that. I told him I wasn't gay and he roared with laughter.

'I know. I know your future. You will marry Sally Ridgeway and will have children, daughters.'

I must have looked stupid because he told me to close my mouth and listen. He said I could only profit by accepting his help, and that in return he would ask a favour of me some time in the future. When I asked what would happen if I agreed to accept his help, he explained that all my problems would be over, the good life would begin and would continue for many, many years. Then he informed me that I had just one hour to think his proposition over.

I didn't need an hour, I just needed to know how he could help, and said I was prepared to listen to what he had to say.

As he talked, he looked around my fairly shabby little flat, and told me I would soon be living somewhere more fitting to the lifestyle I wanted. That he would 'sort out' my current little problem, and that my career would be safe in his hands.

I was convinced. Whatever favour he wanted in the future, I would worry about when the time came. He gripped my hand and shook it hard. A shock like an electric bolt shot through my arm as he told me our bargain was sealed, and I should leave everything to him. My instructions were that I was to telephone the hospital and report in sick for the day, then return to my normal shift the following day. I followed him into the hall but he had vanished leaving me curious, but not really surprised. I felt elated, elated but terrified of what would happen tomorrow at the hospital. However, I did exactly as I was told and made the telephone call.

When I returned to the hospital the following day, the gossip was all about Vince Thompson, a fellow Registrar who had been suspended for negligence for causing the death of the little girl. According to the rota, I had been on sick leave for three days! No-one remembered I had been on duty, and there was no evidence of my involvement at all.

Sally appeared and asked if I felt well enough to be back at work, but I felt wonderful. He had done it! My nameless look-a-like friend had got me off the hook. I was free.

Vince was a nice enough bloke who did not deserve this fate, but it was a done deal and there was nothing I could do about it. I told Sally

I was fine, made the right sympathetic noises about Vince and excused myself. People kept talking about Vince, some sympathetic, but some said he got what he deserved. Of course, I knew that was untrue, but what was I to do about it? I was in the clear and nothing could touch me.

Over the years my career progressed. Whatever I did I excelled in. I could do no wrong. I had the Midas Touch. I thought I caught occasional glimpses of my saviour - still looking like me - at traffic lights, or in a crowd, but they were only ever fleeting moments. Whenever I looked for him, he was not there.

Ten years later I was an NHS consultant, with a very lucrative private practice in Cardiff overlooking the Bay, and I mixed with the elite of London Society. Sally and I married. She was a suitable wife for a man of my social standing; good looking, slim, elegant, intelligent, but most of all docile. We were overjoyed when she became pregnant with twins. My cup runneth over!

With a family on the way, we bought a large, comfortable house situated on a hillside between Swansea and Carmarthen. A beautiful setting, but Sally became sullen at its isolation. She went into a difficult labour on October 30th, a dark, foggy night, and I phoned for an ambulance. Unfortunately, the nearest was over thirty miles away, and there would be a long delay due to a number of serious road accidents. Sally was in trouble. Obstetrics was not my speciality, but I was all she had and they were my babies too. I hoped I would be good enough.

The doorbell rang. A tall, elderly, grey-haired man with a goatee-type moustache, stood there at my doorstep. He introduced himself as Dr Furlice but I recognised him immediately. The face was different - not mine this time - but I knew his smell He was accompanied by a Mrs Owen, a midwife from the next Valley, who for some reason didn't seem to notice his odour. With a brief nod to me, she dashed up the stairs to attend Sally, leaving us alone in the hall.

Once she was out of earshot, he took me by the arm and pushed me into the kitchen and said it was time to pay my debt. He wanted one of my unborn babies. I argued, pleaded with him. The idea of giving him a child was obscene. I offered him money, anything he wanted, but he was adamant. We had an agreement and there would be no reneging, otherwise Sally and the babies would all die. I panicked. What could I do to stop this appalling atrocity that I had set in motion? Desperate, I reminded him that it was me he wanted. I begged to go with him, but would he please leave the children and Sally alone. He laughed and said he was not ready for me yet, and that I would know when the time came. I tried to push him towards the door, determined to get him out of the house, but my hands burned and blistered on contact with his clothes; it was agonising. I searched the kitchen for a weapon. The knife-block was nearby, but he anticipated my intention, and it flew through the air, and out of reach.

Unfazed by my pleading, he asked: 'Are you done now?' I nodded, exhausted, in pain and beaten. Calmly he revealed Sally would deliver three babies not two, all girls, and he wanted the last born. He also reminded me that I had not been so conscience-stricken when I accepted his help. I succumbed. I could nothing else but obey. At least I would have two daughters. Demanding I control myself, and reminding me my wife needed me, he told me to lighten up and led me up the stairs.

It was a little after midnight when the first baby was born, the second followed soon after. Sally was exhausted and delirious which made it easier for him to take the third baby as soon as she struggled into the world. She was smaller, weaker than her sisters and had slipped easily into the world.

Dr Furlice asked me what I wanted to name them. Until that moment I had never really thought about names. I assumed Sally would make the choice when the babies were born and we knew their gender, but he urged me to think of names quickly. Having a great interest in Greek mythology, the name Persephone came into my head for the little one.

While the midwife made Sally comfortable, I examined the first two babies, who appeared strong and healthy, and I named them Phoebe and Phaedra. Dr Furlice showed no interest in them at all, his attention was firmly fixed on tiny Persephone.

When Mrs Owen went to the bathroom, I agreed to let him take the baby, she looked too weak to survive long anyway, and we had the other two. After all, Sally expected to give birth to twins, not triplets, and I was convinced she was unaware of the third baby. I did not ask what he intended to do with the child. I thought it better not to know, it was none of my business and, he was right, I had not concerned myself with his methods before, so I there was little point in starting now. As for Sally, I prayed she would never know the truth, not out of any altruistic motive, I just didn't want her asking questions.

We were startled by Mrs Owen appearing at the door. From her shocked expression I guessed she had overheard us, but she went about her duties again without a word. It was a little after five o'clock that morning when she left. As she headed down the stairs, I assured her I would get Sally and the babies to hospital, and I told her to drive carefully as it was still dark and the fog was now much more dense than it had been when they arrived. It was difficult to see anything more than a metre beyond the door. She gave a polite nod but did not speak to me.

Phoebe and Phaedra slept in carrycots while Dr Furlice wrapped Persephone in a blanket and prepared to leave. I asked him what would happen if Mrs Owen reported us. He shrugged and said the roads were steep, winding and narrow, and the fog dangerous and unpredictable. In this area it hung in the trees and was known to drop without warning onto the roads; terrible accidents occurred in such fogs. With that he left taking my smallest daughter with him. I never saw him again, but I read in the newspapers a few days later that Mrs Owen had been killed in a car accident on her way home that morning. To be honest, I was not surprised, but it wasn't my responsibility.

As the years passed, Sally became depressed and we became estranged, although we continued to live in the same house. As she never mentioned the third baby, I was certain she had no knowledge of Persephone. My conscience did sometimes prick me a little about our missing triplet, and it eased my sense of guilt to convince myself that Sally had no knowledge of our third baby, or that I had paid my debt by sacrificing her.

Phoebe and Phaedra grew strong, were rarely unwell apart from the odd cold, and like most twins were very close. Unlike most twins though, as they grew they seemed to only need each other, in fact they were so close they soon had no need of us.

There was no joy in our family. I found myself working away more and more as there seemed little to go home for. Sally developed a taste for wine and vodka and left me after spending a brief rehab interlude in a clinic. We lost touch and I heard sometime later that she had died. I was sorry she had not been able to have a happier life with me, but I felt no grief.

In their teens, the girls spent most of their time huddled together, frequently changing their conversation when I entered the room. The Au Pair was closer to them than I. However, I had no reason to worry about their education. They were day pupils at a private school and were doing very well, but the Head Teacher did mention once or twice that, although they were excellent students, they did not socialise with other pupils and, considering their age, were unusually serious and studious. I explained that they had always been that way and that this behaviour, although unusual to her, was not out of character for my daughters. That seemed to satisfy her and she never mentioned it again.

Two years ago, when the girls were sixteen years of age, I was invited to join the team at a private hospital in Nottingham, and we moved here to Wensborough. The girls were old enough to no longer require someone looking after them while I worked, so there were just the three of us. The girls did not complain at the move, they did not talk to me enough to complain about anything.

On the other hand, although my career flourished, I was very much alone. Was it all worth it? No. Perhaps if I had confessed after the orchard raid things might have been different. Now I await my fate, whatever it may be.

I stared at the page marvelling at what I had just read. Then the penny dropped. It was Halloween. Luke had set me up and I had to hand it to him; getting George Phillips to play along like that was a blinder. I'd get him back sometime when the time was right.

I closed the book, put it on the passenger seat and looked up.

Something felt different, very different. There were curtains at the windows where there had been vertical blinds before. The drive was no longer paved, it was gravelled! The sky too was much darker than it should have been so early in the afternoon. A creeping fear took hold of me, my pulse throbbed in my head. I took a deep breath, told myself to calm down but my heart pounded in my chest. I slid the key into the ignition, the car started up then died. I tried again but the engine just made a weak whining noise and stopped.

At the door a young woman with long blonde hair beckoned to me to follow her. I had not seen her when I was in the house with Mr Phillips? Follow her? Hell, no, I was leaving! The car might not start but my legs still worked. I grabbed my bag, opened the door to make a run for it, but my feet had a mind of their own, and turned towards the house.

My free will gone. I was unable to resist, and I followed her inside. Funny how you notice things at times of stress. The hall was wallpapered! I was no longer afraid, no longer desperate to escape, it felt perfectly natural for me to follow her into the study where I had not been allowed to enter before. The room was hot and stuffy even though the French windows were slightly open allowing in a cool breeze that gently fluttered the curtains.

I stood at the open door and gazed around the immaculately tidy room, it was then I realised we were not alone. In the far corner, a man was busily writing at an antique wooden bureau, his back to me, his concentration unbroken by my presence. The girl nodded to me indicating I should go over to him. He did not notice my approach, did not look up. Peering over his shoulder, I could see the front cover of the book, it was propped up by his left hand. Embossed into the leather was that same symbol, but, unlike the faded version in my car, this looked very new. I recognised it instantly, and discovered why the writing looped to the left. He was left-handed. This could only be Oliver Bartlett. Doctor Oliver Bartlett! And the text he was writing I had just read! But all this had happened many years ago!

The girl moved closer, her face expressionless as she put her hand on the man's shoulder. He reached up to pat her hand without looking at her.

'Is it time?' he asked. She nodded and turned toward the door where another girl, identical in every way, entered the room. They could only be Phoebe and Phaedra.

Silently, the newcomer walked towards the French windows and opened them wide. The curtains billowed wildly and the breeze blew more strongly through the room, but it was warm, a complete contrast to the cold draught I had felt previously. My thoughts were clear enough to wonder where the warmth was coming from. I moved towards the open windows, no-one acknowledged my presence, or tried to stop me.

At the far end of the garden something glimmered brightly between the trees, consisting of orange-yellow lights that radiated from a fissure in the ground. A shape rose from the earth and drifted just above the ground towards the house, closely followed by others.

At first the shapes had no real form but, as they approached their outlines became more distinct, more clearly human, and the force of the heat increased as they neared the house, one following the other. When just a few yards from the house the figures became obvious.

The man, encouraged by the first girl stood up and made his way to the window where the second girl waited. He leaned towards her and attempted to kiss her cheek but she avoided his embrace and turned her head away.

'Even now, Phaedra,' I heard him whisper sadly. She stared at the waiting spectres and remained remote.

The first apparition drifted closer and it was now evident that these girls were not twins as I had thought, they were triplets. The new arrival was more delicate than her sisters, and so pale as to be almost ethereal; her insubstantial form seemed never to have seen the light of day. Waiting behind her was a little girl of about four years old, a middle-aged woman holding a large black medical bag and a younger, once pretty woman I guessed would have been in forties, behind them stood a young man wearing Air Force blue.

Phoebe led their father outside to meet his youngest, wraith-like daughter while I watched in disbelief. It was like watching actors playing out their scenes in a film. Phaedra moved forward, her cold eyes emotionless as she watched Phoebe hold out their father's hand to the equally silent Persephone.

'Persephone,' he sighed, smiling as the ghost-like girl took his hand and led him through the silent, glass-eyed assembled ghosts towards the fiery glow. They followed him, their feet skimming the grass.

The last person to emerge appeared to be an elegant, tall, elderly man with a goatee moustache. This must have been Dr Furlice. He stood at the mouth of the fissure for a moment then walked through the group towards Dr Bartlett. He stopped, facing the resigned Dr Bartlett and, without moving his lips, I heard his gravelly voice echoing inside my head. 'Well, Oliver, we meet again. Did you really believe that by giving me Persephone, that would satisfy me? It has been a joy to watch her grow as my daughter,' he smiled. I shuddered. 'But you know, you should never do business with the Devil.' He turned and walked back towards the fiery yawning crevice. Persephone followed, still holding her father's hand leading him, submissive, to his doom.

I suddenly had a terrible understanding of what was happening, and cried out a warning. If he heard I'll never know. He certainly gave no indication of it as he allowed himself to be led towards the flames. I screamed at his daughters to get him back, to stop this horror, but then it dawned on me, we were in different dimensions, this had already happened and I could do nothing to make it not happen.

Dr Bartlett and his victims were just a few yards away from the blazing maw when the little girl turned to look directly at me. Her lips did not move but I heard her voice in my head. 'All debts must be paid!'

Seemingly unafraid, resigned, Dr Bartlett walked to meet his destiny and, unable to prevent it, I watched as they all vanished into the fiery abyss.

The young man I took to be Ralph, was the last to disappear before the earth closed over the gateway to Hell, the sky lightened and I found myself alone in the study, rooted to the spot unable to believe what I had just witnessed.

I have no idea how long I stood there staring into the garden, but eventually I walked calmly out of the study. The door closed with a loud bang behind me. Outside the driveway looked just as it had when I first arrived and, as I expected, there were vertical blinds at the window.

I just wanted to go home; get back to normality, but I knew I was unfit to drive, and needed to calm down. My heartbeat slowly returned to normal and I reached for my bag on the passenger seat. The book had gone! I checked the floor and back seat but it was nowhere, it was as if it had never existed. I had no idea what had happened to me, whether it was real or if I had had some kind of hallucination, and I would probably never know.

I dug out my mobile phone from my handbag and called David to let him know I was on my way home, and asked him if he would mind taking the children out instead. I was in no mood for Halloween!

The Spreading Stain

Gary Burn

The author, Sidonie-Gabrielle Colette, claimed that women were tempted towards sexual dalliance with other women out of a desire for equality. The journalist, Geneviève Dorman, disagreed. She believed that 'many young women had entered into marriages of convenience with unsuitable men, then turned against men as a race and sought consolation from other women.' Then again, according to Judith Thurman, 'homosexual adultery had distinct advantages over the garden variety: there was no danger of pregnancy, almost none of venereal disease and it was a "safe" way for women to satisfy their sexual curiosity or take revenge on a brutal or unfaithful husband without risking a scandalous divorce and the loss of their children or social position.' It also, stood a considerable chance of providing women with a partner equally enthralled by the wonders of shopping; at least that is what many men had concluded.

Taken together, it's clear that the world Marcel Proust would soon depict in his novel, *In Search of Lost Time*, where nearly everyone in Paris, male and female, led a clandestine gay life, was not as exaggerated as many claimed. Lesbianism certainly ranked 'high among the chic deviations' for fashionable Parisian women. There was even an exclusive lesbian association, Les Rieuses (The Merry Women) situated in a private mansion, where rich lesbians could dine from dusk till dawn, before retiring to the bed chamber. While the civic authorities were largely in denial with regard to these tender proclivities, the courts prosecuted any journalist who wrote about it: what it was and what they did — "lesbian-love" they called it — fearing the publicity more than the activity itself. The popular explanation among sociologists (all male, of course) was that men had no interest in what their wives got up to in their spare time, nor even regarded them as true sexual beings, given they denied there was such a thing as a female orgasm. To the extent that many husbands thought nothing of spending large sums of money having their wives treated for "hysteria"; by far the most common disorder for which women visited their family physician in those days; the cure for which was a course of induced "uterine paroxysms" — orgasms by any definition.

All this changed almost overnight with the publication of Léo Taxil's book, La Corruption Fin-de-Siècle in 1894 and its stark announcement that lesbianism was 'spreading like an oil stain' throughout Paris, thereby alerting France's patriarchal society to this disturbing truth. And to ensure his warning would be heeded, Taxil claimed that this perversion was being practiced by many well-to-do ladies of good stock, who, looking for 'a partner in vice', as he put it, were even driving through the Bois de Boulogne in open carriages, signalling their sexual preference with 'a distinctive "tell": 'it's the gorgeous poodle', he said, 'a lapdog with curled hair, bedecked with pom-poms and sometimes ribbons, that's always by her side on her strolls and drives.' And those ladies who returned their glances had their own distinctive sign: a 'rapid movement of the tongue and lips' to signal "I go with women."'

The American whisky heiress, Natalie Barney, provided a similar description, although with less emphasis on the well-to-do ladies and more on their professional sisters; the "great horizontals", aka the "unbuttoned"; demimondaines who came to the Bois de Boulogne to enjoy the morning air, 'descending from their carriages to take a few mincing, high-heeled steps along that aptly named "path of virtue"... a sport they "ridiculously" referred to, says Natalie, as "jogging".' And it was here that she first cast eyes on Liane de Pougy and was immediately enraptured, and with Colette to [illegible]

Ironically the publicity that accompanied Taxil's book, pricked the curiosity of many well-to-do ladies who were entirely new to such practices, including a banker's wife who was overheard to say: 'All remarkable women do it. But it is difficult. One has to take lessons.' Although, a bourgeois married woman discovered in a lesbian relationship risked being sent to a mental asylum by her husband, especially now, as male fears of the voracious female, dissipating the financial and the sexual wherewithal of her husband intensified. A fear confirmed when the fashion for wearing trousers among demi-mondaines was taken up by society women, prompting the Minister of the Interior to remind prefectures that 'the wearing of masculine clothes by women will not be tolerated unless for the purpose of velocipedic sport'. Yet, even this exception was condemned by many men, who believed female participation in what had hitherto been a gentlemanly pursuit was great cause for concern. Not only because the humble bicycle provided women with increased mobility and, heaven forbid, greater independence, but, more disturbingly, according to a Canadian medical journal, because 'bicycle riding produces in the female a distinct orgasm.' Overnight, women had become sexual beings, and husbands who happily sent their wives to doctors for induced uterine paroxysms, were getting hot under the collar at the thought of them peddling to sexual ecstasy.

Bicycle Face

While the bicycle proved to be not quite the orgasmatron the medical profession feared, it did lead women towards a greater degree of physical freedom, as it necessitated 'less restrictive clothes, for one thing, and for a woman to open her legs rather than keep them daintily crossed', as the New Statesman so delicately put it. In the 1870s, the invention of the electric elevator forced women to abandon hoop skirts. In the 1880s, the corsetiere, Herminie Cadolle, cut the traditional corset in two, providing the top half with shoulder straps to support a woman's breasts, 'freeing her from the tortuous constraints below.' The Paris Exposition Universelle of 1889 then introduced not one but two iconic structures, to the world: the Eiffel Tower and the first brassière.

Now, garments and undergarments, like split-skirts and bloomers, were in great demand, because without them it would have been difficult to engage fully in cycling without causing a riot.

It was around this time that journalist, Nellie Bly interviewed American suffragette Susan B. Anthony, who claimed that cycling, or "wheeling" as she called it, 'has done more to emancipate women than anything else in the world.' Not only that, she added with gusto: 'I stand and rejoice every time I see a woman ride by on a wheel. It gives a woman a feeling of freedom and self-reliance. It makes her feel as if she were independent. The moment she takes her seat she knows she can't get into harm unless she gets off her bicycle, and away she goes, the picture of free, untrammeled womanhood."

"And bloomers?" Nellie suggested quietly.

"Are the proper thing for wheeling", Miss Anthony confirmed. "It is as I have said—dress to suit the occasion. A woman doesn't want skirts and flimsy lace to catch in the wheel. Safety, as well as modesty, demands bloomers or extremely short skirts. You know women only wear foolish articles of dress to please men's eyes anyway."'

Munsey's Magazine wholeheartedly agreed, proclaiming the bicycle 'a steed upon which women could ride into a new world.' This was dangerous talk, according to Dr. Shadwell, who warned the women of the world, in London's National Review, of the "The Hidden Dangers of Cycling". Such a 'novel and peculiar experiment', particularly the strain involved in keeping the contraption balanced upright, he said, would cause a terrible medical condition called "bicycle face"; the symptoms of which were, 'usually flushed, but sometimes pale, often with lips more or less drawn, and the beginning of dark shadows under the eyes, and always with an expression of weariness'; as well as a 'hard, clenched jaw and bulging eyes.' If that were not enough, in addition to the "horrors" caused to the face, cycling would lead to 'internal

The Dogfight

Brennig Jones

There were two of them; high-altitude bandits. They came at us from inside the glare of the sun; the three of us were blind to their approach, didn't even know they'd been up there, tracking us.

I'd glanced up, caught a movement in the air and threw everything I had into a hard dive. I put one off his aim, he flashed down through our formation. I was caught in his murderous backwash.

I spent moments fighting to regain control as his turbulence threw me around and tried to break my wings off; I swear I heard them crack and groan as I plummeted downwards.

The bandits were diving so fast it was only after they'd flown through us I heard their noise: it followed in their wake as a roar of back-draugh-ted air.

Even as I fought for control, I had an impression of their tremendous power and speed and I thought I caught a glimpse of a face glaring at me, a hard expression set in a mask of hatred, but perhaps that was my imagination.

As soon as I gained control I angled into a dive and screamed down-wards into an inverse loop to throw off any would-be pursuer and to get close to the ground as fast as possible. I thought I was going to tear my wings off, my speed and course was so desperate.

I'd almost reached tree-top height when I pulled up into level flight and checked the horizons. Ginger, who had been on my right flank, had executed a similar manoeuvre but my left flank wingman, Archie, was nowhere to be seen.

Archie: He'd only joined us that week. This was his first operational flight.

When he arrived at HQ, he was ridiculously proud that he had 15 hours flight-time under his belt.

Fifteen hours!

I'd stormed up to my CO and ranted about how they were sending the new recruits out with too little experience and almost no training. He'd simply nodded and taken another drink.

We both knew there was nothing he could do about it.

I looked down for any signs of Archie on the ground but we were so low all I could see were the rows and rows of lush, green, French vineyards stretching away into the distance.

I turned my gaze skywards to look for the enemy and reflected as I did.

It was late spring 1917. We'd been on a routine flight over north-eastern Bordeaux - on reconnaissance over what we'd been told was a green sector.

It was a bright, hot, sunny day; one of those magnificent days when it was hard to imagine a time of conflict, of war, of death and destruction in the skies over that beautiful French countryside.

The three of us hadn't been on patrol long before they'd found us and when they did, they came dealing terrible fury.

I scanned the horizon and reflected on the immense power and speed of these new bandits. Their tactics were so... brutal. It indicated a massive escalation in hostilities.

My heartbeat quickened as I spotted one of them, twenty degrees off my port wing, on a lateral course but about 100 feet above me.

He must have lost me in my controlled earthwards plunge and now my camouflage helped me merge against the tones of the soft French countryside.

I made a mental note of where he was and looked for Ginger. He saw me and waved an 'OK' at me. I grinned back and gestured to the portside bogie.

That's when I saw the other one.

He was underneath Ginger, pulling straight up beneath him on the inside circle of a power climb. I gestured frantically to Ginger, waggled my wings and even shouted his name but it was too late. I looked away, couldn't bear to watch the death of my best friend.

When I looked again Ginger was gone; fragments spiralled down towards the earth and the still-climbing victor was executing a victory roll in jubilation.

Even watching his display, I had to admire his superior speed and deft manoeuvrability.

I glanced around and panicked as I realised that the other bogie was no longer on his station. I scanned the horizon, then searched the sky in quadrants for him. Nothing.

Then I knew where he was; he hadn't lost me at all. He'd known I'd be watching his friend deal with Ginger so he'd inverted himself, flown onto the inside track of a circle and was looping back up towards my unprotected underside like some kind of a missile.

I couldn't take him. In speed alone he had me outclassed. I thought I might have the edge in aerobatic manoeuvrability and probably in flying experience.

All thoughts of standing and fighting were banished. In my mind I had just one priority; to get back to base and warn the rest of the squadron about these marauders so we could put together an operation to track down and destroy their base.

And all the time these thoughts were going through my mind he was climbing up at me, smiling to himself, thinking he had me, waiting until I was in range of his fearsome weapons.

The rush of adrenaline left a bitter taste in my mouth. I wanted to fight; I had to run.

I could sense where he was, below me and slightly to starboard to hide his ground shadow. I could feel his closeness.

I counted; one heartbeat, two heartbeats, three heartbeats, four...

And, my heart feeling like it might burst, I flipped upside down and pulled hard into an inverse dive.

Down, down, down, down to the ground in an attempt to put distance between me and my two adversaries.

The wind shrieked a harsh, almost musical noise as I dived at maximum speed for the ground. I risked a glance backwards.

My aggressor had been caught out and was still climbing away from me, a spent force moving rapidly in the wrong direction. But the other had been on to my move and had followed my dive.

He was now behind me and closing fast as we tore through the air in our haste to plummet to our deaths in the French soil.

The cold air tore at my face making my eyes stream. I blinked fiercely to clear my vision, I needed to be accurate, this was a one-trick move.

When I estimated that I'd left things too late, that I was too close to the ground to pull out of the dive, I threw everything I had into a hard climb.

For an instant nothing happened then gradually the ground shifted as the degree of my dive began to change, became shallower.

I wasn't going to do it, I wasn't going to do it, oh hell please, please let me do it.

I glanced over my shoulder, he was nearly upon me, almost had me in range.

My climb steepened, there was a snap and my port wing weakened, I fought to maintain control.

Did he have me? I flicked a glance behind. No, he was struggling to climb out of his dive, caught in the trap I'd laid for him.

Then I saw it immediately ahead of us. A small barn and getting bigger with every foot.

I pulled and pulled and pulled and yes! I screamed over the terracotta roof tiles, grazing my undercarriage as I ripped through the air and tore away from the barn into a straight and level flight.

My adversary wasn't so lucky. He failed to clear the roof and crashed through the wall into the barn. I didn't stay to see if he survived.

Hugging the ground, I limped home on a damaged wing and with a broken undercarriage.

I kept a careful lookout all the way but there were no further sightings of the enemy.

Soon, familiar landmarks came into view and I began to relax; the abandoned farmhouse, the old mill, the meandering river and there, up ahead was the final marker, the big chestnut tree.

As I approached the landing zone, I hoped my undercarriage would stand up to the strain. Then it was time for finals; left wing weaker so keep it a few degrees higher, lose speed, nose up, up more, three, two one and flare out now.

I touched down lightly, successfully, and sat there.

The CO came over but I didn't move, too tired.

"Trouble?" he asked.

"Two marauders," I said. "New Eagles, they caught us by surprise. Archie and Ginger are gone."

He walked closer and spoke softly.

"Tragedy like this is part of our life but it doesn't make it easy for us." He said, inspecting me. "You're back and we need you. The squadron needs you; you're our most experienced flier. Have you damaged your wing?"

I nodded.

"Go and get some rest, we'll have a look at you in the morning."

I was a good sparrow; I did as I was told, hopped away to my perch.

Tomorrow I'd have to be up there again, flying reconnaissance for the squadron, looking for good food and trying to find those Eagles.

I wondered if we'd ever win this war.

The Nomad

Gary Burn

Misia returned to Paris from her summer holiday in Venice in late September, ready to greet old friends and catch up on all the gossip. So when the couturier, Paul Poiret, invited her to one of his celebrated parties on Le Nomad, his enormous houseboat moored on the Seine and the latest symbol of his success, she accepted with alacrity. These were extravagant affairs: he brought his chef, so the food was always delicious; he plied his guests with the best calvados and pomace brandies. They were interesting soirées too, as he tended to invite artists and enjoyed discussing painting, literature, music, and especially his favourite subject— the "nature of beauty".

The sky was black and a storm brewing as Misia and her partner, the Catalan painter JoJo Sert, took a cab onto the Quai des Tuileries and followed the Seine to where Le Nomad was moored. Once onboard Misia was a little surprised to discover that Ballets Russes remained a hot topic of conversation among the other guests, only now it centred around the question of Diaghilev's criminality rather than Nijinsky's genius. Misia, who in the old days had been most protective of her painters, her vernisseurs, was even more so now of Diaghilev. She would tell them through gritted teeth: 'Poor Serge, who had started by throwing into it all his personal fortune... On himself he spent hardly anything at all. If at the end of a year... he remained with 10,000 francs to spend on his summer holiday in Venice, he considered himself the happiest of men.'

But surely that can't be true, they responded. We've heard the dancers are so fed up with him they are leaving— Tata Karsavina is off to London, Anna Pavlova is starting her own dance company, Ida Rubinstein too. Even choreographer Mikhail Fokine is about to jump ship. Claude

Debussy is also angry with Diaghilev for first commissioning a new ballet from him then cancelling it weeks later. He'll have nothing more to do with the man. This last comment was, unfortunately, true. As he wrote to Louis Laloy, his librettist, on 2 August: 'Our Russian friend acts as if the best way to treat people is to start off by deceiving them... Be that as it may... The main thing is to rise above Diaghilev and his duplicitous Cossacks.' But by then Debussy was in extreme pain; rectal pain and bleeding. As he told his publisher, Jacques Durand: 'For two days I never stopped suffering miserably. Only with the help of a variety of tranquilizers—morphine, cocaine, and other such lovely drugs—was I able to cope, but at the price of total stupor.' He would have to 'endure painful examinations and unfathomable suffering' for the next six years before his condition was diagnosed. And when it finally was, it was not good news.

Only Picasso commanded a higher price than Diaghilev on the gossip index that evening on Le Nomad. Misia had heard that he, together with his girlfriend, Fernande Olivier and their dog Frika, had recently moved house. From his shabby *Bateau-Lavoir* atelier to a chic apartment at 11 Boulevard de Clichy, close to Place Pigalle; going downhill and up in the world at the same time. The removal men had been curious to know how the little Spanish painter had been able to afford to swop a ramshackle wooden hut on the Butte for one of the most bourgeois houses in the neighbourhood; perhaps he had come up trumps at Longchamp. If they had been outside the *Bateau-Lavoir* days earlier when the art dealer, Ambroise Vollard, bought thirty of his paintings for two thousand francs — so many that once he had piled them into the back of a cab, he had to climb up beside the driver for the journey home— they would have understood that Pablo's days as a penniless painter were over.

Misia was anxious to find out more and did not have long to wait, as minutes later she caught the familiar scent of Fernande's perfume and knew Picasso had arrived on board. La belle Fernande was now the "it" girl of the Parisian avant-garde, famous in Montmartre for her hats and veils —'I'm crazy about veils', she said. 'I have quite a collection of them.

They lend mystery to my eyes. This way I think I look more glamorous.' Perfume was her real extravagance though. Rumours abounded that she had paid eighty francs for one named "Smoke" that turned out to have no scent at all, despite its beautiful colour. It was, said Gertrude Stein, 'real bottled liquid smoke'.

Naturally, Fernande was dying to tell everyone about their bright, new, four roomed apartment, with views of the Sacré-Cœur on the studio side and the trees along the Avenue Frochot on the other. As well as the fact that she had replaced all their old fashioned bric-a-brac with chic and snazzy, rustic mahogany; a Louis–Philippe sofa upholstered in ecclesiastical purple velvet and studded with golden buttons, Italian woodwork, porcelain knick-knacks, antique oak buffets, and a large piano on which she would pick out the occasional tune. With the help of Gertrude Stein's cook, Hélène, she'd also found a live-in maid who could make a decent soufflé. A girl, who in return for having her own room, equipped with table, walnut veneered chest, the best of the ugly furniture from the *Bateau-Lavoir* and forty francs a month, was prepared to serve meals, clean rooms and wear a uniform while doing it.

The romantic bobo lifestyle Fernande wished for herself was not one she encouraged her maid to adopt. When the Picassos entertained, as Fernande planned they would do, she wanted their guests to be served by a maid in starched cap and apron. She certainly did not expect to find her in the Taverne de l'Hermitage, located enticingly opposite their apartment, on the Boulevard Rochechouart: a cabaret bar whose clientele included fashionable media stars of the day, celebrity boxers and sportsmen, and the pimps, clowns, acrobats, equestriennes and tightrope walkers, who would soon reawaken Picasso's love of the circus. Not to mention a coterie of women unaccompanied by men, making merry, as a female acrobat, a San Franciscan monk who sang Negro songs and other miscellaneous acts strutted their stuff. In the event, Fernande had a far more intractable problem to surmount. Picasso hated socialising and was reluctant to pursue their new bourgeois lifestyle with the enthusiasm she expected. While they would visit Henri Matisse on Fridays, Gertrude Stein on Saturdays and entertain at home on Sunday afternoons, in a semblance of ordered existence, Picasso was most often to be found back in the *Bateau-Lavoir*, painting with Georges Braque, who had himself recently broken with Matisse.

What Picasso and Braque were doing was analysing objects in terms of their shapes and trying to work out how to paint shifting perspectives, in an attempt to depict the world around them more accurately; a world where what you painted was not necessarily what you saw. 'The squaring of the circle was a phrase that excited our ambitions', said Picasso. More than that, they were in the process of revolutionising western art, even if they didn't know it yet. 'Just imagine', Picasso recalled, 'almost every evening, either I went to Braque's studio or Braque came to mine. Each of us had to see what the other had done during the day. We criticised each other's work. A canvas wasn't finished unless both of us felt it was. I would show my canvases and say "Is that woman right? Can she walk down the street? Is that a woman or a painting?" I would say: "Does that one smell under the arms? What I want is for her to smell under the arms." Or we would say: "No, that one doesn't smell much!"'

They were working so closely together 'we were like two mountain climbers held together by a rope' said Braque. Picasso remembers going to Braque's studio and being shocked at a still life he was painting of a package of tobacco and a pipe. 'My poor friend, this is dreadful,' said Pablo. 'I see a squirrel in your canvas... get rid of it'. Braque took a careful look and, sure enough, there was the squirrel. He toiled for days trying to remove it, but to no avail. He changed the composition, changed the light and the colour. It made no difference. Whatever he did the damned squirrel stayed put, because once it had entered his mind it was almost impossible to remove. But finally, after two weeks, Picasso reported that 'Braque was able to turn the trick and the canvas became a package of tobacco, a pipe, a deck of cards, and above all a Cubist painting.' A habitat that clearly did not suit the squirrel, as it had vamoosed.

Of course, all work and no play makes for dull iconoclasts, so when they needed a break from taking a wrecking ball to renaissance perspective, they went to the cinema or the circus, or were off carousing in Montmartre's bars and cafes dressed as clowns, or to the Issy-les-Moulineaux aerodrome to watch Louis Blériot and the other aviators, whose exploits were enthralling the intelligentsia. There they would run into Anatole France, Maurice Maeterlinck, Gabriele D'Annunzio and Marcel Proust, his "eyes brimming with tears", and his chauffeur-lover Albert. They also made model aircraft together and likened their own enterprise to that of the Wright Brothers, with Picasso giving Braque the pet name "Wilbourg", 'mon vieux Wilbourg' (Wilbourg old boy), after Wilbur Wright, who had become a hero in France. They shared everything: cooking together and producing paintings so alike they had trouble recognising which was whose. They even dressed in each other's clothes, including Braque's army uniform, and took photographs—'Sergeant Braque with a faraway look in his eye, Sergeant Picasso swaddled but steadfast'. They also loved reading stories of Sherlock Holmes, Nick Carter and Buffalo Bill and his buckskin accoutred sidekick, "Pard" (partner); Picasso sometimes even signed his letters to Braque ton pard.

Braque and Picasso had a real affection for each another, a fraternal bond. So much so, as Fernande told Misia now, Max Jacob was jealous. Poor Max, usurped by Guillaume Apollinaire in poetry, by Fernande in Picasso's affections and now by Braque, as his new best-bud. But then, thought Misia, so was Fernande herself, as Picasso had taken to referring to Braque as ma femme (my wife); even if in a joking kind of way. Once, when Braque was hospitalised and Picasso visited him, he was turned away. 'The nurse wouldn't let me into his room', Picasso complained. 'She said Madame Braque was with him. She didn't realise that I was Madame Braque.' He would also say of Braque, somewhat mischievously, that he was 'the woman who loved me best.'

It was the Cézanne retrospective at the 1907 Salon d'Automne, a year after his death that had brought the two painters together, after Braque had initially denounced Picasso's Demoiselles d'Avignon. It was a seminal moment for them both. 'I had to re-think everything', said Braque, 'the discovery of his work overturned everything'. Recent optical discoveries had made Paul Cézanne realise that because we look at the world through two eyes, not one, we receive two views from two different angles, not one, which our brain then combines into one. He then developed a painting technique using repeated brush strokes to build small flat planes in such a way as to portray an object from these different viewpoints at the same time; a blurring or "double exposure". This was why Picasso called Cézanne the 'father of us all'. He had set them on a journey of discovery. They were feeling their way towards a new way of looking at the world, deconstructing the conventions of traditional perspective that had dominated art since the Renaissance, towards what would, according to Apollinaire, be a profound volte-face in how painters and painting depict reality; a radical change in vision itself. As Braque put it, 'the whole Renaissance tradition is antipathetic to me. The hard-and-fast rules of perspective it succeeded in imposing on art was a ghastly mistake which it has taken four centuries to redress.'

It was a "new way of seeing"— a dynamic way of depicting the modern age, where the incredible technological progress of the last forty years had outstripped that of the previous four centuries; an age defined by rapid movement; by the motor car, the aeroplane and, most importantly, cinematography; moving pictures, in other words. One of Picasso and Braque's favourite pastimes was to go to the movies (they even set up a film club), a relatively new-fangled entertainment, fashioned out of what was, in effect, a profound change of form and vision, a revolutionary depiction of space, time and motion. Picasso had begun this experiment two years before, when in creating Les Demoiselles he rejected a fixed point of view and harmonious proportion, in favour of multiple perspectives and dislocation, and disturbing images of primitive art that desecrated much that had been held sacred in art up to this point.

In doing so he had cleared the decks for what was to come: a freedom to create a new pictorial language. Braque followed with his 1908 painting, Maisons à l'Estaque, depicting houses with square extended roofs. Matisse had remarked to Louis Vauxcelles that Braques' houses were 'made of little cubes', and even drew a sketch of 'two ascending and converging lines between which small cubes were set depicting "L'Estaque of George Braque"' to demonstrate his point. When Vauxcelles reviewed the current state of Parisian art for the newspaper Gil Blas, he wrote that Braque 'reduces everything—places and figures and houses—to geometrical patterns, to cubes.' The term stuck and this revolutionary method of painting came to be known as "cubism". Much to the irritation of Braque and Picasso, who complained: 'When we invented cubism we had no intention whatever of inventing cubism. We simply wanted to express what was in us.' And later, when a reporter from Paris-Journal asked Picasso about cubism, he replied: 'Il n'y a pas de Cubisme [There is no cubism]' and went off to feed El Mono, his monkey. So, just as Marx had famously denied he was a Marxist, so Picasso and Braque denied they were ever Cubists.

While Misia sat talking to Fernande Olivier she felt a definite melancholy pervade their conversation. 'I've never liked Sundays, they have an oppressive, unpleasant character', Fernande complained. 'They are wearisome days, with a smell to them.' Just then it began to rain again and with the sound of the drops pounding on the roof of the boat her face brightened. 'But I love it when I get caught in a summer rainstorm that turns me into a streaming creature with hair dripping down my neck', she added, staring straight ahead for some moments, as if in a trance. 'To feel the water dripping down my neck, and to feel the water seeping between my underclothes and my skin, so that I can't move because my dress sticks to my body and hampers my legs, and to feel my face varnished by the rain, water in my eyes, my ears, my neck and then, when the rain stops and a rainbow shines across the newly washed blue sky, to let myself slide on the glistening glass and to feel myself drying under the strong rays of the sun, back in his heaven.'

Fernande had, perhaps, had too much to drink and was soon telling Misia secrets that she should have kept to herself: Apollinaire could only make love fully clothed sitting in an armchair to avoid wrinkling his bed covers, such was his penchant for neatness; "his bed was sacred" he said. His former girlfriend, Marie Laurencin, had never experienced an orgasm. Max Jacob's preference was for Republican Guards with moustaches. What she did not reveal was that her relationship with Picasso was in trouble. He had made numerous portraits of her in the new "cubist" style. She was the first of seven important women in his life (two went mad, two committed suicide) and only later did it became clear that when Picasso was falling in love he painted the object of his desire to make her look beautiful. Conversely, when he was falling out of love he did the opposite. In Fernande's opinion, the paintings he made of her during the summer of 1909 made her look ugly. But, as Pablo explained, 'I was experimenting with perspective.' She was also certain that lurking in the Demoiselles somewhere was 'her image as a whore'. That wasn't surprising, given that Picasso had "jokingly" told his friends that she was, indeed, 'one of the girls in the brothel.'

'Life is miserable. Pablo is morose and I can't look to him for any moral or physical support,' Fernande told Gertrude Stein. Once he had been so jealous he locked Fernande in their apartment whenever he went out. 'Out of a sort of morbid jealousy,' she recalled years later, 'he forced me to live like a recluse. But with tea, books, a couch, not much housework to do, I was very, very happy.... I was, I admit, extremely lazy.' Those days were drawing to a close. Now Picasso was irritated and bored with 'her little ways', he said. She told him he was 'as stupid as can be', and knew nothing except how to paint; that he was a spoilt child genius and not much more. He complained about her constant complaining. He would finally end their relationship on the pretext that she was having an affair with an Italian Futurist. But then, as he admitted: 'For me there are only two kinds of women, goddesses and doormats". And they were most often the very same woman seen from two viewpoints, two perspectives, on two separate planes of time.

It was getting late so Misia and Sert got ready to leave. Just then they were approached by a babushka, an old woman with a wrinkled face and a prominent mole in the middle of her forehead, dressed entirely in brown, who spoke to Misia in Russian, explaining that she had just returned from St Petersburg where she had seen Serge Diaghilev, who was not at all well. Sweat, she said, was running off him like fat off a cooked goose. Misia was taken aback at this. She turned to speak to Sert and then turned back again, but the woman had vanished. When she didn't reappear they left and as they stepped off the boat the rain fell ever more heavily; like a pissing cow, as the French say. Looking back, it seemed to Misia that it never stopped raining after that. As their taxi wound its way back along Quai Henri IV, she thought about Diaghilev and wondered if Paris would ever enjoy the Ballets Russes again. 'Sometimes, Diaghilev is his own worst enemy', she had told the impresario, Gabriel Astruc. 'Not while I'm still alive, he's not', the Frenchman replied.

Just Words

Frances Thimann

Eleni said: 'Tonight - you would like to come with me, perhaps?'

Eleni's kitchen was warm with sweet-smelling bakery. They were sitting together there, talking, drinking coffee, as they so often were; but Cathryn was too depressed this time to be good company.

'Will I enjoy it? Will it be *fun*?' she muttered, and she stared gloomily from the window as the December sky cast arrows of sleet onto the pavements. Eleni looked at her friend for a while without speaking, her dark eyes thoughtful, searching: pitying also. Then: 'I think it will be good that you come,' she said. 'It will take your thoughts from... these things that are troubling you.' There was still a trace of her own southern country in Eleni's voice, as if there were soft wine on her tongue.

At the last moment Cathryn decided that she would go - but it was only to escape the emptiness of another evening. She had nothing better to do.

The email - the latest email - had come just before Christmas. 'We very much liked your novel, but just at the moment...' Or perhaps it had been: 'Unfortunately we are unable to accept any new submissions for at least six months...' - she had hardly bothered to read it. The publisher was clearing his desk of unwanted manuscripts before the holiday, Cathryn supposed. She - and the email - was one of hundreds, no doubt.

Cathryn had written two novels, a romance and a historical mystery; this was her sixteenth letter of rejection. Each marked another notch in the measure of her dejection and self-pity. She brooded miserably over her failures: those love scenes in the first novel - they were too timid, too... restrained, she saw that now. The plot of the second one, the mystery, was no doubt obvious from the start. But she was tired of revisions and rewrites, and each comment she received from editors, or from agents, seemed to contradict the previous one.

She dragged herself through the big city store - it was piled high with Christmas gifts: *Latest Best-Sellers*! T*hrillers A-Z*! *True Crime*! But the books she saw did not seem better than her own. 'It's rubbish, most of this,' she thought angrily, looking over the shelves and tables, the special offers and half-price deals. Not for the first time, but more bitterly now than ever before, she questioned herself: 'Do I want to be a part of all this? To be a special offer - a deal? Do I have to... to compete...?' Always at this time, and now especially, she felt the aggressive marketing, the commercialism, most acutely, as if its only purpose was to hide the meaning of this season behind all the layers of glitter and glamour.

More bright and buzzing titles promised happiness and well-being, and she surveyed them with weary eyes: *Looking Great, Feeling Great*! *Live Better, Live Longer*! they carolled. *Cooking to Stay Slim*!

How To Make An Attractive Window-Box!

Christmas presents for those who needed nothing? *Real Lives*! *Fantasy Worlds!*

The event had been organised by the local Refugee Centre - Eleni worked there as a volunteer - and was to include readings by some of the refugees themselves. Cathryn had passed the church many times and never entered. Inside it was plain, and quiet - only half-full now. It was beautiful in its plainness, she thought - red brick and wood, with a scent of new polish and old textiles. It was very warm, surprisingly so, and she stripped away her coat and scarf, then her jacket. Other layers slipped away too; she was a child again, with her parents on a Sunday morning, looking at the colours and light of the windows, making her own stories from the figures pictured there. She sat patiently now and allowed the church's simplicity and peace to reach her, feeling the resentment and dejection fall slowly from her. And there was something special here tonight; she could feel a sense of anticipation in the audience, but also of uncertainty, of not knowing quite what might be expected of them.

The readers sat together in the front pews, feeling something similar, perhaps.

The director rose to welcome them all. He told them something of the work of the Centre, how it was developing, and of this small writing group which had started only a year ago with a local teacher as leader. 'It has taken great courage for our readers to speak and write of their experiences - they've all been through very difficult times,' he concluded. 'One or two are still waiting even now to hear what their future might be. But they'll tell you more themselves in all the pieces they have written.' Then he turned and shared a few words of support and a smile of encouragement with the readers.

The first, a young man, stood and turned to the audience. He was from Eritrea, he said, and his name was Girma - he was small and slight, obviously very nervous. He explained that he would recite two of his poems:

Rain
It is my enemy
It drives against me
It makes a barrier
It conceals what is before me
It makes me forget what is behind me.
It is my friend.

Night
I cannot sleep
I cannot think
I only listen
The sounds come back to me like stars
Glinting and sharp
Painful
Coming out of memory in the dark night.

Cathryn was astonished; had she expected clumsy rhymes or long-winded prose? Exotic scenery? Poignant recollections of childhood?

The audience were not sure how to respond - but some applauded, and others called out their praise.

The next speaker was an older man, middle-aged, from the Democratic Republic of Congo - his name was Amadu, and he had been a lawyer, he explained. He wore an ill-fitting suit and glasses:

Queues

I had heard that the English like to make queues. (The audience relaxed a little here and began to smile, pleased with the familiar joke, and glad perhaps that the evening would not be all difficulty and gloom.) That they will make queues in the cold, in the wind and snow, that they will not ask the reason for their wait. Sometimes they will talk together while they wait, I had heard. And I have found that some of that is true. I have found they have made a queue for me, and for so many others, I do not know how many others, nor who they are, nor how long will be the wait to know my future, and there is no-one I can talk to in this queue...

The audience were quieter as he continued, and at the end, the laughter was gone, but the applause was steady, and sympathetic.

A younger man, perhaps from the Middle East came forward - he had more confidence and spoke more fluently than the others:

'My name is Zahir, and I am a writer,' he told them: 'a poet and a journalist.' Cathryn sat more upright in her pew. 'Your poet Shelley believed that poets were the true legislators of society. I believed that too, and I tried to write the truth when I could, but that became impossible where I lived - eventually I had to get away. My piece is called 'Punishment' - it is partly my own story but it could be the story of many of my friends':

Punishment

I saw everything that they did to my parents - my mother, first, while we were all forced to watch, and then my father... then they

> were dragged away. I have never found out what became of them. And it was because of me that it happened - because I wrote an article for a magazine in the town. They did not punish me, not at that time, but my mother and my father instead. But then my own punishment began... And I was punished by my loneliness too, my hunger and fear when I escaped, and now it happens again not once but so many times, over and over, in my memories, and in my dreams. I am safe here at last but the punishment continues. I do not know if my family and friends are safe, as I am. I would endure more punishment if I could know that. I think that the punishment may be for ever.

The audience were silent, though there were murmurs amongst them. At last an uncertain ripple of applause spread through the church. *True Crime*! thought Cathryn, remembering the bookshop labels. Live *Better, Live Longer*!

There was a short interval then; cakes and biscuits were served, with cups of tea and coffee - but the audience were thoughtful and constrained. Most were moved and impressed, as Cathryn was, and wanted only to hear more of the readings.

A tall, striking young woman stood waiting for them. There was a dignity and a peace about her which spread somehow to the audience; her stillness drew them back to their seats.

'I am Sarah,' she told them, speaking quietly and calmly. 'I took that name when I became a Christian.' Her dark eyes held silver as she spoke and moved, as though from the brightness of belief within her. 'In my country it was not allowed to be a Christian, and I had to escape, to leave my home and family. It was a difficult journey for me, very terrible, and very long, but at last I am here, and I have heard that I can stay. I can sit here when I wish, in this church, safe, and quiet, and equal, an equal person, not something to be beaten or thrown into prison just for what I am, for the things that I believe. I would like to become a teacher one day, to teach your language to other people, perhaps to children. To me words are like jewels that I can hold up to see that they sparkle and change their colour in the light. This is what I have written. It is about all the women, everywhere in the world, who are treated badly just because they are women. It is the best I could do':

Just

Not just a girl to be cut and spoiled
Mutilated
Not just a daughter to be married too young
Frightened
Not just a wife to be bruised and beaten
Used and misused
Just a woman
To be safe, to be quiet, to be equal
To be at peace
To be free.

Just words.

Before the audience had any time to respond, the very last reader stood up. Joseph was only a youngster, and so shy at first that he could hardly look away from his paper. He managed to stammer that he had seen a beautiful mobile in the shopping centre, butterflies of many colours made by children from a local school - he gestured suddenly with his hands, fingers fluttering, unable to describe it in any other way:

Butterflies

I saw the butterflies
The butterflies in the park
The butterflies in the shopping centre
Made by children -
Flying.

I remember my friends, children like me
Made to kill
I hope they are free now

Like butterflies -
Flying.

Some members of the audience stood to applaud. The boy was surprised at first, then he laughed quickly, as a child does, on the spur of the moment, and with his long fingers he made the fluttering movement he had made before. Some of the audience began to do the same, copying him, laughing too, and for those few minutes it was as though the church was full of butterflies set free by the boy with his words, the changing colours and the light of their wings flickering above the pews, by the windows, in the roof.

Others remained still and quiet, like Cathryn, with tears in their eyes.

And afterwards, she saw how the readers were changed, that they were calmer, somehow taller, somehow filling more space. She watched as they shook hands, embraced each other and the staff of the Centre.

There was a pause then, no-one quite knowing what should follow. But after a minute the teacher who led the group rose and spoke to the audience; she told them how it had started, how it had changed during the year and how important it was to them. And then they all joined in, thinking and speaking at the same time, glad to say how it had helped them.

'It was good to describe the loneliness and the fear, to release it,' Amadu said, slowly. 'When it is released, it is made less. It makes something good - something better, at least - out of something very bad. And people should know how it is for us.'

The teacher turned to Joseph, touching his shoulder gently. 'I can speak better, more confidently now, I am not tongue-tied,' Joseph said; and Girma felt that he had learned new and important things, that might be useful for the future. He added: 'I can think more clearly and I can write more clearly. One day I would like to write a novel about my country.' 'I would like to read it!' someone called out, and there was laughter, cries of 'Hear Hear!' and more applause.

'It is like a new life for me,' Sarah told them, very simply. 'My writing, it is my companion, my hope. It is... I think it is a future for me.'

The director came forward again then, his face showing all his pleasure and pride in everything that had happened during the evening.

'You've heard enough by this time, I'm sure,' he began, 'you've seen what it has meant to our readers - but I would like to add to everything they've said. We know now about wars and conflicts in every corner of the world, but there's not so much understanding of the day-to-day lives of the people who are affected most at the time, and long afterwards too, even when at last they've reached a safer place. But only in this way will we be able to improve the services and treatments that are available for them - and there's so much more that we still have to do. So I want to thank the readers for their pieces, and the teacher who has worked so hard with them. And I want to thank you all for coming tonight.'

Cathryn sat on in the church, hardly listening, huddled at the end of the pew as other members of the audience left. There were tears in her eyes still. She was experiencing a kind of double vision - she saw the bookshop, glossy and garish, with its shriekßing titles: *Looking Great, Feeling Great*! *Cooking to Stay Slim*! and this quiet, plain church, the stories and poems she had heard: 'I was punished by my hunger and fear...' *Live Better, Live Longer*! -'The punishment will be for ever.' '... Painful, glinting and sharp, out of the dark night...' 'Children like me, made to kill...' - *True Crime*! *Real Lives*!

Eventually Eleni roused her, her eyes soft and wide and concerned. 'Cathryn - you OK? We must close the church now. Will you come tomorrow - we will have some coffee, we will talk?'

'Could I be a volunteer, Eleni? Help with their writing? Or something?'

'Tomorrow - you will come?' Eleni said.

This tory was fi st published in 'The Clock Museum and other stories', Chaffinch Press, 2021.

Sailing To Zanzibar

Frances Thimann

20th January, 1990

I think evening must be the loveliest time here. Yesterday, after we arrived and had rested for a while, we walked through the old town to the seashore. There are about twenty of us in the tour group. Beyond the harbour wall the sea rose up to the horizon just like a great peacock's tail, fanning and swaying, turquoise and violet. Along the waterfront the local men were preparing food for the evening meal — the whole town seemed to be gathering there to eat. We watched as they crushed long sugar canes in ancient mangles, squeezing out colourless sweet juice (we tried some, and it was delicious) or fri d octopus and squid (we didn't dare try these!) in shallow wide pans, slicing strange-shaped vegetables and fruits into the oil. The scent of wood-smoke and spices drifted round us.

Boys ran shouting and laughing, diving from the wall into the water, and their heads appeared again like currants, bobbing and dipping at the surface. Then the sun seemed to fall, quite suddenly, rather than to set in a calm and sedate fashion, as it does in England. It burned a path downwards to the sea, and somehow it was like a great tragedy that everyone watched, from the shore, or from their balconies, as if it were happening on a wide stage.

The sky was golden and scarlet beyond the palm trees. Far out to sea, a sail appeared at the horizon and turned in to harbour, its spar slanting, moving quickly on the last wind.

Then the colour disappeared all at once, and it was night.

January, 2008

Gwen stands in her narrow hallway, steadying herself for the difficult climb. In the darkness, the familiar surfaces and spaces of the daytime have become a labyrinth of shadows that move unpredictably as wild creatures.

Since her illness, her balance has become unsteady, her sight and her hearing are weaker. Sensations within her body have become confused with those beyond it, so that she feels she is crumbling into the world around her.

With painful fingers she touches the night-time switches once more, the locks and chains and bolts, all the little devices for her safety. She moves slowly along the hall.

24th January, 1990

I chose this place, Zanzibar, from all the others in the brochure, because it sounded so different, so exotic, so far away! And I have decided to keep a diary during my stay here. I've not done this since I was a teenager, since before I became engaged to Bill, all those years ago! — but it's easy to forget, especially as one gets older, and I should like to remember everything that happens during this holiday. It's a wonderful opportunity for me to escape for a while, at least, after all the sadness and worry of these last few months and years.

Now that Bill is gone — and dearest Bill was never fond of travelling! ('I don't want to become discontented, Gwen,' he would say, and I never found a reply to this) — now that he is gone, I have to get used to being on my own. But the other members of the group seem very pleasant.

Even after several days here, we find the labyrinths of the old Stone Town confusing. The narrow lanes twist and turn behind the palaces of the waterfront and the grand houses where the famous explorers of earlier times — Livingstone and Stanley are the best-known, I suppose — lived and planned their journeys, and where they returned, sick and exhausted, but enduring bravely till journey's end. The Stone Town is crumbling these days, its stained balconies and fading walls are decaying in the humid climate. The gorgeous wooden doors are often split and broken-down, though they are still most striking. The island is famous for these doors, often beautifully carved with foliage and animals, and it's almost as if they are 'magic casements', inviting us to step through to find a better life. But we found them in the poorer streets too, less fi e of course, and sometimes there was nothing behind them at all, just damp and dirt and emptiness.

In one of those tumble-down houses, miserable and wretched, we saw three small children playing, all alone, the oldest would have been about six, maybe. I dropped behind the group for a while, thinking that I'd like to speak to them, to reach out and help them in some way, but they stopped their play and stared at me with their large, grave eyes, until I became uncomfortable, and went on.

Later, a little boy ran up to me, very daring.

'Where you from, lady?' he called out. 'You English lady?' Then he ran away again, laughing at his daring, without waiting for my answer.

They are such beautiful children, thin, malnourished I suppose, their knees protruding like match-heads above their skinny calves. It occurred to me that in a way they are like Zanzibar itself. Their eyes and teeth, their ragged shreds of clothes are so brilliant and bright, but their streets and homes are dark and poor.

I thought of my little grandson Joe, pale and polite and serious — already he has everything that he could ever want.

Later we visited a museum, built like a mosque, of pure white stone, and dedicated to the history of Zanzibar. Amongst all the things I saw there, I remember Dr Livingstone's medical bag the most clearly. It was hardly bigger than a handbag, and it held only a few small bottles and rough-looking implements, all that he had with him as he travelled through Afric .

'It's less than anything a modern tourist might take, even for a short holiday in Europe!' I exclaimed to our tour guide, Freddie.

'You're quite right, Gwen,' Freddie remarked, glancing at me as if he had not thought of this before. 'He was a brave man.'

I should have liked more time there. Stupidly, I hadn't realised that the island was connected with the slave trade — I am learning so much here already — but another excursion had been arranged for us in the afternoon. We were taken to see a workshop where local people demonstrated and sold their crafts, and we were able to buy gifts and souvenirs. Perhaps there'll be an opportunity later in the week to visit the museum again.

January, 2008

She struggles up the stairs, as she does each night, setting herself to the task, bent forward, concentrating on each movement. Her old bag is slung around her, shoulder to hip, her stick clicks along the banister-rails. This step creaks, that one has somehow become taller than the others since the previous night; at the curve of the staircase there are new and dangerous loose threads in the carpet. The shadows trick her, and she tries to ignore them — a second's distraction, and she might fall again. The landing is full of sharp corners too, hard-edged furniture, heavy doors and handles — dangerous ground to cross before she can enter the soft safety of her bed. Gwen knows that this is the proving point of her life, that she should not look back, she should not complain. She must go bravely, like the great explorers she had learnt about so many years ago, journeying to the edges of their world without maps or markers.

26th January, 1990

Yesterday was disturbing and strange, it gave me much to think about. In the morning I slipped away from the tour group, and from Freddie. I wanted to see things for myself, to explore the town, for I may not have another opportunity to travel in this way again, at least for a while. I suppose I'm afraid of everything that lies ahead of me, afraid of growing old. My son is married and gone away, and little Joseph is going to school in France now. Sometimes I look after him in the holidays, and I look forward so much to his visits. Of course I hope that one day perhaps they will return for good.

I was searching for an old Turkish bath, which was marked on the map I had found for myself in the local tourist office. It appeared to be in one of the very poorest parts of the town, not much visited by foreigners, and I wondered if it might have been demolished, or crumbled away long ago. Soon I was quite lost, the lane I was following became just a puddled track between empty buildings. Ugly waste land and heaps of rubble lay ahead of me, and a stained brick wall with no way through that I could fin .

Other ruined buildings mouldered all round me. For once, in this crowded island, there was no-one there, and for that moment I felt very alone, and a long way from home. Everything was different and rather frig tening.

Eventually I found a small shop, and the man there gave me directions back to the hotel. Before I went on my way, he pulled out an old wooden chair for me, brushing the dust away with his fi gers. I was tired and hot, glad to rest for a little. I felt no anxiety.

He offered me a pale-coloured drink in a smeary glass.

'You drink, please, lady,' he said. 'Is good for refresh. Is from coconut,' and it was sweet and cool.

I sat there for a little, amongst the loose batteries and packets of matches, dented cartons of washing powder and piles of bananas. The man was thin and small, and the skin of his face and hands was like the bark of an old tree, cracked and broken. But his eyes were very kind, and he treated me as if that little shop were his kingdom, and I an Arabian princess, from the 1001 nights, maybe.

I thought afterwards, for some reason, that the man might be about Bill's age, but it was impossible to tell or to compare. And I couldn't help wondering whether Bill would have been so kind, if an exotic lady from Zanzibar had arrived on his doorstep one day, seeking directions!

Of course, I arrived very late for lunch, the others waiting, looking at the clock, and Freddie most annoyed with me, his charm and his smile quite gone, disappeared like the Turkish bath.

'You must not leave the group again, Gwen,' he scolded me. 'We didn't know what had happened to you. There are places here where it's not safe to go alone.'

Freddie is responsible for us all, of course, and I didn't want to upset him again, nor the other members of the group. I sat quietly on the lawn after lunch, under the canopy — the sun is so hot in the afternoons. Suddenly I am missing Bill very much.

Later, in the early evening, we visited a pleasant spot along the coast, where there had once been a Sultan's palace. It had been burned down, now just a few parts of it remain, and it was peaceful there, the ruined buildings surrounded by gardens and palm trees. It was cloudy that day, and the sky was just beginning to lose its colour, but at that moment it was like pearl or opal, ivory and cream and pink, as if all those colours of the palette were melted together, smoothed and softened by the feathery palms. And yet it was so similar to an English country churchyard! I couldn't help feeling that this would be a tranquil resting-place — though when the time comes, of course, I shall be with Bill in our little village at home.

It's strange that one can travel so far, and discover a place that seems at fi st so very different — the trees and flowers, the buildings, even the air were foreign — but the atmosphere, and the feelings and thoughts I experienced there, were the same as if it had been England.

But it is England that is beginning to feel far away and foreign to me, and I know that it will be damp and cold there now.

January 2008

On the landing Gwen pauses, short of breath, the familiar pain forming around her heart. From the window she sees the winter sky like an iron vault, bare black trees beneath, a colourless string of moon dropped between the branches: small sharp stars, very distant. Sometimes, in her loneliness, she feels that she is standing at the peak of a great mountain range that stretches far into the distance, or that she is becalmed at the centre of a silent sea. Sometimes she feels that time too has become endless, every minute has become an hour or a year.

She feels that she must hold fast to a chair, a door, so that she will not be brushed away.

28th January, 1990

Freddie is keeping an eye on me, I think! — but I don't have any wish to explore again on my own just now, I am glad to rest for the moment. The hotel is air-conditioned, not hot or humid, and it's situated almost on the beach, so that I can sit and look through the window at the sea as I have breakfast. Fishermen go by, and I saw an old woman returning home with the goods she had bought at the market, all stuffed together into an old string bag, a wretched chicken squirming at the bottom beneath all the cans and tins. Tomorrow there will be a coach tour to a different part of the island, and we shall visit a spice plantation, then stay for two nights in a chalet on a coral beach, before returning home.

I've been thinking about this holiday, now that it will soon be over. There were days when I felt that I was learning about the people here and about their history, but I know that I've not been very brave, I haven't been much of an explorer!

I should like to have travelled more, but there has always been someone to look after, someone to care for, and I think it becomes harder when one is older, and on one's own.

But I have this record, and I shall read and think about it all again in the years to come. The island is the most beautiful place that I have ever visited or could imagine, though sometimes it is mysterious, even frig tening.

And of course I hope that one day I shall be able to come back, and rediscover all those things that I have found here, and other things too perhaps, and understand them more completely.

January 2008

She leans against the landing wall, waiting for the agony to pass, her lungs empty and rasping as if she were breathing the thin-stretched air of the desert, or saturated thickets of jungle. At last she turns at the doorway of the bedroom and fumbles with the lamp; but something strikes at her heart, and she slips, falling hard and heavy against the bed. She does not move.

Her eyes are filled with brilliant colour, scarlet, gold, and crimson: she hears a sound of water, and the air is warm, and fresh, it lifts her — and she is sailing now, sailing on a fine wind, sailing, sailing to Zanzibar ....

On the shore, the men are gathering to prepare the evening meal, and dark-skinned boys run and laugh along the harbour wall. There is a scent of wood-smoke, and of spices, and the sun burns its pathway downwards through the sky, spinning, to the surface of the sea.

Thisstory was fi st published in 'Cello and other stories', Pewter Rose Press, 2008.

Fiona Linday

Finding the Sublime in Nature Writing

As someone who finds observing nature sublime, I acknowledge it is an important way God speaks. Regularly, I shriek excitedly as a gaggle of geese fly in a V shape. I advocate for wellbeing from nature as He reveals his majesty by showcasing mind-blowing sunsets. Recording my nature-watching journey reassures me there's a masterful creator who inspires habitat protection for future generations. As a grandma to five, I am well motivated. Balancing the content of my creative writing to raise awareness of environmental concerns effectively is my aim. Living next to the Grantham Canal is a blessing, with swans, ducks, swallows, coots and bats regularly swooping by. Equally, we reared our own lamb and kept hens for fresh eggs on the table at our smallholding. So, I widely share my enthusiasm of countryside life experienced in short stories and poems. It is an authentic way to tip the reader off about the precariousness of wildlife habitats by championing the wonder of wild species to encourage their preservation. My purpose is to celebrate and praise the spectacular free gift of nature by writing eco-stories to gain perspective.

Here's where my wild creature advocacy stems from, real-life inspiration- An extraordinary event happened around the millennium when paddling in the warm Red Sea with family. As I waded into the sea to pat the wave surface while watching my children swim, a couple of dolphins came up behind me. There was an echo of 'Wow!' as the magnificent mammals glided either side to do a swim-by. They had escaped from an area of paid-for experiences to swimming with dolphins. I was too flabbergasted to grab hold of their fins, though. What a privilege! My father snapped up a photo of my shocked face being ushered deeper into the waves by the cheeky dolphin duo. Some extracts from stories and poetry written to engage young people and adults in considering their unique environments and sustainability are in my *Count Our Blessings*, collection, *Onwards & Upwards*, 2021 below. Thus, I wrote about a similar event in The Real Me story where the protagonist is diving:

"I'm saved by this spectacular mirage which begins with a clicking sound. My heart races as the swell of a huge, grey fish moves me. For a few seconds, I hold my breath, enjoying the dolphin's hypnotic gaze. During his ballet, this fantastic creature checks me out as sunlight bejewels his body. Playfully he turns, flicking his tail..." Again, in *Finding Myself as the Tide Turns* I use my experience of the splendour of the Lindisfarne coast to connect with sea creatures as the young adult, Sarah, revels:

> "Waiting, my feet sank into the tiny shells on the shore, I almost missed nature's treat of a shoal of silvery tiddlers swimming by. Together, we rippled the surface of the sea, forming our temporary peaceful spot. Only when the ghostly seal pups stopped barking from behind the rocky outcrop, I de-stressed by following on into the lapping waves up to my knees."

Now, I fully understand how God shares glimpses of the wonders of His creation to lift my spirits and equip me to tell others. When I worked as a Teaching Assistant in Primary school for many years, we particularly highlighted the awe and wonder of the seasons and weather. A favourite activity was taking the 'Afternoonies' for a listening walk. We often left our desks to gather mahogany glazed conkers- fallen from nearby horse chestnut trees to mark autumn's arrival. Locally, conkers are still baked, then drilled and threaded for hours of smashing fun. Or, to enjoy winter's crisp bright snowfall, we'd hat and scarf up for snow-angel making on the iced, grassy pitch.

So, there were subtle cues to an improved environment in my first YA-winning short story, 'Off the Beaten Track' that told of an honest rural existence of fowl keeping:

"One day this mud will be a meadow of tall buttercups. I know it. Right now though, I have to collect the eggs. I despise those chickens. I despise the way they're turning our yard into a grey, slippery, mess. It's horrible. Still the eggs are lovely."

Writing about global warming comes with responsibilities and challenges. There, I comment upon alarming weather changes but try not to traumatise the reader. That came after learning lessons from some over-enthusiastic apocalyptic writing, Paradise Lost...Not! That is where there's an Asian volcano eruption:

"There was a scorched line where the foul magnum cooled. It oozed from the fiery centre, reaching to the surface of the earth. Crackling flames enveloped the defiant, dragging the last of them back, screeching. I covered my ears. They left claw marks, etched forever in the ground - a terrible reminder of the time..." Lately, I realise this doom narrative backdrop from my early writing days was not as effective as showing the glory of our natural world.- Offering possible solutions before tragedy a more wholesome aspiration.

Later, I wrote for young adults more sympathetically, avoiding climate disasters. Instead, my tale was about the effect of melting icebergs in Iceland with a carbon footprint-aware holiday story called Dancing on Thin Ice:

"Naturally, huge lumps of ice break off into the lagoon; we adapt it into sculptures by keeping it frozen artificially... environmental activists are highlighting their concerns over the ice melting earlier each year..." There, I attempt to describe the outstanding Aurora Northern Lights despite ever witnessing the phenomena. Using an artistic license is essential when imagining better worlds. However, I did suggest a starting point for two young girls to engage in sustaining their local environment: "I let her sign us up to the next village litter pick." By quoting expert opinion from Ben Okri in a 2021 Guardian report, I validate my point of view in 'Daydreaming':

> "Artists must confront the climate crisis-we must write as if these are the last days...We need a new art to waken people both to the enormity of what is looming and the fact that we can still do something about it."

Also, that story discussed the COP26 Conference and storm Arwen's flooding. Therefore, with all that signposting, I was commissioned by Arts Council England support to facilitate a project culminating in the *Making Our World Better* anthology, edited by me, Dahlia Publishing

Ltd, 2022. I wrote as part of the stimulated active learner challenge delivered to a few previously marginalised groups across Leicester University. The foreword was by Michael Attenborough CBE. D Litt, and it said:

"Climate Change has brought us to the brink of self-destruction. We now need, as a matter of urgency, a creative response from humanity. .. a civilised society is one that is in constant dialogue with itself, one of evolutionary discovery and growth. This exciting new anthology is one vital part of this creative movement." I was happy to have this validation for my *Making Our World Better* facilitation efforts at the Attenborough Arts Centre, where Michael is the patron. In that anthology, a couple of my poems reflected on lockdown and how engaging in nature helped improve our wellbeing. Firstly came 'Turning Over a New Leaf', explaining a walk in the park:

"The branches knew about vital social distancing,
even then when humans were sniffling the bitter pandemic scent.
Ash trees grew longer roots to help prevent their dieback,
so we can learn from how these wise, adapted fir trees bent..."

Then in 'You'll Find Me' as an Essential Worker gave a hint of my legacy starting with:

"You'll find me at Belvoir Vale; it's tree-lined.
That's the perfect place for my family.
At Leicester's greenest place to abide
Happily buzzing around kith and kin,
I'm there championing our hopeful story."

Again, I do try to take the command seriously to subdue the earth and the animal life and have mastery over all of it. That acts to give direction for caring for all creation and habitats. And I promote the same approach in readers, where possible. Our small home used solar panels to harvest the sun as a clean energy solution. We enjoy growing our vegetables in a large frame and greenhouse. For decades, I've used charity shops to recycle and make do with pre-loved clothes and reuse household items. So, I attempt to practise what I preach. Closer to home, reflecting upon familial inherited health issues, I wrote *A Dot*

Leaf Legacy with more than a hint of truth. That life writing showcases exotic endangered species and a fantastic trip to Costa Rica inspired the wonders of health tourism:

"Guanacaste coast... a protected rainforest running adjacent to the coral-filled Pacific. Warm memories came flooding back of clever, camouflaged insects ... and vibrant neon birds... a couple of green and red toucans and feeding hummingbirds honey... we need to protect the forests to avoid more species disappearing."

Reorganising resources to share harvests and resources with those in need is worthwhile. As part of dealing with social injustices, I often pen possible solutions in story. In a recording for Leicester's 2023 *Human Rights Arts & Film Festival* my Ukraine tale keeps the reader aware of the ongoing horrors of war using the everyday pleasures of eating home-grown vegetables. Showing the contrasts of life with a juxtaposition of food availability since the invasion from before the war, *Love Hopes for the Best* attempts to empathise with those caught up in the conflict:

> "We usually had an abundance of produce. My face burnt. Last night, Dido foraged for potatoes and wild field mushrooms from the dampest part of the community orchard. When he brought the ingredients in my belly churned, 'An army can't go to war on an empty stomach,' I clapped. As several chickens roamed our town since the bombing caused mass evacuation, I asked, 'Oh, no meat yet?'
>
> 'You'll be lucky! Oh, what a treat meat pie would make!' my husband salivated. 'Sorry, I'm too slow to catch a chicken for May Day.'"

So, my anthology and collection writing has a crossover target audience, which I serve in accessible literature and by doing readings, also being broadcast online and on the radio. A few years ago, as a member of the Wildlife Trust, I read my apple poetry at one of their local events. At my Random Acts of Wildness reading to establish identity, I read poetry called Rosy:

> "A set-aside garden patch boasted the Old Reverend type apple
> Onto whose strong twisted bough he knotted a used lorry tyre.
> Only just up the road from Newton's nature gravitation

Where stands the famous Flower of Kent eating variety.
I expected you wise apple tree to teach us much
About valuing our long roots & the importance of family."

Since working as a creative mentor with children these last few years, I've drafted picture books to reach the youngest audience and their carers. These enchanting dummies, printed in short runs, tell tales from my *Wild Animal Splash Landing* series. The first was *Sofia Swan Flies the Nest* the second, *Felicity Frog Finds Her Way*. There I offer positive identity affirmations by showing respect and wonder for water-born wildlife. I aim to use nature to model healthy attitudes for toddlers to emulate on their independence journey. These have been read to local Early Year's groups and my younger mentees.

From 2024, there is a self-published seal picture book story normalising foster care, called *Who Cares About Superheroes*. Those words came after visiting a seal sanctuary at Donna Nook, Lincolnshire. There I touched upon my concern for sea life. A follow-on dolphin story is being created, too. I seek an illustrator to collaborate with for that project. That unpublished porpoise picture book story was stimulated when I was briefly a writer in residence at Scotland's Cove Park. I seek a publisher or illustrator to bring my text to life. As part of my writing collaboration, I regularly engage with other artists to share our love of nature. There, I took encouragement from a Burns poem on their shelves from 1787, courtesy of Michael O'Mara's 'A Red Red Rose and other Poems: On Scaring Some Water-Fowl in Loch Turit- A Wild Scene Among The Hills of Oughtertyre'. Of the tenants of the lake, Robert indicates his wish to preserve water birds.

Earlier, I took notice of this famous poet's historic warning to appreciate the birds. Other nature writers and showcasing artists collaborate with offering an eye-opener to the planned actions for sustainability and recovery. Sadly, since bird flu hit, the songs of many local small birds are much quieter. Environmental concerns are not new; my meagre efforts and suggestions are realised by numerous green and eco charities actions throughout the world. I try to repackage some of these concerns into bite-size pieces; reflecting snippets when I experience the call to showcase our responsibilities.

From believing God created the seasons in our world, His faithfulness and provision give us stability. The baton of providing care to protect our endangered wildlife and their habitats is passed onto the next generation through hope from continued artistic spotlights. My most recent anthology called *Moments of Grace* I edited in 2025. It is a collection of poetry and flash prose non-fiction from my Southwell Writers' Group, *Scriptorium*. This small volume shows how many writers unveil the subtle ways God's presence can transform their reality through personal testimonies. Readers are encouraged to dive into those heartfelt reflections to discover how grace shapes their paths, encouraging us all to share our own moments of grace.

To anticipate another sunrise for all about the community anthology *Making Our World Better* Dr Harry Whitehead, Director of the Centre for New Writing at the University of Leicester wrote: "Even in the darkest times the artist glimmers on." I do try my best!

The Highcross, Leicester, Planet Earth
The Other Side of the Universe

David Parkin

The outside sitting area is busy with smokers, but I see the alcoholic regular in his usual spot, and there at his feet is the tired old Alsatian.

The dog is here. I thank the universe. The dog is here.

I might just get some drinks down without it being too loud and exhausting. I step inside. The bar is rammed, it's going take a while to get served. A swirling overload of voices. I squeeze my eyes shut and start counting in my head.

1, 2, 3, 4, 5, 6, 7, 8, 9…

The Highcross is my local but I wanted somewhere quiet to get the first few pints down. But everywhere was full. The shuttle launch has really captured the public's imagination. Like the World Cup and the Olympics, people want to watch it with a mate and a pint. People want to watch it in a crowd.

I am not good with crowds.

…156, 157, 158, 159, 160, 161, 162, 163…

'Yes mate?

'I'll have a pint of Stella and a double Scotch.'

'What Scotch?'

'I don't care. The cheapest … no… the strongest.'

The young barman gives me a weary look. He knows my face and he doesn't think very highly of me. He thinks I'm an alcoholic. He is wrong.

I am not an alcoholic.

If it wasn't for alcohol I wouldn't get out of the house in the morning. I don't remember how I ended up in this small city but I'm here now and today I want some company. If it weren't for booze I'd still be in that cave in the woods.

I can handle most people on a one-to-one basis. I can quickly work out if someone is an idiot or not. I'm just not good with crowds, but I can cope with them when I'm drunk. The booze deadens the onslaught of raging thoughts. And yes, I suppose I am little curious to see what people will make of this package holiday to space.

I bustle outside, manage to get a seat and set to the matter at hand: drinking fast and focussing on the dog. Things quiet down as the booze sets in. The dog is sleeping. I love it when dogs dream.

He is a puppy running through a field of deep grass. The smell is intense and warm. That aroma, that delicious tang, is the smell of happiness for him. The scent of what he still thinks of as home. His tail and paws twitch and suddenly the sky is alive with birds of all different colours. For a moment his heart is full of the joy of flight. A sky of colour and sound. A sky of dizzying movement and possibility.

He wakes up with a jolt and I am jolted too. I hastily finish the drinks and stare at the dog. He pants, eyes half closed and thinks *warm sunshine. I like warm sunshine.*

I slowly get a handle on things. I close my eyes, compose my thoughts and listen to the church bell chime.

Bong.

Okay.

Bong.

Breathe.

Bong.

Calm.

Bong.

Let's get another pint.

The dog has gone and I'm inside with the crowd and the TV. Things have calmed down. People are talking quietly so they can hear the television and I am nicely tipsy. It's getting to the point where I can only hear thoughts if I want to. I focus on a young couple holding hands.

She is beautiful and he is painfully aware of this. He keeps taking little sideways glances and then nervously looks around the pub.

He is thinking, hoping, that this will turn into a shared memory. Something that they will look back on fondly and maybe tell their kids about. I watch him, full of young love and hope and insecurity and dreams.

I turn my attention to her. She watches the TV intently and thinks *I wish I was on that flig t, I wish I was on that flig t.*

There are things I remember and things I don't. I remember the first animal I met, all those years ago. I was bloodied, lost, broken ... slowly scrambling out of the crater. My mind was awash with young panic and confusion. I got to the lip of the hole, pulled myself onto the grass and there it was. Some kind of flightless bird. It stared at me, cocking its head to one side in surprise. Like the dolphin and a few other animals, its beak had a specific shape to it. It looked like it was smiling. It just blinked at me and thought *Oh hello. You won't hurt me, will you? I have just laid an egg. I am very happy.*

Then it scuttled off and its thoughts disappeared just as quickly as they arrived. Suddenly I didn't feel so lost. I watched its waddling tale and felt that I might be okay. I could have crashed on worse planets. The world, and its inhabitants, had a lot of simple charm.

I looked at the blue sky and the green trees and listened to the explosion of bird song. I would find a way to work things out. I wasn't a mechanic but I had picked a few bits and bobs up from my dad's lectures. How hard could it be?

I have looked through the books and I still don't know what species of bird that was. Its time on this planet must have been very short. It's so extinct that nobody knows it was ever around to become extinct. Except me.

I watch the TV ... the rocket slowly getting smaller in the sky. A trail of smoke against the blue.

I was sitting in my backyard yesterday watching the swifts in the evening air. A beautiful display of how to really get about in the sky. They occasionally swooped down close enough so I caught a thought or two.

Flies! Flies! was the overall gist, but also, *I love flying!* And (this made me laugh so much I choked on my wine) - *Wheeeeeeeeeeeeee!*

Swifts live in the moment. Flying is not just something they do. They know they are blessed, so every day is filled with the joy of fantastic aviation. The sky is a playground for them, and they love it. Happy ... eating flies ... being swifts.

Then, high above them, an aeroplane made its heavy way across the sky. Long white smoke tale and a low mechanical hum. A resolute straight line. Powering forward, weighty and inevitable. I concentrated on the plane. It was high above the clouds and I could only hear a low murmur. Most of the passengers were depressingly average. They thought of their luggage or the film they were watching. There were some (and these were easier to hear) whose minds were filled with a sort of commonplace fear and panic. The bad flyers. But there was one voice that came through strongly. A child looking out the window with wonder.

Wow, flying, she thought. *I feel like a bird.*

And there, in a nutshell, we have humans. Humans looked at birds and wanted to fly. But as the airplane thrummed above me, I was struck by its ugliness. Metal, machine, noise. Where was the grace? Where was the style? I can't decide whether this desire to fly, and how they have done it, makes the human race terrible or brilliant. Maybe a bit of both.

So, humans have this urge to fly. They want to take to the sky. They want to travel to faraway places. Humans are never happy where they are. And neither was I.

I go for a wee and spend a long time looking at myself in the mirror. Nothing about me says "alien". All over the universe, it would seem the monkeys have been the smart ones. The monkeys have been getting there first. My eyes are drawn and sad. I'm a good-looking man but the years have tinged those looks with melancholy. I stare at myself in disbelief. All the things those sad eyes have seen. I try hard to remember. For thousands of years I was alone but happy. The nature and the animals were beautiful and astounding. And the animal's thoughts were *simple.*

They were desperately alive and, although that could be pretty fraught at times, their thoughts were straightforward and not invasive.

When the monkeys came down from the trees, I was hopeful. Here's someone I can maybe have a chat with, I reasoned. For a while the monkeys were nicely simple. Then they started making tools and their thoughts got louder. Then weapons. Really noisy thoughts now. Then they called themselves people and decided that some people were better than others. A cacophony of gibbering voices. Then they started killing each other because of *ideas* and I just threw my hands up, headed into the woods, found a cave and became a hermit. I grew a long and impressive beard.

People would visit me and be astounded when I would tell them what they were thinking. They would leave food and treasures and I'd feel guilty about taking advantage of these babbling grown-up monkeys.

I'm not a mystique or a holy man, I thought. *I'm just telling you what you already know. Now just get on and act on it, you morons.*

Still, it was a good beard and the food was great.

I stare at myself harder. Such lonely eyes.

When you have done everything it soon becomes nothing.

I've done it all. Been a hermit, a duke, a beggar, a marine, a king, a scientist, a concert pianist ... but with the endless years the meaning always disappears. Then there are the vast periods of forgetting.

My eyes. I have my father's eyes.

On my planet we have three moons. One is always a soothing amber, another is made of ice and a cold sheen surrounds it, the last moon is made mostly of gas so is constantly changing colour and hew. Swelling and tightening, depending where it is in the sky. There are different phases when the moons align or make shapes. The Triangle, The Perfect Line ... The High Cross.

I would sit out when the gas moon was melting and building. In the right alignment our sun would swell the moon with its rays. Then the ice moon would freeze it back into shape. The moon of gas, constantly growing and shrinking. Alive and then dead. This would happen every ten days. I would sit under it brooding. I felt like the gas moon ...

trapped. My parents were strict. They were busy moulding me into the man they wanted me to be. I didn't want to be that man.

So, I sat and sulked, young and grumpy, under one of the true spectacles of the universe. The moon went through its regular changes, one moment large and fiery, the next small and cold. All I saw were the changes and other bodies shaping this helpless moon. I didn't see the colour. I didn't see the beauty.

I sat under that fantastic sky and thought, *I want to get out of this dump.*

'Alright mate?' Terry sits down next to me with a bump and some spilled pint.

Great ... just great, I think. 'Yeah, I'm alright, how are you?'

'Not too bad. Just finished work. You know where I work, right? The building site off Queens road. Leicester. Great Britain. Earth.'

I AM BEING FUNNY! his brain screams at me. He always does this. He always goes straight into it. The problem with managing my mind with booze is when I overdo it. A good five pints dampens the thoughts, the babbling nonsense of other people's brains, and allows me to read minds if I want to. The problem is that then I am drunk. And I often find that when I am in that position, I want to get more drunk. That's when I start telling the truth. Gibbering to strangers about three moons and how to achieve light speed.

'Any word from home yet?' says Terry with a grin and raised eyebrows. He also makes a V with his hand. The gesture from Star Trek. The Vulcan greeting. I'm definitely not in the mood for him today.

'Well,' I say. 'I know my father is dead.'

'Oh yes, of course!' Terry says happily. 'Just remind me of the date?'

'About three hundred years ago.' I look down into my pint. 'But it still hurts.'

'Of course, 'cos grieving can take a long time.' He suddenly sits up straight and looks right at me with wide eyes. 'What am I thinking?'

'Terry,' I say wearily. 'You're not the brightest man and you are drunk. So most of what you think comes out of your big mouth.'

'Alright ... alright ... there's no need to be stroppy.'

'Okay … you are thinking about the tiles being put up in your bathroom.'

'Outstanding! Outstanding!' Terry is delighted and looks about, wanting to share this miracle.

I'm feeling really grumpy now. 'I'll tell you something else about that tiling you're having done.'

'Yeah,' says Terry, happy and expectant.

'I bumped into your missus the other day. And I have to say her thoughts were quite an experience.'

'How'd you mean?'

'Swarthy chap doing the tiling, is it?'

'Yeah … Italian. Franco.'

'Well, she seemed to be thinking about him quite a lot. I got images of him and her in … well … compromising positions.'

'What … huh?'

'But don't worry. They were probably just fantasies … and we're all allowed to dream, right?'

As Terry gets up and strides off yammering into his phone, I feel very naughty indeed. But I'm enjoying it. I know I'll feel bad about it in the morning, but this is now. I think about the swifts revelling in their aerial acrobatics. Tomorrow I'll feel guilty but right now I'm wickedly chuckling into my pint that I down *swiftly*. Back to the bar!

My father ran out of the house furious, as I took to the sky in his favourite flying device. I could feel his outrage and grinned to myself. As I rocketed into the heavens, I'm sure all he could feel was my stubbornness, anger and bewildering youth slowly disappearing into the sky. That was the last time I saw my father.

Probably getting a little too drunk now. I look up at the TV. The ship lands and the pub cheers. This only makes me angry and I set about finishing my pint.

'Hello sad eyes,' she clumsily sits in the seat opposite and smiles lazily. She is a little drunk too. 'Why you looking so fed up?'

'I don't know … this flight to the moon…'

'Yeah, it's weird isn't it?' she says. 'What's the big deal? The only reason I can think of going to the moon is so you could look back at the earth. I mean, what's on the moon?' She thinks for a moment and although I know what she is going to say, she delivers it with a lovely aplomb.

'I tell you what will be on the moon before too long.' She looks up. 'Advertising slogans! This lunar cycle was bought to you by Pepsi!'

I laugh and remember why I like this girl so much. She has a brilliant mind. I look at her and grin. Scruffy clothes, a bit chubby, lip pierced, hair a little frayed from too much bleaching, cigarette stains on her fingers ... but her smile and her eyes and her thoughts are filled with such warmth.

'Hey mister,' she says with a pretend pout. 'You didn't phone, you didn't text, what's a girl to think?'

I shouldn't have slept with her. I, of course, was drunk and she had the most original, sparkling mind in the pub. That night was too good. Some people's thoughts have a certain temperature to them. There are the volcanoes, the icebergs and then there are people like this girl. As we had sex her mind was so open and comforting. Her thoughts were like a warm embrace. I can't do all this again.

'Listen,' I say to her seriously. 'I'm not normal.'

She laughs, 'Who is?'

'No ... I'm really not. I'm not for you. Find yourself a nice normal man.'

She is still grinning. 'Who wants normal? Sod normal!'

I think of all the people I have loved. I think of all the people I have watched age and die.

Time.

Time destroyed the people I loved and each time it destroyed me.

I put my hand over hers. 'Please ... listen to me. You need to leave me alone.'

I can't take the empathy in her eyes or in her thoughts. I'm going to have to be harder than this. 'Can you please just ... go away?'

She is taken aback and looks at me with a scowl ... then she softens. Like a mind reader she knows I don't mean it.

'Alright sad eyes,' she says standing up. 'If that's what you want. I'll ... go away.'

She gently kisses me on the corner of my eye and walks off.

Closing time. Really drunk now. I'm seeing the TV in double. People noisily leave, talking and thinking about saving up for a flight to the moon.

'Don't go,' I mutter. 'Just stay here and look around'.

I am sad and full of wishes, all of them impossible.

I wish I could cuddle my mother.

I wish I could say sorry to my father.

I wish I could fall in love, grow old and die with the person I love.

I wish I could fly like a swift, soaring and swooping to the other side of the universe.

I wish I could go home.

A Hop Too Far

Andrew Taylor

K's nervousness welled in the pit of her stomach, the excitement welled in her throat. It was a peculiar combination of sensations that she wasn't prepared for. K knew full well that the scientific approach would have been to go back a couple of days, perhaps just a few hours, and see if the Goliath frog got there and safely returned. She was also a dreamer though and being thoroughly confident in her idea, the computer mod-elling and the device the dream won and she let herself be a bit more ex-travagant.She went straight for a much earlier epoch, sixty two million years earlier. This was the time when the dinosaur age had come to a close and the era when the furry rodents that had been watching their demise had filled the void they left. This was when the age of mammals had begun. K was curious to study an earlier time that life on Earth had suffered a catastrophic jolt, then had recovered, the Palaeocene Period. She knew there was a whole lot more science needed than a three minute frog sample but this was just the start. K was letting her dreams fly, as well as testing her time machine, Itneha-1, she endeavoured to see what results she could get from one of their signature frogs. For their ecological analysis K never usually named the animals they printed out, this was more than field work though, this was a time travel experiment, the worlds first time traveller had been named Marty.

K reset the graphene membrane tissue identifier, the Grametide, rechecked the programme, downloaded it to the controller, removed the safety tag and initiated the control sequence. The Grametide neatly deployed from its container, wrapped itself around the frog, confirming to Itneha-1 what it was to take through the wormbubble. In a logical sequence, but quicker than her eye could follow, K saw all of the tags flash green on her display, indicating that everything was functioning as she had intended, the frog went into a blurred spin and vanished.

K knew the physics but was still a bit disappointed about the lack of drama of what she had just seen. Fictional time travel that K had enjoyed involved a tense build up, a catastrophe indicating alarm silenced by a bit of comedy improvisation, too much lightning and usually a few dying flames. Excited that everything was looking good, and underwhelmed by the lack of special effects, her nerves jangling K started pacing. Three minutes was an eternity when you're waiting for your pioneering frog to return from the first ever journey through time.

Marty, having never seen any of the movies or read any of the books that had shaped the non-scientific parts of K's brain, didn't have any preconceptions of what it would experience, he was unsurprisingly oblivious to what time travel might involve. The significance of the role he was about to play at the forefront of scientific achievement was something he was ill equipped to appreciate. His journey backward came to an end with a similarly low level of drama. Just as K had hoped he hadn't moved in Space, and just as K had also hoped, he had moved in Time. But, he hadn't arrived precisely when K intended.

Having no knowledge that he had found himself in an earlier age to that which K had sent him out to sample, he cruised about, with no real purpose, in the Cretaceous period water into which he had fallen. He very loyally, and without any instruction, used his own in-built respiratory processes to take water composition samples for K. After three minutes Itneha-1s control sequencer reached the automatic return sub-routine and powered up. Just at this moment the frog became, in one gulp, an insufficient snack for a plesiosaur which was much more purposefully cruising about in the same water looking for food. The grametide sensor deployed, found both frog and plesiosaur and formed the wormbubble to perfectly encompass both beings and transport them on a journey towards a time a little more familiar to the frog but quite alien to the plesiosaur.

This particular journey through time culminated at twilight of an autumn day in the year 565AD, quite startling an Irish monk, who incidentally was to become Saint Columba, and was fishing at the mouth of the River Ness. Without knowing it as a plesiosaur, he was startled by a huge dark shadowy creature that was forming arches with it's immense body in the loch from which the river flowed. Frozen to the spot, the monk tried to scream, but no scream came. He tried to comprehend what he saw, but no comprehension came either. All he could do was make the sign of the cross and resolve to tell people a story. If only he knew what was really playing out in front of him, now that would be a story.

He totally missed the far less frightening sight of a large frog cruising, still with no real purpose, towards the shadows of the loch bank. He also missed the graphene sensor retract into its protective shell and Itneha-1 sink through the water to the sandy bed of the loch.

A convincing monster story was going to be tricky enough, though he had an inkling that it might gain some traction. A time travelling frog just might have seemed a bit far fetched to his sixth century congregation.

Success can be partial, and in many respects K's time travelling experiment had succeeded, a frog had travelled back in time and, unintentionally with a companion, had travelled forwards. Any degree of success though is meaningless if no one is aware of it. K was completely in the dark about any of the events of the previous three minutes which had now more than passed, some fuming had been added to her pacing, K was frustrated with herself for indulging her childish fascination of time travel instead of taking a more measured and scientific approach to the first steps. She knew also that she knew better.

It dawned on K that the only being that had any knowledge of the trip through time that she had designed, engineered and executed was a frog called Marty, she was completely unaware of the adventure that the plesiosaur had found itself a part of. Applying any scientific rigour in order to scrutinise what had happened was out of the question. K realised that amongst the brilliance was a pretty dumb decision, the frog could only provide her with information on the atmospheric conditions of the Palaeocene, if that was where it had gone?Even had it returned he wouldn't have been able to tell her anything about the time travel.

She gathered her composure and started to take a more considered approach, she had to devise how to test her time machine in a way that meant she could measure what was happening. Another set of parts was now needed too, K hadn't considered losing Itneha-1, she thought it would come back. Now she needed Xue to assemble another. Should she just tell her what she was working on?Xue will be curious.

K was aware that the frog had been on a journey, right now she could only theorise that it had moved through time, all she was certain of was that it was no longer present in the time she was, or the space she was or possibly her ideas were way off and that it had moved through both time and space. It could be having an experience that a human would struggle to describe just as much as a frog. The amount of energy involved in creating the wormbubble was vast, it wasn't impossible that all she had achieved was to have built a failed time machine and had vaporised it and a frog.

Vaporising a frog and Itneha-1 would leave a signature, in the vicinity of where it had happened.

Detecting the constituent parts would be simple to someone trained in understanding biological material at a quantum level, and K was exactly that. K also knew full well that vaporising a frog here in their buildings would have been a fair bit more destructive and meant visual special effects along the lines she had imagined for the time travel. So she suspected it wasn't what had happened.

Being a simple test, and as it could prove that this could be eliminated as an explanation, it was the first thing she did. K added the SpectrAN bead to her IIHTD instrument interface device and ran the scan,Data streamed and she started to interrogate the results, shaping the holographic display with her hand. No beryllium from Itneha-1s fusion cell, and none of the tough carbohydrate proteins from the frog mucus.

K hadn't vaporised anything. At least she could be sure that she had ripped a hole in SpaceTime and thrown a frog through it. So where, or when was Marty?

Still struggling to accept her stupidity at wasting all that hardware on an overly extravagant experiment, investing everything without being able to see any of the results, K started to form a strategy to properly test for time travel. A few hours to start with, and in a way that meant that she would be able to see and interpret the results.

K found Xue in the workshop checking through their field equipment.

"Hi K, you ok?Need some help?" Asked Xue

"I need some more of those components printing off, did you get enough rhodium for another set?"

"Yes, there's more, I'll check, what have you done?Which ones do you need?"

"All of them" K said cagily.

"Was that fusion generator a bit too powerful?"

"That's gone too, do you know where there are any more?"

Xue was a bit lost at how anyone could lose one of those.

"We can scan for the beryllium containment casing or the lead-lithium possibly?I'll find it."

"No, it's gone, entirely gone, scanning won't help".

"You've not left the compound since I put the assembly together, it's here somewhere".

Telling someone that you've lost something in Time but not in Space is bound to raise eyebrows, it can only mean time travel that generally isn't going to be taken particularly seriously. This was the only thing left to K who had no real option but to go through the story of her attempt to send a frog back in time, then to bring him back. She would also have to explain her lack of thought into how she might afterwards demonstrate that it had even happened, after all, if it had all worked, what would she do?Show Xue a frog?"She'd think I was out of my mind!" K said to herself and, resigning herself to not explaining things in any other way but a moment of stupidity. She chuckled.

"It could be here, somewhere, but I'm not sure how close. I also have no idea when it is".Xue didn't look as puzzled as K thought she should but she'd focussed on that last comment.

"Those components you manufactured and assembled, I've added a Grametide, and coupled it with a nuclear fusion generator. I was trying to travel through time."

Xue pieced together in her mind what she had built for K, it had been a nice little project while she was getting used to life back at their home base.

"That accelerator unit and those amplifier streams, I could see you were concentrating a lot of power for something, a burst like that would momentarily rip open SpaceTime."Xue explained back "I did kinda wonder."

"Exactly that Xue".K knew Xue would have had a bit of a stab at what the device was for, she was a smart cookie."Focusing all that energy for a mere instant in time, precisely around a living being, rips open SpaceTime.The Grametide determines what is travelling, and the detected being travels through it. How far it travels depends on the amount of energy made available for that one short burst."

"So what have you done K?Have you travelled in time?"Xue was getting a bit more animated as she realised the magnitude of what she was maybe becoming a part of.

"I haven't, but Marty has" explained K, being playful and a bit cryptic. "I tested it on one of the signature frogs, had named him Marty."

"And where is Marty now?"

"I don't know, I can confirm he is no longer in this time, I believe he is in this space, but it's possible he's in neither. I can confirm that I didn't simply vaporise him. It looks as if everything functioned, I just can't be sure, it looks as if he left for another time, but I've no idea if Itneha-1 triggered for him to come back."

Stranger in Sight

Rosanna McGlone

My mother wears no knickers. Instead she wears a back-to-front dress and a puzzled expression. I rush to greet her; she stands on the doorstep, seeing but not recognising who she sees. I introduce myself and fix a bright smile on my face; a smile that remains in public for three long weeks (at least in public). The lady on the doorstep was once my mother. Her wafer-think skin sags loosely over once proud cheekbones.

And who am I? I am the prodigal daughter, the one who sought a better life but who cannot keep away. Of course, when I left my mother was like your mother, like all of the other mothers in the world. She baked and laughed and wrote long, entertaining letters. But now she is an agitated stranger plucking at a wad of toilet paper held tightly between plum-coloured fingers.

Much has changed since my last visit. Sixteen months is a long time when you're in your 80s. Yet, perhaps for my mother it is no time at all. Days and nights merge into one, punctuated by the comings and goings of others whose lives touch my mother for infinitesimal moments and then are gone.

When I last saw her she was confused and lonely. She understood too much about the deterioration taking place in her mind and cried out in despair. She was a woman fighting the ravages of age. It was a battle that she could not win. At least she is no longer lonely. Rather, the table is littered with bread rolls with their tissue paper fillings, waiting for a party that will never happen, for friends who will never come.

My mother is confused. She swears that there are strangers in her house. I am confused. There are strangers in her house. A constant parade of them. Joan and Margaret and Cathy and Marion; Jane and Sue and Eilleen. This is the Independent Living Programme; the one designed to keep my mother in her own home, the one designed to retain her dignity.

It is a strange kind of independence. The knobs on the cooker have been dismantled and hidden. My mother is now a hazard to herself. Instead she must rely on others for sustenance. Eight o'clock: it must be Joan (or is it Marion?)

The grease on her chin has barely time to congeal before the arrival of lunch. The Meals on Wheels lady means well, they all do, but there is no time. She sets the table and pushes the unappetising foil containers towards my mother. "Eat up," she calls cheerily as the door slams behind her, caught by the wind. And some days my mother will open the cartons. (She enjoys the desserts.) Other days the meals will be found squirrelled away beneath a pile of nightdresses or at the back of the Welsh dresser.

In the fridge is a box of shrivelled mushrooms and a jar of apricot jam. My mother hates apricot jam. I am suddenly enraged that these people who profess to care for my mother don't realise that she hates apricot jam. Yet, why should they? Who will tell them? My mother will simply smile that enigmatic smile that would far outdo the Mona Lisa and say nothing.

It is not just my mother who has changed. Cobwebs hang beneath the stairs; upstairs my mother's bedroom is shawled with dust. In some ways, it is this that is most upsetting. My mother, always so houseproud, sits oblivious to the filth. I wonder if this upsets me so much because it is all that I can focus on? I phone and question the supervisor who speaks of personal care. Is my mother not washed and clothed and fed? I try to explain: To my mother cleanliness is next to Godliness, and my mother is very, very devout. I fear that I will upset the supervisor and then what will happen to my mother when I return to my adopted land? I murmur that I'm sure she is doing her best and, gripping the receiver hard, express pathetic gratitude.

Throughout all of this my mother sits in her armchair, her eyes fixed on a patch of green that beckons in the distance. Sometimes the view is obscured by rain, sometimes the sun shines in, casting shadows in this twilight world. These are the vagaries of my mother's life. It is by these that she would set her clock if it had not stopped many years ago.

Carers are not the only ones to visit my mother. Now she speaks of visits by people long dead and of her hopes. It is time, she says, to go upstairs. The metaphor does not reduce the pain. I try not to let the tears start, knowing that if they do they will never stop. I hold her leathery hand and stroke the softened nails, cracked with age. I phone my sister Brenda. "Why didn't you tell me?" My head is thick with sorrow and anger.

"You wouldn't have believed me," she replies calmly. "I thought that you needed to see for yourself."

I hate her for sounding so reasonable as I in turn cry and berate. Yet I know that she is right.

I even think of returning home, to all I escaped from all those years ago. "Don't come back," says my sister firmly. "What could you do?" she mutters.

I wonder if she is embarrassed? I know I'm not being fair, but I don't care. My sister has just recovered from another heart attack. The doctor thinks it's stress. Of course he's right. And that is why she tries to warn me and insist that I don't forsake my other life of barbecues and publisher's parties and glasses of chardonnay quaffed with the papers on a Sunday afternoon. My mind crawls with guilt.

There are happy times. We take my mother to Newstead Abbey, Lord Byron's home. She marvels at the flowers and the beauty of the world and we marvel with her. I ask if has other outings and she says no, that she can't be bothered, but I don't believe her.

Then it is time to leave. An old lady stands on the doorstep watching curiously as a visitor departs, just one of many. I turn and smile brightly, my heart wet with tears. Inside this stranger, deep inside, is my mother.

First published in *The Weekend Australian* August 15-16th 1998.

(Im)Pure Fiction

Rosanna McGlone

Nottingham it was and romantic it wasn't. Nottingham is Players and Raleigh and Pork Farms. A heaving mass of factories belching acrid smoke are not necessarily conducive to a passionate encounter. Barbara Cartland romances are not set in Nottingham, but mine was.

A small student bedsit provided the setting. The walls were speckled green with mould; the carpet-stained. I think best not to know. In one corner an electricity meter whirred, on the mantlepiece a mountain of 50p pieces had dwindled to one.

He was 20 and spotty; I was 21 and desperate. We met in the university library one dismal afternoon. He was into metaphysics, I was reading law. We touched minds; bodies followed at a polite distance. Hours spent poring over textbooks in a dimly lit room both concealed and revealed.

I hid my desperation behind Halsbury's *Laws of England*; Patrick's blemishes softened beneath the mellow glow of a 30 watt bulb. Innocence blended with desire. So many times it could have happened, but the vortex of Catholicism dragged guilt across our eager union.

There is a peculiar passion to Nottingham, a grittiness, an earthiness. Ask Lawrence, ask Sillitoe. It is not a pretty city and I was glad of it. A sun-kissed landscape somehow would have been wrong, too flippant for such a momentous occasion.

It was a Sunday. A mutual friend had died and in discussing his life we discovered our own. Life is precious and life is now. In the background Leonard Cohen moaned dolefully of love and hate. Having just eaten our 100th meal with mince we raided the cupboard for the ubiquitous long-life milk. Snuggling up on the sagging settee, we drank cups of Nescafe, our only luxury.

Suddenly the electric meter gave a final whir and we were plunged into a merciful darkness. With a last mangled moan Cohen fell silent. When it finally happened we buried ourselves beneath covers of a different kind. All props abandoned, our morals lay tossed on the floor beneath our garments. Contraceptives were strictly forbidden; we were Romans, after all.

The sky was slate grey, and the rain sheeted down. A rhythmic drip could be heard in the far corner of the room where it licked through the ceiling. No birds sang. Grindingly, the 37 bus changed gears to climb the hill and through the open window, which never quite closed, a blackened chimney burped forth its load. None of this mattered to us.

Finally it was over. A statue of the Virgin Mary gazed down at us from above the bed. I think she understood. Later, as I lay in the comforting tenderness of his arms, I heard the factory siren disperse its workforce; other women just like me. We talked of life and love and what was to come. Everything of importance was contained in that bed.

It mattered then and it matters now, as it has moulded what, many years later, I have become. Whenever I see a slowly unfurling python of smoke it brings back memories of Nottingham and of love.

First published in *The Independent on Sunday* March 2000

Love at First Sight

Rosanna McGlone

Love at first sight? It doesn't exist, does it? I was sixteen when I first laid eyes on you and I've been thinking about you ever since. My parents insisted on splitting us up. 'It's for the best,' dad. HUGE WAIL, me. 'There, there, love,' mum. Welcome to Holyhead.

A blink of the eye and we were at a different dock, this time Southampton.

We stood on the deck, looking out at the sea of humanity, cameras clicking. "Arthur!" "Rose!" "Over here!" Streamers were thrown, ephemeral strings of hope. Lots of yelling and crying and loud laughter, you know the sort that hides the pain. And then the horn sounded, a long rude toot, farting out our past. I stayed on the deck until land had disappeared and I knew you were finally gone. I clung to the railing, my eyes shining brightly.

Then we were sailing towards God's Own Country and a new life filled with kangaroos and coloured milk and other exotic delights...like Graeme.

We met at a barbie overlooking Manly Beach, amongst the palm trees and the sizzling smell of snags and spitting fat and the screams of nippers jumping the waves. Later, we caught the ferry back to Circular Quay and later still, we kissed. I could still taste the sausage as the jacaranda's purple rain gave its blessing and twilight smeared the horizon.

It wasn't just me against the world anymore. I had never sensed the aching loneliness, until Gray came and took it away. He held me and I breathed him in, like a baby sucking milk. We could tell each other anything. Nearly anything. We planned a house overlooking Turramurra, a garden for the kids, deep within the scent of frangipani and the clatter of cicadas at dusk. It never happened.

You were always in the shadows, but finally, I was happy...

And then he died. A stroke. Cancer. A car crash. It doesn't matter. All that matters is he is dead.

Suddenly, out of nowhere, it came. My mind was filled with you. I longed to hear your voice. I began to write, long rambling letters. Every week I pushed my hopes and dreams and fears into an envelope. Every week, I slid it into the drawer, the ink smudged with love. How could I disrupt your precious life, with the selfishness of mine?

Years passed.

Then, out of the blue, you wrote to me. 'Can we meet?' Terror squeezed my throat, even as love beat at the door of my heart. I felt sick. I felt scared. I felt delirious.

The plane's about to land. My stomach lurches.

'Please wait for the seat belt sign ....' Sudden panic. This is a mistake, isn't it? I try to breathe; jerky little puffs escape my lips, like tiny prayers.

I scan the crowd. You look nothing how I remember, yet I know you instantly. You move towards me and at last I hear your voice: 'Mum?'

First published in *Orton Collection* 2021

Plus Ça Change
or
The Ring

Rosanna McGlone

When you are young, you don't understand that 'Till death do us part' is a hope, not a promise.

I am sitting in a National Trust Cafe at Quarry Bank Mill submerged in a sea of Joules and Boden and White Stuff. We have seen how poor children were exploited every day of their tawdry little lives, crawling under the machinery to untangle the woollen fibres amid the clattering cacophony of the looms, and now we need flat whites.

It
Is
Our
Second
Date.

I watch you, standing at the counter, pushing your tongue deep into your cheek the way you do in moments of indecision. You nod and a pair of silver tongs move seamlessly over the chocolate fudge cake and the lemon drizzle. You return with coffee and a piece of flapjack shelled with dried cranberries; a tiny superfluous fork curled beside it.

" What a coincidence. I love flapjack!" I beam at the unexpected pleasure.

"I know," you smile, " you did the first time too."

My mind flashes back to 1984, another life fresh out of university and fresh into love. I lifted my eyes from Halsbury's Laws of England and there you were. Me with my big hair and big dreams, you with your green leather jacket and mud splattered Yamaha 750. (Is there any greater love than selling a throbbing bike, for a clapped-out Simca in order to teach your girlfriend to drive?)

We moved in together, that is to say I moved my two, battered suitcases and three cardboard boxes into the £4,000 end terrace you had bought in Stoke. Stoke, let that sink in. Now, that's love.

We lived in sin opposite The Church of Our Lady, the Blessed Virgin, the irony of which didn't escape me. Like all Catholics, I had received an infusion of guilt into my veins at birth and spent the rest of my life performing lifesaving transfusions on myself in dark corners.

We lasted three years; years which spun by with The Eagles and Dire Straits and Fleetwood Mac; years where we sat in miners' darkness, singing along in the flickering candlelight neither of us on key, yet totally in tune; years where a chippy tea from The Plaice Above was enough.

At

First.

As the months somersaulted by, my heart grew still. I had longed for your proposal, but now it was too late. Something had changed, not in you, but in me. I had sutured my gaping heart and tightened the thread.

" No one will ever love you like I love you," you said.

Afterwards.

I left you for another country. The other man was incidental. Unexpected cargo.

"Can passengers for flight QA874 to Sydney, please make their way to the boarding gate?"

I didn't turn or I would have seen you behind the shiny glass, an arm half raised, like an act of surrender.

As I wove my way unsteadily from the Jumbo, I already knew that the jet lag was a small price to pay for the sunlit uplands. The Sydney sun and the snags and the overwhelming scent of eucalyptus filled my senses. I was captivated by the sheer blue openness. The Manley ferry transported me beyond Sydney, beyond life as I had ever known it.

The first missive arrived a fortnight after my arrival. "I didn't think you'd mind," my mother said defensively, and I could see her lips pouting, down the wire. One by one the pale blue aerogrammes tongued through my letterbox, as regularly as my monthly period, but remained cruelly unread. Stuffed into a draw I never opened, like dormant rattlesnakes, waiting to be prodded. Gradually they declined, eventually they stopped.

Boyfriends came and went, figures in a Swiss weather house where every day was summer. My twenties hurtled into my thirties. You were pushed to a tiny synapse of my brain, amidst The Battle of Hastings and photosynthesis and amo, amas, amat.

I
Heard
Of
Your
Wedding
Through
A
Mutual
Friend.

We both married other people, had other people's kids, led parallel lives. You don't know the journeys you had to make until you've made them. Some people will never leave and never know. Perhaps you are one of these, shrouded in the blanket of suburbia, not daring to look out because what is outside has the dangerous pungency of the unfamiliar. Or maybe you were just waiting for me to bring it in?

An embarrassment of divorces followed with an accompaniment of tears, guilt, regret and, yes, relief. And then, like shipwrecked mariners, clinging to driftwood, we found each other on the other side.

They say there's one who kisses, and one who turns the cheek, but they are just two parts of the same whole.

All those years ago, I wanted you to propose, but now I've realised it doesn't matter. We can marry, but it doesn't mean anything. Once I thought it was a sign that nothing could part us: Excalibur in the stone. But now I understand that all of the nuptial niceties and fancy finery won't matter in the end. The duplicity of the vows renders them unrepeatable, their sacredness scattered through the winds of time like blown confetti.

The flapjack sits between us as I look up at you,

And
Outside
The
Sun
Is
Shining.

First published in *Annie's Journal* 2024

A selection from

Metamorphosis of Psyche

A book of twenty-four poems by

Jack Blackmore

with eight paintings by
Clare Shaw

Copies of the book, and of a CD or download
are available from jackdblackmore@hotmail.com
or clarefrancesmary@gmail.com

METAMORPHOSIS OF PSYCHE

as we disintegrate
how should I compose?

only our bellies grow

as we revert into the future
you and I

    spinning a cocoon

    to chrysallize
    the butterfly spirit

SPRING MANIFESTO

I would have you flower
under my gardening hands

tentatively
proliferate

I would dig up weeds
and replace those areas gone to seed in your memory . . .

I had conceived of you as
of a piece with the spring

with bluebells rife
in the echoing woods

but the form we thought natural
has proved ephemeral

gone shapeless in a mother love
for the lost child of those trancelike times . . .

come into the womb
of my hands

PHILIP LARKIN

It's not their nights he envies much, if at all,
But their excuses: breakfast complications, kids, bills in the hall,
Anxieties about the immediate future, which obscure
The single man's dreaming desolation, the chaste moon's lure,
    And the somehow pregnable vacancy of books.

With eagerly cynical student's eye I've seen him twice,
Or three times: once buying whisky, another being nice
To some old fart, absently saying apropos parents 'how unjust
One is to them'—the last time you seemed nonplussed,
    Catching my eye sidelong on the street,
    Your face crumpled suddenly, as if caught by the wind.

THE MIND'S EYE

dark is a dream;
a vision is of light.

    dream and vision:

between these states
the mind's eye oscillates

    until words and imagery abound

and paradise is lost and found
and paradise lost is found.

OBLIVION

There everything's contiguous and warm;
Music, maternal and his own, makes him at home;

The beating of his mother's heart, his own,
And silver singing of her voice, all keep him calm

—Yet never will his blood so purely rage,
Yet never will he revel in such bold changes

*   *   *

A world in miniature, a world enclosed,
And workable as an orrery; a world in isolation

—Yet never will he be so un-alone
So radiant in unfolding transformation

*   *   *

With each change, his memories erase themselves,
Like a meteor shower on a summer night;

Familiar with forgetfulness, he has memories
But no recall; he is unaware that he has lived.

ESTUARY MUSIC

Easy to sense the way the world's adrift,
Harder to shift one life from its course;

Repetitious mornings, afternoons,
And the orbiting of the moon

Soothe and smooth away
The agitation of uniqueness . . . .

Never cease to glide, or to elide
Earth's dark, gravitational waters

With the incoming salt sea tide
Against the outgoing river slide

Between waking and sleep . . . .

Returning at the ebb, the wading birds
Will find with me rich pickings

Sifted from the burden of the silt
Left on the glistering mudbanks.

MID-AIR ONCE MORE

The cold particulate fog, the fish dock's heatwave stench
And the ferries have departed in the decades since we left,
Rendered redundant in a range of modern ways—
By containers that condemned port industries,
The cod war defeat against a nation no larger than the city,
And by the most beautiful bridge,
    A span to almost nowhere save the airport,
    Whither I'm in flight, to the other side.

Mid-air once more above this once luminous
And mortal city, for real this time; the pilot banks the plane
Over a privileged perspective of avenues and streets,
Mapped in saturated orange light
Upon a blue-black canvas in the urban night;
    And I feel a savage nostalgia,
    An urge to press emphatically in dots the sight,

Not otherwise than as an aboriginal might,
Seize the usurper's brush and paints to populate
And repossess his desecrated nation's
    Emptied, and no longer numinous landscapes.

LARKIN REVISITED

Ten thousand bombs and more descended here
But silence fell over the wounded and the dead.

A university and a hospital then sprang up
Where the poet worked, and where he died.

He frequented the green cemetery;
He scanned the breadth of estuary;

And wrote an uneasy celebration of the bridge,
Being more comfortable with what distances.

The squared streets packed with oblivious lives
That made him sad, made me feel more at home.

I wonder now what made him crave
More than mortality, exemption from the grave.

He illuminated a book of his hours
That lies open to the centuries.

THE COMMON BLUE

After the long wait,
The effort made to pupate,
The inward metamorphoses,
The two of us unfurl
Into the imago state.

Such beauty

A moment of union, of joined
And dispersed possibilities—
Blind and blighted or blest by fate,

And no reason not to fear,

No reason in this moment
Not to celebrate.

The Empty Wall

Gary Burn

JoJo Sert, the Catalonian painter, visited the Louvre most weeks, often to look at just one painting in particular, and a favourite of late was The Counterattack of Michelotto da Cotignola at the Battle of San Romano by Paolo Uccello. He would go there on the way to his atelier on Rue Barbet-de-Jouy, as he did on the morning of Tuesday 29 August 1911; the first opportunity he'd had since he and Misia returned from their summer holiday in Venice. Although, on this occasion he'd gone specifically NOT to see a painting! When he arrived he found himself in a queue. This in itself was surprising, as a queue outside the Louvre had never been known before. When the visitors began streaming in, it became clear that most had come, like Sert, to look at one thing. All around hung famous paintings, priceless paintings, but the visitors ignored them all and walked into the Salon Carré, to stare intently at an empty space. 'Unwittingly', as the writer Jérôme Coignard put it, 'the Louvre was exhibiting the first conceptual installation in the history of art: the absence of a painting.'

This was no ordinary space, however. This was where Leonardo's Mona Lisa, painted on a 77cm by 53cm wood panel made from Lombard white poplar, hung on four hooks between Titian's Allegory of Alfonso d'Avalos and Correggio's Mystical Marriage, until, well... it didn't! Most likely eight days earlier, on Monday 21 August. Nobody was entirely sure, because it was only the next morning when a talentless artist called Louis Béroud arrived to sketch the painting and found it missing. He assumed the photographers had her and joked with the guard. 'Of course, when women are not with their lovers, they are apt to be with their photographers', he said. When she hadn't returned by

11am, the police were summoned and they found the glass frame into which the painting had recently been placed for security reasons, in a service stairway, empty.

Jean Théophile Homolle, director of museums, had assured France before leaving on his summer vacation that the Louvre was secure. 'You might as well pretend that one could steal the towers of the cathedral of Notre-Dame,' he said. Now, just weeks later, the world was told that the "impossible" theft had, indeed, taken place. It was embarrassing. The empty space had become a "Mark of Shame" for Parisians and France. Never mind, 'we still have the frame', sniggered the Petit Parisien, while in Montmartre's cabaret-bars, topless dancers were can-canning around wearing the face of Madonna Lisa, and comedians asked the vital question on everyone's lips: 'will the Eiffel Tower be next?' It seemed that only the Dutch painter Kees van Dongen wondered what all the fuss was about. 'She has no eyebrows and a funny smile', he declared. 'She must have had nasty teeth to smile so tightly.'

Scapegoats were needed, especially as all the Sûreté's moustachioed star detective, Inspector Robert, had to go on was a single fingerprint left on a wall. The far-right Action Française blamed the Jews, naturally. Although, Prefect of Police, Louis Lépine, believed it to be the work of international art thieves. While a psychology professor suggested the culprit might be a sexual psychopath who would enjoy 'mutilating, stabbing, defiling' La Joconde, as the French prefer to call the painting. Either way, something had to be done and quick. Yet, it was only after the Paris-Journal offered a 50,000 franc reward, no questions asked, that suspects came to light. That they might be innocent, mattered not a jot to dogged Inspector Robert.

It was all Guillaume Apollinaire's fault. The surreal poet had his head full of dreams of daring-do and the exploits of a fictional criminal mastermind, the elusive Fantômas, when he befriended Joseph-Honoré Géry-Pieret, a dashing bisexual Belgian thief who had a penchant for stealing Iberian statuettes from the Louvre. Knowing Picasso would be interested in acquiring one, Apollinaire acted as go-between and a deal was struck. All might have been well had Géry-Pieret not sold his story to the Paris-Journal for 250 francs, which they duly published, while keeping their promise to protect his identity, referring to him only as "The Thief".

When Apollinaire and Picasso heard this they decided to throw the statuette into the Seine. So Picasso's girlfriend, Fernande Olivier, found them a cheap suitcase large enough to hold the incriminating evidence and at midnight 'pushed them out of the door'. The two iconoclasts lugged it down the hill, looking over their shoulders at every turn, until an unexpected noise sent them scuttling under an archway, their hearts thumping madly. They continued on, until something in the shadows scared them so much they hurried home terrified, trudging up Rue Foyatier, the steep hill of Montmartre, puffing, breathless, exhausted by their paranoia as much as anything. When Fernande opened the door at 2am, the two men stood, white faced, still holding the suitcase, she said, like 'contrite, frightened children.'

Two days later, on 7 September, Inspector Robert, accompanied, perhaps, by Inspector Juve, and believing the same thieves were behind both Louvre thefts, arrested Apollinaire and took him to the Prison de la Santé, where he was stripped of his belt, tie and shoelaces, and handcuffed. As he said: 'It seemed to me that, from that moment on, I was somewhere in another universe and I was going to be destroyed.' Given he had already come to the attention of the police as a 'cultural provocateur' and undesirable alien, he certainly had good reason to be worried. He was one of the "Wild Men of Paris", painters and poets who mocked traditional art. Young, brilliant and ruthlessly ambitious, they strutted through the cobblestone streets of Montmartre and filled the cheap cafes, defining themselves as well as a new creative idiom, breaking the rules to free art from art history. He called for the destruction of all museums 'because they paralyse the imagination', and he championed Picasso, "as a young god who wants to remake the world"; or so his police file declared.

Picasso stayed indoors, 'out of his mind with terror' said Fernande, hoping the nightmare would blow over. It didn't. Apollinaire, in an effort to save his family, his mistress and, above all his mother, incriminated his friend and at 7am, on 8 September, police hammered on Picasso's door, which was opened by a sleepy Fernande, wearing a diaphanous dressing gown. Picasso was arrested and taken by bus to Halle-aux-Vins in tears, all the while proclaiming his innocence. Once inside the Judge's Chambers, his protestations were brought to a sudden end when a door opened and in walked Apollinaire, 'pale, haggard, with red eyes and two days' growth of beard', according to Fernande, 'with his collar torn, his shirt unbuttoned... a lamentable scarecrow.'

Picasso began to tremble. Do you know this man?', asked the judge.

'Nnno,' stuttered Pablo. 'I've never seen him before in my life.'

Picasso was released, while Apollinaire was locked up for four more days in a stinking cell in the Souricière, aka the "Mousetrap", as the Palais de Justice holding cells were called. When he was finally released, he discovered that his muse and lover, Marie Laurencin, his "twin soul", his 'little sun, a feminine counterpart of himself,' he said, had left him out of disgust at what he'd done. Although, Picasso claimed it was because she was bored with him in bed. While she told Misia that she had never had an orgasm as a consequence of his best attentions, or what she assumed were his best attentions. Either way, she used this as an excuse to end their relationship. Apollinaire's friendship with Picasso would survive, but was never entirely the same again. Apollinaire and Laurencin would remain estranged too. But then, they didn't have much time left. He died relatively young in 1918. He survived action on the Front but not the flu epidemic that followed. She lived to a ripe old age. When she died, in 1956, she asked to be buried in Père Lachaise with a rose clutched in one hand and Apollinaire's love letters to her laid across her heart.

A Quoi Bon Dire

Frances Thimann

Most Sundays it is the same. They invite her for lunch, the old lady, though it is a trouble to call for her, take her home again, down the long country lane at the end of the village. She still lives in the little lopsided cottage on the farthest corner, half-slipped into its own wild garden.

But she is alone now. Her husband passed away long years ago, no-one is sure quite how many years. Some of the people nearby can just remember him - tall and fine-looking, they say.

The village has changed a great deal since those days – though at the far edges, where the cottages are tumbled together and more over-grown, and the lanes wander into the fields, it is probably still the same as it has ever been.

It is Barry's turn to fetch her this Sunday, while Mum is at home cooking for all the family. His girl Sian, with her blue eyes and soft honey skin, is with him. It is special today – they have just become engaged. He is bringing Sian for lunch, and calling for the old lady as well.'Two birds,' he says.

It is August; the air is blue and gold and glows as they do. They climb out of Barry's rusty car and walk down the path to ring the bell, waiting on the door-step to hear the old lady's slow faint tread. She always takes a while. They wonder what she can be doing; she knew when to expect them.

'She's just finishing the chapter.'

'She's lost her keys.They're not where she put them last night!'

'The cat!Where's the cat!

'She's checking the kettle's turned off.'

'And all the taps! And ....'

'Love you Sian,' he says as they wait, and the sun shines on her upturned face; he touches it with his fingertips, tracing the patches of light there. 'Always. Even when you're an old lady like this one' – and he smiles and gestures towards the cottage door, which is so overgrown he wonders how it might ever open again. Sian reaches up to run her hand through his hair:it is corn-brown, very fine, streaked gold now in the sun, and he wears it long, so that it touches his shoulders.

He has a habit of shaking his head back, freeing the hair from his face. She does it for him this time, makes it fan through her hands.

'Only ever you since I was six,' she murmurs. 'Guinness Book of Records,' and they hold a long close kiss in the sunshine, forgetting.

They spring apart a little awkwardly when the door opens, though he is half-smiling still. 'Sorry,' he mutters to no-one in particular, his face bright.

After lunch she is quiet, the old lady. Sometimes she sleeps, in her chair in the corner. But Barry notices that later, with her cup of tea untouched before her, she is awake again, though her eyes are very far away, faded, cloudy and grey with all the memories, he thinks. Then they are silver too, and there is a little spillage of silver on her cheeks. Her lips are working, though she does not speak;her old hands, a crumple of bone and wrinkle and grey vein, move on her lap, as if they remember something that they touched once, how soft and fine it was.

'What's the story, Mum?'Barry asks, after he has taken the old lady home again.

Seventeen years ago you said
Something that sounded like Good-bye;
And everybody thinks that you are dead,
But I.

So I, as I grow stiff and cold
To this and that say Good-bye too;
And everybody sees that I am old
But you.

And one fine morning in a sunny lane
Some boy and girl will meet and kiss and swear
That nobody can love their way again
While over there
You will have smiled, I shall have tossed your
hair.

Charlotte Mew [1869-1928]

This story was first published in 'A Change of Direction',
Mantle Lane Press, 2019.

Author Biographies

Antonia Reed When Antonia isn't developing her own stories, she helps others as a writing coach and editor. Her work has been published by Disney and Dark Horse Comics, The Mechanics' Institute Review and performed at Green Ink, as well as being featured in Loose Muse, Emagazine and other journals. www.antoniareed.wordpress.com

Christy Fearn, 'The Girl with the Byron Tattoo', has written and performed literary presentations about the Romantic poets and Mary Shelley; the 'Characters of Cranborne Chase' project; and 'Mary Shelley - Mother of Monsters'. The excerpt is from *Notorious* the sequel to Christy's debut novel *Framed* about the Nottingham Luddites.

Mark Eklid is a Derby-based former award-winning sports journalist who writes crime thriller novels set in his home city of Sheffield.
https://markeklid.com/

Jasmina Svenne historical fiction writer was born in Derby to Latvian parents, but has lived most of her life in Nottinghamshire. To date she has had one novel and eleven novellas published, as well as several award-winning or shortlisted short stories, mostly set either during the late-Georgian era or WWI.

Moira Hodgkinson writes both novels and non-fiction with a theme of witchcraft and the paranormal. Her work has featured in multiple anthologies and magazines and she is now working on her first paranormal thriller. She lives next a thousand trees in Nottinghamshire with her family and too many cats. Find all her books at https://www.amazon.co.uk/stores/author/B084ZY12XJ

Mark Jacobs is preoccupied with the poetry and thought of the poet Laura (Riding) Jackson (1901-1991). He was a member of her Literary Board. A Fellow of Trent University, he established an archive of her correspondence and work. He has been a college lecturer and later a teacher in special education. Https://lauraridingjackson.org.uk/

Trevor Watts is a Nottinghamshire, UK writer. He has 20+ books published in three genres. He has also published many reader-friendly non-fiction books and articles, mostly about exploring active volcanoes around the world, and searching for fossilised dinosaur footprints on Yorkshire's Jurassic coast. In the 1980s, he pioneered the use of computers in the education of children with profound learning difficulties. Now retired, he writes, walks the local footpaths; curses his computers; and loves his wife, the cat and his kids.

Julie Malone (pen-name Jae) writes fantasy adventures, historical novels, children's bedtime stories. She has organised literary events, workshops and creative writing competitions for schools and community groups. She is an experienced public speaker, and a regular guest on local TV and radio. Her newly released adult crime novel is *In Too Deep* (978-1835636114 by New Generation Publishing). www.jaemalone.co.uk

James Ellson was a police officer for 15 years, starting in London and finishing as a Detective Inspector at Moss Side in Manchester. He now writes crime fiction (the DCI *Castle* series), gives talks, and manages a smallholding.
https://jamesellson.com/books/

Brennig Jones has been struggling with fictional characters in his animal-friendly writer's garret for more years than he'd like to count. His latest work is the four-novel thriller series *Tempest*, *Storm*, *Hurricane*, and *Tornado*. He's currently wrestling with a telepathic dog in a new project. The dog might win.

Trevor Locke was born in Portsmouth but now lives in Leicester. He has just completed the first draft of his seventh novel. He has also written a large number of poems and is now embarking on a series of short stories. Now retired, he was previously a journalist and report writer and has authored one book about the Criminal Justice System (published by Longman.) Some of his work has been published on his website www.writertrevorlocke.com. Trevor also writes reviews of music and concerts in the Leicester area.

Frances Thimann has published five collections of short stories - the latest, 'Sweet Thames, Run Softly', was published earlier this year. In 2017, her piece 'Shells' won the Society of Authors' Tom-Gallon Trust short story award. She has also published individual pieces in magazines and online. In 2006 she completed the MA in Creative Writing at NTU.

Fiona Linday facilitates lifelong creative writing alongside practising multi-genre writing with prize-winning short stories, plus a YA novel. She sparked and edited a couple of ACE supported commissioned anthologies, too. Recently, her life reflections collection is *Count Our Blessings*. There's more in Scriptorium Group's anthology *Moments of Grace*. Her wildlife picture book is *Who Cares About Superheroes*. www.fionalinday.co.uk

David Parkin is an author, theatre maker, musician and installation artist. His work is fiercely autobiographical or silly and speculative, from his children's book and musical *The Nose That Nobody Picked* to his 'clinical depression concept album show' *Good Friday*. Whatever it is, his work is always thoughtful, moving and funny.

Jack Blackmore had a long career in social work before publishing on various subjects, notably on the poet Laura Riding. Last year, he and James Green collaborated on *Prometheus in Chains*, an adaptation of Aeschylus for the modern stage. The poems in this anthology emerged out of a memoir of his early life, *Out of Oblivion*.

Andrew Taylor, an engineer who has always enjoyed the creative side of solving problems. That imagination needed to look at things differently is now stretching itself beyond the real world and learning how to craft science fiction novels. Email: andygoesforth@icloud.com

Rosanna McGlone is a writer and journalist for publications including: *Th Guardian*, *The Sydney Morning Herald* and *The Weekend Australian*. Her recent book, *The Process of Poetry* -which explores the redrafting of poems by leading UK poets- was number 1 on Amazon and featured on Radio 4's *Front Row*. *Feisty Females*, a book of short stories celebrating medieval women, is her latest publication. Follow her @rosannamc-glone.bsky.social or explore her work here: https://rosanna-mcglone.sumupstore.com/products